Devastation

Shay's sculpture studio had been trashed. The glass door was smashed. Tools lay in mad heaps. Her current project was crushed into shapeless blobs of clay. Three months' work gone.

On the table lay a small clay sculpture. Mickey's calling card—a sculpture of male genitalia, pierced by one of Shay's Exacto knives. Shay's daughter called her name. Shay moved to hide the clay piece, but Kelly had already seen it. The girl gasped in shock.

"Why won't he leave us alone? Mom..." she started to cry. "I thought he was so cute..."

"He isn't cute. He's trying to scare us and I won't have it," Shay said grimly. "I'm going to call the police."

"I hate him! I hate him so much!" Kelly shouted.

Hidden outside, not far away, Mickey watched Shay and Kelly. He saw the police arrive. They would never find him. They would never stop him.

Also by Julia Grice

The Cutting Hours
Jagged Light
Suspicion
Tender Prey

JULIA GRICE

THE CUTTING HOURS

A TOM DOHERTY ASSOCIATES BOOK
NEW YORK

This is a work of fiction. All the characters and events portrayed in this book are fictitious, and any resemblance to real people or events is purely coincidental.

THE CUTTING HOURS

Copyright © 1993 by Julia Grice

A Forge Book
Published by Tom Doherty Associates, Inc.
175 Fifth Avenue
New York, NY 10010

Forge® is a registered trademark of Tom Doherty Associates, Inc.

ISBN: 0-812-51092-5
Library of Congress Catalog Card Number: 93-26916

First edition: December 1993
First mass market edition: January 1995

Printed in the United States of America

0 9 8 7 6 5 4 3 2 1

For all those who have been so loving, especially. . . . My wonderful sons, Mike and Andy Grice; my lovely daughter-in-law, Nancy Gibson; and those others so close to my heart, my parents, Jean and Will Haughey; my sister, Jean Temme, my brothers, Russ Haughey and Bill Haughey, and dear friends, Margaret Duda, Elizabeth Buzzelli, Roni Tripodi, Don and Lorraine de Baptiste, and Joyce Hagmaier. But always deep love and grateful thanks to my husband, Richard Fitz.

THE CUTTING HOURS

ONE

The voice of the Channel 7 anchorwoman awoke Shay Wyoming from a full-color dream in which she and her sixteen-year-old daughter, Kelly, were sky divers free-falling in space, separated by a malfunction of Kelly's parachute.

Pull the cord! she kept screaming to the terrified teenager. *Pull the cord!*

She jerked upright on the old couch in her studio and looked around blankly, for a few dreadful seconds still caught in blue space, her child's scream of terror ringing in her ears.

Damn. She'd fallen asleep.

Glancing at her watch, she saw that it was 11:20 P.M. The news broadcast, emanating from the twelve-inch portable she kept on a nearby work table, was almost finished. Kelly hadn't called—again. What was she going to do about her daughter?

Blinking, she gazed around her sculpture studio,

which she'd added on to the house last year; part of her divorce settlement had paid for it. It was a dream of a room, thirty-by-forty, windows on three sides hung with Levelor shades that gave ideal light control. Shelves held sculptures she was saving for her next one-woman show.

On a work table, still in the soft-wax "sketch" stage, was her latest project—a strong, ovoid sculpture of a burly Detroit auto worker. It was a commission for Entech Services Ltd., a temporary-employment firm, for which they were paying thirteen thousand dollars—amazingly high pay for a struggling sculptor.

Coming from the TV set, the voice of anchor Carmen Harlan penetrated Shay's consciousness.

". . . the second victim, ten-year-old Stacy Kennelley, was hit by ricocheting bullets from police gunfire as she sat watching TV in her living room in the house next door. Stacey was pronounced dead on arrival at Beaumont Hospital. . . ."

Shay's stomach gave a clench. It was every mother's worst nightmare, wasn't it? The powerlessness. The inability to protect. And if your child was a teenager, the worry intensified. You simply could not accompany her everywhere she went, could not always keep back random violence, rapists and psychos, because your vigilance could only be part-time.

She flicked off the TV as EMS attendants were carting away the corpses of other women's children in body bags.

In the kitchen, she cleaned up the mess from the popcorn she'd made earlier for Matt, her feisty, adorable six-year-old. She dumped unpopped kernels from the air popper into the wastebasket, put their two dishes in the dishwasher, and put the popper away. She wasn't a spit-and-polish housekeeper . . . her artist's temperament, she assumed. But she didn't like food on the floor, so she swept the kitchen for stray kernels and wiped up a sticky place where Matt had spilled his Hi-C.

Where was Kelly anyway? Worry caused her mouth to tighten. She remembered the crazy year she'd had after her own parents were killed. Once she and eleven other kids had crammed into a boy's car and gone hurtling down I-75 at a hundred miles per hour. Not a one of them wearing seat belts.

Shay switched off the kitchen lights and walked through to the family room, where poster-sized photos she'd taken with her Nikon formed an eye-catching wall display. On a foggy day she'd posed Kelly standing in the split of a huge, 150-year-old tree in Rochester Park, a pensive wood sprite in a flowing lace dress.

She studied the photograph. They'd been fighting that day, and Kelly's expression looked wary, reserved. Her daughter had battled the divorce bitterly, and had never quite forgiven her for filing. Shay felt she'd had no choice.

For her the marriage ended the moment she rushed into the emergency room and saw her battered daughter lying on a gurney, sobbing at the pain of her broken collarbone. Randy, a problem drinker for years, had totalled the car while drunk, with Kelly in the passenger seat beside him.

Now the telephone rang, and Shay hurriedly answered it.

"Hello?"

Her stomach tightened. Maybe there'd been another accident. Maybe this was a call from some police officer, or a hospital. . . . Then she heard the sound of rock music, a pounding heavy-metal beat jumped up with synthesized guitar.

"Hello? Kelly, is that you? Who *is* this?"

The jarring music continued for a second longer,

then the phone clicked in her ear, and she heard the dial tone.

Annoyed, Shay hung up. These calls had been coming, off and on, for about a year now, often with rock music in the background. Maybe the caller was her ex-husband, Randy. Randy liked "Fox Radio," a rock station—especially when he was drinking.

Or maybe it was just someone who'd dialed their number at random. There hadn't been any heavy breathing, any obscenities—yet—but Shay was arranging with the phone company to have a device put on her phone to trace the calls.

The phone rang again. She snatched it up. "Yes?"

"Mom . . . Terry's car broke down; it's the battery or something. He left the lights on when we were at Chi Chi's, and now he's trying to find someone with those cable things."

Kelly. Shay felt a vast, welcome wave of relief. "You mean jumper cables?"

"Yeah, those. . . . Mom, I can't help it if this happened. I did call you." Kelly had a Gidget kind of voice, breathy and sweet.

"Kelly." Shay drew in a deep breath and expelled it carefully. "I told you to be home by ten, honey. It's nearly 11:30."

"I couldn't help it."

"You could help it. You didn't even leave Chi Chi's until just now, did you? Kelly, when I tell you ten o'clock, I mean *ten o'clock,* not eleven, or twelve, or any other time."

"Okay, *okay.*"

"And don't get that tone in your voice, young lady. It's not as if our house rules come as any great surprise to you. Now, if you aren't home in thirty minutes, you'll be grounded for the next two weeks."

"Mom . . . . He can't find the *jumper* cables. . . ."

"Let him go and ask the restaurant manager, then. Someone who works there will have cables. Count on it."

Kelly uttered a sob and hung up. Shay stood holding the phone, frustrated. These days, Kelly was touchy and difficult. She knew she couldn't establish rapport with her daughter by scolding her and grounding her, but what else was she supposed to do? She couldn't let the girl just run loose, without any sort of structure. Not if she loved her . . . and, God, she did.

"I didn't mean to be so late. I *didn't* do it just to bug you," Kelly protested twenty-five minutes later. She had arrived home with five minutes to spare, dropped off by a vehicle that blasted M. C. Hammer from its souped-up stereo system.

Kelly loped into the kitchen, wearing frayed jeans and a matching jeans jacket, which she had decorated with painted flowers and silver metal studs. She was a striking girl, at 5'10" several inches taller than her friends, a height that intimidated most of the boys at Walton High School. Her hair was the color of clover honey, worn moussed and curly. Her skin was porcelain clear, without pore or flaw. She wanted to be a nurse, she said, and take care of preemie babies.

"I am bugged," Shay said dryly.

"But we were still *eating* at ten, Mom. I couldn't help it, some of the kids were late. They just got off work, and we couldn't order right away, and this guy Heather likes, he was *so* late, and—"

Kelly went on with a long, involved explanation of teenager logistics, interspersed with rummaging in the refrigerator. "Don't we have any more Pepsi? God . . . tacos make me *so* thirsty. And we had extra hot sauce. I could drink one of those big bottles, the whole thing."

"There's an open bottle of 7-Up in the door."

"It's not fizzy."

"That, my dear, is because you left the bottle cap off."

"Oh, yechhh." Kelly took the bottle out of the refrigerator. "Do I *have* to drink non-fizz? Every time I swallow it, I just want to gag. Did Dad call?" she added.

"No, was he supposed to?"

"He was going to get Heather and me two tickets for Taylor Dayne at the Palace," Kelly explained. "Are you sure Dad didn't call? He told me he'd check with you about the tickets. You didn't have the answering machine on, did you?" Kelly added suspiciously.

"I was working, honey. I was in the studio."

"Where you never hear the phone. Mom, you *never* hear the phone in there. And you keep forgetting to switch the machine on. You don't want me to see Dad, do you? You hate me seeing Dad."

"Of course I want you to see him," Shay protested automatically. But did she really? Wasn't she secretly afraid he'd have another accident with Kelly in the car?

"Well, I saw Dad today after school, and he said you don't give him any kind of a chance at all. You just tossed him away like so much trash in the dumpster."

"What! Oh, Kelly!"

"Well, I mean it, Mom. You hate Dad, and I don't think it's fair." The girl poured Diet 7-Up into a glass and added a handful of ice cubes. "He wants to get back together with you, Mom, and you won't let him. You won't even talk to him. You're being very, very cruel."

The accusation hurt more than Shay wanted to admit. She sat down at the kitchen table, staring at a bouquet of peach-colored roses sent her by Ben Lyte, the man she'd been seeing for four months, a teacher at Kelly's high school who was also a published author.

She supposed Kelly's anger had to do with Ben, too, the fact that her mother was dating another man.

"Kelly . . . your father walked out of the alcohol treatment center two times. He didn't even want to try. I'm sorry, I know how much this hurts you, but I can't live that life any more. I just can't. I was an enabler, honey—for years and years I covered for his mistakes. Well, I can't do that any more."

Kelly tilted her head angrily. "You didn't *love* him. You didn't *care*. That's why you divorced him."

Shay bit her lip. How could a sixteen-year-old girl understand what it meant to live with an alcoholic? To come downstairs at 2:00 A.M. to find your husband passed out on the floor in his underwear. Waking to the sound of loud voices downstairs and discovering that he was entertaining a group of barflies he'd picked up at The Gathering Place. Being blamed because alcohol had affected his arteries and he could no longer get a firm erection.

"Kelly," she finally whispered. "There are things . . . things about my relationship with your father that are private."

"But he says if you would just go out with him, just go out *one time*, Mom. . . ."

Out in the street, a motorcycle suddenly roared past the house, revving its motor to blast away the suburban quiet. Kelly stopped what she'd been going to say, freezing delicately. A red flush spread across her cheeks.

"Someone you know?" Shay inquired.

"Oh, just a kid from school."

The popping of pistons faded, then increased in volume as the driver circled back. Shay reached the living room's bay window in time to see the biker, a boy clad in black jeans and leather jacket, wearing a black helmet with a black plastic visor pulled down over his eyes. Was he staring at their house?

"Kel? Who is that boy? I think I've seen him ride past here before."

"Oh, nobody."

"Nobody? By the sound of that motor, I'd say he's definitely somebody, or wants to be."

Shay returned to the kitchen. Kelly was poking around in the refrigerator, peering at plates full of cold chicken, leftover spaghetti. Her voice emerged reluctantly. "Oh, he's just Mickey McGee, that's all. I think he lives near here. Maybe on Portsmouth."

"Mickey McGee. That name sounds so familiar. Mickey McGee. . . ."

Kelly giggled nervously. "He was in that art class, Mom. The one you taught at Walton last year. The kid you said was so good."

"Oh," Shay said. "*That* Mickey."

Memory flooded back to Shay. The previous year, she'd taught a week through the Michigan Council for the Arts "Artists in the Schools" program. Twenty kids were hand-picked for a two-hour sculpture seminar.

Mickey McGee had stood out from the other kids with their nice, middling talents like a cheetah in a cage full of house cats. In a high school where kids possessed plenty of money for trendy clothes from the mall, Mickey wore biker gear. A Harley T-shirt, the works. Shay hadn't expected much from him, despite the screening process. She'd been shocked when she'd walked around the room, examining the clay sculptures molded over the wire armatures she'd shown the class how to make.

Mickey's statue of a man and a boy fighting had been of professional caliber—nearly gallery quality.

She'd told him so, after class.

"No shit?" the boy said, staring at her with opaque olive black eyes. However, there was an expression growing on his face . . . an eager, incredulous yearning that Shay found touching. Of all the kids in the class, he was the last one she'd expected to reach.

"Oh, yes, you definitely have talent, and I think you should try to cultivate it," she began, trying to ignore the curse words. "I have several excellent contacts at the University of Michigan. One of them is Noah Ransom, a very well known sculptor who also is a personal friend of mine. I think he could—"

The bell rang, cutting her off in midsentence. Mickey McGee's eyes immediately glazed; he broke eye contact. With a hoodlumish scrape of his boot heels on the floor, he sauntered out of the art room and disappeared into the crowd of kids changing classes in the hallways.

"That's the way it is with some of these kids," the chairman of the art department, Janice Goldman, had told her later. "Some of them make a whole career out of being difficult."

Shay still remembered the spasm of disappointment she'd felt—her regret because she'd had him, then lost him. Was this boy now interested in Kelly? Was that why he kept buzzing his bike past their house?

She wasn't sure she liked that at all. Could Mickey be the person making the anonymous phone calls? Sighing, Shay returned to the present.

"Okay, baby, but Portsmouth is more than a mile from here, so why would he pass our house on the way home? This is definitely the long way around."

"I don't know," Kelly muttered.

Shay stabbed a wild guess. After all, she'd once been sixteen, too. "Does he follow you around sometimes? Take you for a ride on his bike once in a while?''

"Just once."

Shay didn't hide her dismay. "Oh, Kelly. . . . You were in that art class. Don't you remember what kind of work Mickey was doing, how angry it was? He's not a—he's got some pretty serious problems, I think. Maybe it would be best if you didn't encourage him."

"I'm not *encouraging* him, Mom," Kelly cried. "I've only said about ten words to him all year. I can't help it if he drives past here. I can't help it if he's in my art class."

"Kelly . . . I didn't mean to interfere—"

"You never mean to! But you always do! You act like I'm some kind of a baby, like I can't do anything. Well, I'm not a baby and I hate being treated like one, and I hate the way you won't even *try* to make it up with Dad, and I hate, oh, I hate just everything. And now I'm going up to bed and I'm going to go to sleep because I'm just *tired*. Tired of everything, and especially tired of *you*, Mom!''

"Kelly," Shay gasped.

But the girl turned and rushed out of the kitchen. Shay heard her thumping upstairs toward her room, then the slam of her daughter's bedroom door.

She stood there, fighting a feeling of hurt that she knew was unrealistic. Anger was normal after a divorce, to be expected.

But what if Kelly's anger was *more* than normal? *What if Kelly never forgave her?*

For a brief, wild second Shay considered calling Randy, her ex-husband, and casually making a date to see him, to talk. But immediately she dismissed the idea. It would only raise Kelly's hopes unfairly. Nothing short of remarriage would satisfy her daughter, and Shay knew she couldn't go backward, back into a marriage with an alcoholic who refused to change. The relationship would only fail again.

On the street the motorcycle made one more pass, the sound of its motor insectile, vaguely disturbing.

TWO

Kelly slammed her bedroom door, feeling a surge of satisfaction at the loud noise it made, a surge that turned to consternation as she realized that she'd probably awakened her six-year-old brother.

She stood frozen, waiting for Matt to cry out, but the boy was silent. She didn't need Mattie right now, wandering in in his PJ's with his hair sticking up, begging her for a dinosaur story.

She switched on the overhead light. Her bedroom was her safe place, her haven, and she guarded its privacy fiercely. The wallpaper, patterned with pretty pink rosebuds, was nearly obliterated by the New Kids on the Block posters that were plastered everywhere. In the smaller spaces, she'd taped photos she'd clipped from *Teen Beat* and *Bop*, showing Donnie, Danny, Jordan, Jonathan and Joe—her idols.

Her desk was stacked with more pictures she hadn't yet put up, a catalog from Madonna University's nursing program, and her sizeable collection of compact disks, many bought for her by her father. A shelf held her portable CD player and more CDs. She slipped in *Step by Step*, programmed it to repeat, and turned up the volume as far as she dared.

Their voices filled the room, creating a sweet-boy, woozy comfort, that lapped at her ears in sugared waves.

Kelly threw herself on her bed, on top of the pink flowered comforter.

Did her parents think she was a fool? She knew she'd caused the divorce. She'd begged her father to take her to the mall to return some of her Christmas presents. He'd hit a guy turning out of a tire store. She'd dislocated her collarbone and her mother had totally freaked.

Kelly knew her dad would never hurt her on purpose. He'd even cried, he was so sorry. So what if he drank—weren't you supposed to love someone no matter what they did?

She kicked off her Reeboks and stretched out on her back, locking her hands behind her head and losing herself in the New Kids music. Her window was open, and the early May night air drifted in, humid with spring. She could hear tree frogs peeping in the pond at the other end of the street.

The sounds made her feel funny, somehow. Restless. As if she wanted something, only she didn't know what.

Then she heard the motorcycle again.

Kelly felt her heart give an enormous squeeze. Mickey! The cutest and baddest guy in school, so biker cool. He reminded her of Jordan. Nearly six feet tall, Mickey had a mop of heavy black hair that fell over his forehead into his eyes, but was shaved close at the sideburns. His black eyes *burned*, and his lower lip pouted.

There was something unsafe about Mickey, Kelly sensed. A rebel quality. She knew she wasn't the only one who felt it. She'd overheard Mrs. Goldman, the art teacher, calling Mickey *"a real hard core case."* Mrs. Goldman, a grown woman, was a little bit afraid of Mickey, maybe because he always ignored her in class, just doing what he wanted, and using whatever materials he pleased.

But that only made him more fascinating to Kelly.

She flopped onto her side and reached for her pink princess phone, punching out Heather's number.

Her best friend answered on the second ring. "H'lo?"

"God," said Kelly, thumping out a huge sigh. "Are you as bored as I am? I mean, my mom went all paranoid again just because I got home a little tiny bit late."

"My mom wasn't even home," Heather complained. "She had a heavy date with some guy named Hank. He's got a big fat stomach; he looks like he's pregnant."

"Ugh! Eeechh," Kelly agreed uncomfortably. *Her* mother was dating Ben Lyte, her English teacher. It was a totally embarrassing situation as far as Kelly was concerned.

"That guy drove by here on his motorcycle again," she told her friend, changing the subject to what was foremost in her mind.

Heather didn't sound thrilled. "You mean Mickey?"

"Yeah, him."

"He's kind of crazy," Heather said, giggling.

Kelly felt a delicious shiver. "Yeah. This is about the fifth time this week he's ridden past the house. I wonder what it means. I wonder if he knows someone on this street.''

Like her.

Heather giggled again. Six months older than Kelly, she was getting very boy crazy. ''Oh, he's probably got girls all over. Biker chick girls, who wear those tight Harley Davidson tops.''

''Sure.''

''Anyway''—Heather lowered her voice—''I've got to tell you about Terry. After you left, we got in his dad's car, and did this really heavy duty kissing. He French kisses just wonderful . . . and that's not all he does either. I took off my blouse and let him see my breasts and he just loved them, Kel. Boys *love* to look at a girl's boobs. I mean, it's incredible how really crazy it makes them.''

Kelly hung on to the phone, listening to Heather go on and on about Terry Griffith, a senior who played on the Walton basketball team. Heather had lost her virginity several months ago, and since then she'd changed. She talked about sex all the time, and was full of remarks that let Kelly know she was slow and inexperienced, missing out on a part of life that all the other girls were enjoying.

Restlessly she listened as Heather gave every detail of the heavy petting she and Terry had done that ended with her performing oral sex on him. Kelly knew if she didn't have sex soon, she'd lose Heather. They would still be friends, but not best friends, because Heather would be too sophisticated for her.

''Kelly? Kel? Are you listening? You haven't been listening to one word I've said,'' Heather accused.

Kelly jumped. She realized she hadn't even said *mmmmmm* in several minutes. ''I've heard everything,'' she protested.

''No, you haven't. You just pretend you're listening. That's because you don't know about sex yet, and you can't relate."

Kelly felt a wave of hurt feelings that she tried unsuccessfully to hide. After all, Heather *was* her best friend. "I was listening," she repeated.

"You know, you ought to think about trying to get a *real* boyfriend. I mean, most of the girls we know aren't virgins anymore. They just aren't. And if they say they are, they're lying." Heather giggled. "Except for you, Kelly. If you say you're one, *you're* telling the truth."

Kelly hesitated. "You think," she remarked.

"What?"

"I said you think I'm telling the truth—but maybe I'm not. Maybe I've got a boyfriend and I'm not telling you about him because he's too, too cool."

"Yeah, right," Heather groaned disbelievingly. "I'm *so* sure. What's his name?"

"I'm not telling . . . now."

"You don't have anyone, so don't lie to me, Kelly Ann Wyoming. If you were having sex with someone, *I'd* know."

As Kelly was getting undressed for bed, she heard the familiar, buzzing roar of Mickey's Harley Davidson.

Again. How many times tonight? Five? Six? It was the most times he'd ever ridden past in one day.

She paused with her sleep shirt in her hand, wearing only bikini panties. *He was outside the house . . . right now . . . looking for her!*

But when was he going to talk to her? She'd only spoken to him two or three times, counting the one time he asked her to ride on the back of his bike last May. Kelly still treasured those fifteen minutes of heaven, gripping Mickey around the waist from behind, the wind roaring in her ears.

Suddenly she knew what to do.

God, why hadn't she thought of it before? She had to show him . . . send him a signal.

Her heart pounding, Kelly hurried to the window and pulled aside the chintz flowered curtains, leaving only the white, semitransparent liners in place. She'd seen this done on VH-1, on a music video.

As the Harley sounds grew stronger, Kelly began swaying to the sexy beat of the music still playing in her room. She undulated her torso, pretending she was in a Madonna video. She'd seen the front of the house at night and knew that she was silhouetted from behind, her body dimly visible through the curtains.

She leaned her head back, arched her spine and shook her hair, feeling incredibly silky and female. She wondered what she looked like from the street. She wondered if she looked exciting to him, beautiful to him.

"Kelly?" her mother called through the closed door. "It's almost one o'clock! *Please* turn your CD player off and go to bed."

Kelly jumped, freezing in midshake. She grabbed the sleep shirt and threw it over her head, wiggling it down over her nakedness.

"Okay, Mom."

"Are you all right?" came Shay's voice. "You sound, I don't know. Funny."

Kelly felt another wave of sick, excited guilt. "I'm . . . just exercising."

"At this hour? Did you hear that motorcycle? That boy's out there again. He's waking up the whole neighborhood. I can't believe he could be so inconsiderate when there are people sleeping."

Kelly didn't answer. She padded over to the window and pulled the chintz curtains over the sheers.

"Honey?" Shay knocked, then pushed Kelly's door

open a crack. She was dressed for bed in a pale peach silk T-shirt, and looked very elegant. Her blond hair shimmered in the overhead light. Everyone said Kelly and Shay could be sisters, not mother and daughter.

"Look, I know I came down hard on you," Shay said. "But I just want things to be right for you, and I want you to have good values, and—I love you. Sleep tight, honey."

"I love you, too," Kelly responded after a long, poignant beat.

Mickey McGee aimed his Harley around the block, feeling his body almost explode with sexual pressure. He straddled the bike, one hand rubbing frantically at his groin.

The slim form in the window, dancing for him. . . . Bitch Kelly. Mickey knew no girl who danced like that could be innocent. She was a whore, yeah, she was gloating to herself as she showed off her body to him.

The night air, whipping against his face, tasted of green leaves, lilac blossoms and damp grass. Expensive houses flashed past him—colonials and a few ranches, yellow lights glowing warmly through windows. Inside one house he glimpsed a TV set's blue flicker. A man and a woman sat on a couch watching, a teenager sprawled on the floor.

Savagely Mickey's hand jammed on the accelerator. Family stuff . . . shit. *He'd* never had any family stuff. His old man had taken care of that with a ten-inch meat cleaver, barricading himself, his mother and eight-year-old Mickey into their house on Wyandotte Street, in Royal Oak, for fourteen hell-packed hours.

"*Danno! Danno!*" his mother kept screaming. "*I'll do anything, anything. . . .*"

Mickey closed off the memory of what happened next. He never thought about that any more. *Never*. It made him feel sick and weak, trembling with the pre-monition of some impending doom, something that was *going to happen whether he wanted it to or not.*

He found himself circling the block, approaching the Wyoming place again. Over the last year he'd become obsessed with the Wyomings' house, mostly because of the large addition that had been built onto the back—the blond bitch Shay's sculpture studio.

Mickey stopped the bike, straddling the seat as he balanced the heavy machine. He glanced angrily toward the dark windows, thinking about all the things inside—the finished sculptures, tools, equipment, sinks, kilns, and huge built-in shelves crammed with bags of plaster, wax, and other things.

All the things he didn't have, never would have. He was stuck with where he was and who he was. Yeah, he wasn't going anywhere and he knew it. Oh, one day Shay had told him that he had talent, but Mickey knew he had to have good grades to get into art school, and his grades sucked. He only liked one thing, art, and the rest of school he just let go.

Glancing up, Mickey saw that the curtains had been pulled shut in Kelly's room. But he could discern two shadows moving across the cloth—they were up there in that room, Kelly and her blond mother, Shay. Talking, probably . . . about him.

Gradually Mickey felt the fantasy come upon him—the stylized sexual fantasy he'd had for so many years he couldn't remember when it had first begun. It was always the same, varying only in small details. In his right hand he held a knife, its handle already slippery with blood, whose blood he didn't know. There was a flowing tenseness, heat in his body, between his legs. A girl was with him. She was crying and scared, begging him to fuck her rather than kill her.

The more she sobbed, the harder his erection became.

There was a man, too. His face was blurred but he was strong and powerful. Sometimes the man would be a male teacher or a probation officer, sometimes his father. Occasionally it would be a woman, someone on his shit list. But that didn't matter. The important thing was the cutting.

He lunged forward in a beautiful killer's dance, jabbing with the knife blade, teasing out the pink, writhing organs. Thrusting into dark red flesh that resisted the blade at first, then drew it in silkily like a woman spreading . . .

Mickey arched his pelvis upward, his orgasm so violent that it made him buck against the steering column of the bike. He flowed with it, groaning with unholy joy, while the charged-up night spun around him.

THREE

Ben Lyte switched off his car radio, which had been playing Bonnie Raitt's mellow languishments.

"It was a nice play," he said in his low-timbered, sexy voice. "And you are even nicer, Shay. I love sitting next to you. I love holding your hand in the theater. Your hands are so smooth considering what you do. You should consider doing hand lotion commercials—you could make a million dollars."

She smiled at the fancy. "It was a wonderful play," she agreed. Both of them loved the theater, and Ben had season tickets to the Birmingham Theater, where they'd just seen *Driving Miss Daisy* with Debbie Reynolds making a special appearance.

Shay gazed at the man she'd been dating for the past four months. Ben was forty-eight, his black hair lightly salted with white. He had a square, rugged, rough-hewn face that looked as if it belonged to a builder or trucker rather than a high school English teacher who had published three paperback thrillers. She wondered what to do about him. He was falling in love with her—of this she felt positive—and it was creating ripples of complication in her life. Was she ready for romance? Frankly, it terrified her.

"Well?" Ben said huskily. "Are you going to invite me in, or are we just going to sit here and try to neck across the console? I'll do it if you want, but I confess I find a couch more comfortable."

"Oh!" she said, startled out of her reverie. "Oh, I'm sorry, of course you can come in." She reached for her door handle, but Ben jumped out of his side and hurried around to hold the door for her. Under cover of darkness, she made a tiny, amused face. She could use a lathe, an acetylene torch, and a chain saw, and often lugged around hundred-pound bags of dry plaster. But Ben sometimes coddled her as if she were very, very feminine.

Together they walked to the front door. She knew he wanted to make love to her, but she'd begged off, telling him that she needed more time. He was kind and loving, but something in her would not open up.

Shay unlocked the front door and the deadbolt, and they went inside. The sound of gunshots and screams echoed from the family room TV set.

"Great," Shay groaned. "Matt's still up. I told Kelly to put him to bed at nine, and no scary movies."

Shay put her purse down on a hall chair and led the way to the family room.

Matt was perched on the couch in front of the TV, one fist pounding his pajamaed knee as he watched *The Blob* on HBO. He was a blond, little-boy version of Kelly, with the same clear skin. The teenager was nowhere in sight.

"Hi, kiddo," Shay called. "Where's Kelly?"

The boy ignored her, gazing mesmerized at the

screen where an adult male was being sucked down into a restaurant sink drain, his head being bloodily dissolved, limbs crushed.

"*Matt!*"

"Hi, Mom," her son said automatically, fist pounding his knee.

"Matt! Why aren't you in bed, honey? Kelly shouldn't have let you watch that. Where is your sister? Is she upstairs?"

"Yeah, she's in her room, she's taking off her clothes for the window."

"What?" Shay said, perplexed. "You mean undressing, Matt."

"Yeah. . . . There's this blob," the six-year-old told her. "It's pink and it eats people and then they've got their faces in it and they look out of the blob and they scream."

Shay slid a Muppet Babies video into the VCR and switched it on. "Sorry, Matt, no more Blob tonight." She glanced at her watch. "You can stay up for seven more minutes—then it's bedtime for you."

She led an amused Ben up the four steps to the living room. They sank down on a long, oatmeal-colored couch. The room held five or six of Shay's sculptures, some in treated plaster, others cast in metal. On the coffee table was a rounded mother and child, the mother holding up her baby and gazing into its eyes. It was one of Shay's favorites, a piece she had done when Kelly was an infant.

"Don't feel guilty about the TV," Ben remarked, taking her palm in his. "Television is a real dilemma, I think. If you stop your kids from watching what all their friends watch, you're separating them from their own generation. No child wants to grow up not having the experiences every child they know has."

"I know that. But I grew up with the Waltons."
Shay sighed.

Trying to relax, she leaned backward and snuggled
into Ben's shoulder. The scent of his aftershave mingled with the faint, musky saltiness that was his own
odor. Smelling him gave Shay a sharp, lonely feeling.
God—how long was it since she'd had sex? At least
eighteen months—since Randy. Her celibacy was
sometimes painful, sometimes ridiculously easy, but
she knew she didn't want it to go on forever. If she had
sex with Ben, would she be committed to falling in
love with him? Maybe she already had fallen in love.
She was absurdly terrified by all the ramifications that
would be brought about by the one, not-so-simple act.

Ben had sensed her mood. "Shay, I don't have to
linger tonight. I know it's late and—"

"It's only five minutes to eleven," she said, forcing
a laugh.

"Shay, Shay, Shay," Ben said, reaching out to
stroke her neck with one blunt fingertip. "I know I'm
rushing you a little, and I'm sorry. I don't want to
make you uneasy or scare you off."

"I guess I am a bit scared."

"It's okay."

She allowed his finger to stroke her neck, then
move to the soft blond hair at the back, her vulnerable
nape. By the way he stroked her she could tell that he
would be a devoted and caring lover, focused on her
own pleasure as well as his.

"It's just that this isn't very fair to you, Ben. I've
come out of a difficult marriage. I never thought I'd
ever get divorced. I always thought marriage was for
life. And Randy hasn't handled it well. I have a lot of
guilt, Ben."

"Alcoholism is a disease. You don't have to feel
guilty because he's got a disease."

"But if it's a sickness I should have stuck by him!" she burst out. "Kelly certainly thinks so. But I couldn't. Maybe I'm too damn selfish, but I could not stick it out. And when he hurt Kelly in that accident, something inside me just died."

They sat quietly talking, and when Shay heard the grandfather clock in the hallway start its bonging, she went down the steps and shooed Matt off to bed.

"Bedtime, Mattie . . . now. Hurry! It's eleven o'clock. I can't believe you could stay up this late and not have bleary eyes."

Her son, still buzzed on adrenaline from the exciting movie, made a ferocious face at her, pulling back the corners of his eyes with his fingers.

"Ugh," Shay murmured. "Don't do that. What if your eyes stick that way?" She gave her son a kiss. "Scoot, Matt—and don't forget to brush your teeth. I mean that. No more wetting down the toothbrush with water. I can tell when you've used the toothpaste."

As she started up the stairs with the small boy, the motorcycle racketed by on the street again.

"There's that dumb mo'cycle again," Matt commented, going into the bathroom reluctantly.

Shay frowned. "Again? Did it come past here before, Mattie?"

"Um, yup."

She supervised his tooth-brushing, thinking that Mickey's interest in Kelly was a bit too obsessive. She didn't like it.

The child's lids were finally beginning to droop. She led him to his room and tucked him in. He settled under the covers with a cozy squirm.

"Mom? Does the Blob ever come to Walton Hills?"

"The—no, honey, of course not! It's only a movie."

"But if the Blob did come—"

She put a finger lightly over her son's small, rose-bud mouth. "Hush, Mattie. That was just make believe. Just a story, honey. There aren't any such thing as Blobs."

She switched on his night-light, soothed him until his eyes fluttered shut, then left his room and went down the hall to Kelly's room.

The familiar syrupy sounds of *You Got It (The Right Stuff)* were emanating from her daughter's CD player. How could she stand to listen to the same lyrics hundreds of times? Or maybe, Shay figured, she used the repetitive sounds as background and no longer listened.

She knocked on the door. "Kelly?"

There was a sound that might have been permission to enter, so Shay pushed the door open. Her daughter was sitting on the bed, looking flushed, her baggy sleep shirt pulled haphazardly over her head, as if she had grabbed for it and jumped into it just as Shay was opening the door.

"Kelly? Did you and Matt have a good evening?"

"Um . . . yeah."

"I thought I asked you not to turn on any more horror flicks when Matt is watching."

Outside, the bike drove away with a racheting sound of pistons. Kelly pulled the cotton shirt over her knees, her eyes sliding once to the window. "We were zapping the remote and there wasn't anything good and he wouldn't let me watch MTV. And we had a big fight about it, and finally I let him pick and he picked the movie."

She shrugged as if that settled it. Shay noticed that her daughter had drawn only the sheer curtains, not the heavier, cotton drapes. She walked over to the window and drew them. Enclosed, the room felt safer somehow.

"Honey, Matt is too young for movies like that. He's only six, he has trouble distinguishing between fantasy and reality. He thinks the Blob might come to Walton Hills."

"Oh, Mom, he's such a baby."

"He *is* a baby," Shay insisted. "And babies do not watch *The Blob*. And one more thing. What about that motorcycle? Has that boy been driving past here again tonight?"

"Oh, *Mom*," Kelly cried, leaning over to touch the volume lever on the CD player. The New Kids surged even louder, effectively drowning Shay out.

Shay suppressed a wave of anger. But she didn't want to fight with her daughter tonight—not with Ben sitting downstairs waiting for her to return. Troubled, she walked out of the room, closing the door behind her, and went back downstairs.

"Damn," she said to Ben as she entered the living room. "I think Kelly has some sort of admiring swain who keeps driving past the house on his motorcycle."

Ben frowned. "You don't mean that bike that just went by?"

"Why, yes, I do."

"I recognize those pounding pistons; . . . engine needs a little work, and the timing's off. Oh, brother. I hope that's not the bike I think it is."

Shay sat down, kicking off her high-heeled pumps. "It's Mickey McGee. Kelly told me that much. Do you know him?"

"I had Mickey last year for English, and believe me, he's no one you want cruising past your house making eyes at your daughter."

Troubled by Ben's reaction, Shay said, "I taught him, too, last year when I did that sculpture class. He was the most talented kid in the class. I couldn't believe the work he did, it just burst with life. But it was so angry. One day I had this feeling that he was actually going to talk to me—then the bell rang and he raced out of the classroom and that was the end of it.''

Ben nodded. ''That's Mickey, all right. You always think you're just on the verge of reaching him, only there's no way in hell you're ever going to reach a kid like that. He's got a records folder about four inches thick.''

''Oh?''

''He's got a juvenile record, Shay. What he did, I don't know, since those records are sealed to give the boy a fair chance of making it without prejudgment. He did two years at a juvenile facility near Ortonville and now they've mainstreamed him back into the general school population. Dr. Vigoda handles him.''

Dr. Eleanor Vigoda was the overworked school psychologist.

''Great.''

Ben sighed, rubbing black hair away from his temples. ''The trouble is, he's really a good-looking kid, kind of baby-faced, and that means he gets more leeway. And another thing, he's got this artistic talent, all the case workers have commented on it. He's not exactly your run-of-the-mill juvenile delinquent.''

As they talked, the motorcycle returned, then the motor noise died. Shay jumped up, and hurried to the living room window. Yes, there he was, seated astraddle the bike, a sinister-looking figure in black. The helmet, its visor tilted upward, gave him a futuristic appearance.

''Why do motorcyclists always look like Darth Vader?'' she queried sharply.

''It's part of the mystique.''

''He's watching Kelly's bedroom window.''

Ben nodded. ''I wouldn't be surprised. Teenaged boys are a case of walking hormones.''

Shay recalled the thin curtains drawn in front of her daughter's window, the way Kelly's sleep shirt had appeared to be just thrown on, the guilty flush on the girl's face. And Matt's remark about Kelly "undressing for the window."

"Oh, God, Ben," she said. The breath left her throat. "Oh, God . . . I think my daughter's been—"

She turned abruptly and headed for the stairs.

She hadn't had good feelings about Mickey McGee from the beginning, and now Ben had confirmed her worst fears. If the boy had spent two years in the facility, then whatever he had done was certainly unsavory and possibly violent. Oh, God, was it rape? Arson? Robbery? Drugs? Muggings?

Shay knew she was prejudiced, but even the words *juvenile delinquent* made her shake, especially when it was connected in any way with her child. How could Kelly be attracted to a boy like that? Was her self-esteem that low? Of course, Mickey was handsome, and teenaged girls tended to romanticize boys, never looking beneath the surface.

Anyway, maybe she was getting upset over nothing. Maybe Kelly had simply been waving to him out of the window. Shay had done that as a sixteen-year-old—she'd even climbed out her window once to meet a boy on the corner.

Reaching Kelly's bedroom with its closed door, rock music pulsating from underneath, she paused. She also remembered how she'd hated having her mother invade her room.

But this was not 1968.

This was 1993, where young girls like Kelly could be and were raped, abducted, even murdered. It was on the TV news every night.

With only a second's hesitation, Shay flung open her daughter's door.

In the flash of a second, her eyes took in the startling tableau. The heavy curtains had been reopened. In front of the gauzy sheers, her daughter danced and swayed like a sexy MTV video star, wearing only bikini panties. On the floor lay a discarded heap of cotton—the sleep shirt Kelly had been wearing only minutes ago. Kelly's head was tipped back, her eyes shut, lips parted as if she were in the middle of sex.

"Kelly!" Shay cried.

"Mom," the girl yelped, covering her breasts and reaching down to grab her sleep shirt. She held the shirt in front of her. "Mom . . . what are you doing in my room?"

Shay strode to the window and angrily drew the curtains. She reached for the CD player and switched off the New Kids in midnote. She was trembling.

"He's parked right out in front," she snapped. "Watching every move you make. You're silhouetted in the window like a damn peep show. Why, Kelly? Why?"

Kelly sank onto the bed and crawled between the covers, huddling there like a waif. Big tears began to roll down her cheeks.

"Honey," Shay said, feeling sick. Her anger seeped away to be replaced by a helpless love. "Kelly . . ."

"Mom," Kelly sobbed. "I d-don't know why I did it."

Shay sat down on the edge of the bed, wondering what to say, how to retrieve the situation. Finally she reached out and stroked her daughter's honey-gold, glossy curls that Kelly had recently streaked with even lighter blond. Trying to calm herself, she recalled several articles she'd read about teenaged exhibitionism.

Girls experimented with their new sexuality, not realizing the full implications of what they did.

But the boy Kelly had shown herself to certainly did, Shay knew. A boy with a juvenile record knew the score. On the street, Mickey kick-started the motorcycle to life. The show was over and he was going away—for tonight.

Shay searched for the right words. "I think it's a mistake to show yourself to a boy you don't know, honey, a boy you don't know anything about. It's not safe to—"

"Mo-o-om," Kelly moaned, burrowing under the covers. "Don't make me feel guilty."

"You're such a beautiful girl. You have no idea of the effect you could have on a boy like Mickey. Kelly, this boy has—"

"No! I don't want to hear!"

"But you have to be realistic—"

Her daughter pulled her face out of the covers and screamed, "You don't know *anything!* You don't know him and you don't care! You don't care about Daddy and you don't care about me! *You just don't care!*"

Shay descended the stairs, her daughter's accusation ringing in her ears. *You don't care about Daddy and you don't care about me.* How unfair when just the opposite was true. She cared so much it was painful.

"I'm sorry, I couldn't help but overhear some of that," Ben said, getting up as she approached. They walked into the kitchen. "The acoustics in this house are excellent."

"Oh, God!" Shay breathed, leaning against him for a second, allowing his body to create some comfort. "I'm sorry. I know this isn't relaxing for you."

Ben shook his head. "I had a few go-rounds with my youngest son. In fact, there was one year when he ran away from home twice. But I tell you, it will pass."

"I can't believe it, Ben. I mean, her anger! Kelly really hates me for breaking up the family. She's so unforgiving. I just can't reach her." She sighed.

"She'll work it through. It'll just take some time, some maturing. Remember, teenagers always see things in black and white. There aren't any gray areas for them."

Shay gave a short laugh. "Don't I know it. And now this—I found her undressing in front of the curtain, Ben. Undressing for that boy."

Ben raised one eyebrow. "Well, it's probably not going to happen again. Kelly's basically a fine girl, Shay. She's going to do just fine." He paused, then changed the subject. "How about a sandwich or something? I could use a real Dagwood if you've got the fixings."

"A sandwich!" Shay stared at him, then began to laugh. "God, I didn't even offer you a cup of coffee, did I? I've been so rude—"

"You can redeem yourself with a kiss," he said.

They went into each other's arms, their hips bumping against the refrigerator door. Ben's kisses were deep, slow and sweet, his hands gently caressing her back, careful not to stray too far down. He was a sensuous man, but was holding himself in check for her sake. Shay tried to relax and enjoy the light necking, but her mind kept returning to Mickey McGee.

He was dangerous, she sensed.

FOUR

She dreamed she was running through a white lake of wet plaster, falling, dragging herself up again, struggling to reach some unknown and terrifying destination. But the plaster was beginning to harden. In a few seconds it would solidify around her like a body cast, immobilizing her . . .

The ringing of the telephone penetrated her nightmare.

Shay lay for a few seconds, gasping. Every muscle in her body was sore from the physical effort of fighting the plaster. Who said dreaming wasn't hard work? Finally, on the seventh ring, she turned on her side and fumbled blindly for the phone.

"It's me," said her ex-husband, Randy.

She said nothing.

"Now, wait, Shay, before you hang up on me . . . please . . . can we talk?"

"Randy," she sighed. She blinked open her sleep-sticky eyes. The room was filled with glaring morning light. Sun had found the cracks in her curtain, and fell in a thick, warm bar across her bedcovers.

"Please. Shay, please, just talk to me. Please. I haven't been to bed yet, I've been up all night, thinking, and I just need to talk to you. Please," he repeated.

By the sound of those slurred *pleases* she knew the whole story. Randy had been drinking all night and was now in one of his self-pitying, guilt-making jags. God, she really didn't need this—not after her daughter's accusation last night that she "didn't care."

She sat up in bed. "Randy, it's Saturday morning and I work Saturdays. I've got a busy day ahead. I've asked you not to call me like this."

"Shay . . . little Sheila . . ."

The familiar pet name, derived from a fifties song, brought a choking sensation to her throat. "Don't, Randy."

"Little Sheila . . ."

"I said *don't*!"

There was a moment of silence, then Shay heard Randy clear his throat. She could see him in her mind's eye—a good-looking, forty-year-old man who owned a successful life insurance business and served on the alumni board of his college, and who lived each day from drink to drink. "Baby . . . you know that divorce is just paper. Just a piece of paper."

"A court-ordered piece of paper," she reminded him.

"It's not a divorce in my head. I'm still married to you, Shay. We're still married. I don't know how to go on without you. I don't know what to do."

This was the way he pleaded with Kelly, too, crying and being pathetic. How could a sixteen-year-old girl deal with that? It was extremely difficult even for a grown woman. Shay felt her stomach begin to clench.

If he would only sign himself into a substance abuse center, and stay there. Then at least something positive would come out of their divorce. But he'd tried quitting before. He'd stayed in the clinic only seven hours the first time, two days the second.

"I can't talk now. Good-bye," she said, hanging up.

For a few seconds Shay sat with her fingers clenched around the plastic phone. Damn . . . he could still get to her. Maybe there *were* still pockets of love for him left in her. Maybe she'd only been kidding herself that she didn't love him, and maybe Randy sensed that and tried to take advantage of it.

But Shay knew she couldn't give her life to an alcoholic who still drank.

She got out of bed and moved to the master bathroom, where she stripped off her sleep shirt and stepped into the shower. As the warm water beat down on her face and chest, she arched her shoulders and tried to release some of the tension in them.

Let it go, let it all go. She intended to work most of the day in her studio, and she didn't want any negative energy to interrupt her creative flow.

As she emerged from the shower she heard the motorcycle again—Mickey's bike. Annoyed, she tugged a towel around her dripping body and hurried barefoot through her bedroom to the window that overlooked the front part of the house.

Parting the curtains, she peered out through the crack.

There he was—in jeans and a black Harley Davidson T-shirt, straddling the bike, both feet thrust out for balance, helmet cradled in one arm. The sun caught his thick black hair, mussed by the helmet. He stared at their house, scowling.

She gazed at Mickey, feeling a sudden fascination.

When she was sixteen, boys like him had thronged the halls of Royal Oak Dondero High School—the "hoods." The James Deans and Johnny Depps, angry in their jeans and boots with metal toe covers. Could a boy be born knowing how to act like a hood? she wondered. Or was it a way of distancing himself from a world that had already hurt him too much?

Oh, terrific, she thought. Now she was feeling some sympathy for him.

The boy rolled the cycle forward several feet and Shay realized that he wasn't focusing on Kelly's window this time, but on her own studio. That was strange. Why would he look there? Why did it hold such a fascination?

Mickey's breathing quickened as he rolled the bike, in neutral, the few feet necessary to give him a better view of Shay Wyoming's sculpture studio.

He drew air deep into his gut, and let it out in a soft whistle. The place knocked him out. The studio was about the size of a three-car garage, just the size Mickey himself would have chosen. It had windows on three sides, tall windows that would let in all the light, not like the shitass basement where he had to work at home.

Unlike himself, Shay Wyoming had everything she needed . . . everything! Mickey had poked through the Wyomings' garbage on several occasions, and had found invoices from a place called Sculpture House, in New York, and an outfit called Shearman & Company Ltd., in Devon, England.

She bought plaster in *hundred-pound bags.* Brands called Hydro-Stone and Denscal ST, Ultracal 30 and Densite K-5. He'd been fascinated even by the names. She had no right to own so much.

The anger flooded him again, choking him. A huge

studio like that was meant for huge work. Shay didn't use it right, didn't see the possibilities. She should have made the roof a story higher, leaving room for the serious big stuff.

He could do a big work, something really impressive, much better than the dinky, small, clay sculpture he'd been forced to fuck with in high school art class.

And Mickey already knew exactly what he wanted to sculpt. He wanted to do a huge set of male genitals—thirty feet high. He'd have to climb on a ladder to finish it, climb up a huge cock and balls, almost become part of them.

Yeah, that's exactly what he wanted. To show the world he was king . . . King Mickey.

And he knew he wasn't going to get his desire. Not in a hundred years or a thousand either. He and his mom lived in an old lady's cramped basement, and he only had a few feet of space to work in. His stupid mom spent all their money on her tuition at Marygrove College, where she was studying to be a paralegal.

He hated Shay for her good luck. She'd probably lain on her back to get her studio, he speculated. Panted and moaned. It was what his mother did to get things out of men. Only they usually never gave her anything much besides a hit upside the head.

If his dad had not gone to Jackson Prison, then gotten out, jumped parole, and disappeared, then *he* could have his own studio. He'd also have the money to rebuild the engine on the fifteen-year-old Harley, which desperately needed it. His dad had really fucked his whole life up.

He blamed Danno, his dad, for everything.

Without his even realizing it, Mickey's hand slid down to where the four-inch handle of the butterfly knife created a bulge in his Levi's. A lot of bikers carried butterfly knives; you could buy them at any motorcycle show. But Mickey's knife wasn't bought at any show. His dad once owned it.

Now Mickey had it.

He knew how to twirl the blade, too, in the famous "butterfly wing" pattern that street fighters used to put on a fancy show.

Mickey waited several more minutes to see if Shay was going to turn on the lights in her studio, but when she didn't, he stomped down on the bike's starter. He had to use his entire weight. After five tries, the cycle rumbled to noisy life.

Yeah, he needed the noise so people in cars would know he was coming. He twisted the throttle and felt the machine finally surge under him as he peeled away from the Wyoming house in an explosion of rubber.

Upstairs, the noise roused Kelly from her Saturday morning sleep and she stumbled to the window.

There he was . . . Mickey!

She watched the bike disappear down the street, her heart pounding thickly in her throat. Mickey loved her. There was no doubt in Kelly's mind at all. This was the most exciting and scary thing that ever happened to her.

But why didn't he talk to her, in art class? Why didn't he pay attention to her, or ask her to ride on his bike again, as he'd done that one wonderful time last spring?

She sat by the window for several minutes, wondering with a shivery thrill if he would drive past again, but he didn't return. Finally she got up and walked to her mirror, where she stared at herself in the glass with disgust. She was too tall and gangly. Her boobs were too little, and her perm had begun to grow out, her fine hair turning limp again.

.Had she been a fool, dancing in front of the curtain

last night, showing off for him? Maybe he thought she was easy and cheap. Or, much worse, maybe he hadn't found her pretty enough.

Wanting comfort, she reached for the phone and dialed Heather's number.

"Cripes, Kel, it's the middle of the damn night," Heather groaned in a sleepy, bleary voice. "What time is it, *nine?* I don't have to get up until noon. What'd you wake me up for?"

"He's driving past my house again!" she told her best friend triumphantly.

"He? Who do you mean?"

"Mickey! Mickey McGee!"

There was silence, then a loud, sloppy yawn. "Oh, you mean bad Mickey."

"Mickey, yeah. I think he likes me!"

"Shit," groaned Heather, dropping the phone receiver with a clatter, then picking it up again. "There's lots of stuff I heard about that guy; . . . you don't want to know it."

"What don't I want to know?"

"God," Heather moaned. "I don't want to get up; . . . I hate mornings. My mom says I'm a night person, you know? I never do *anything* in the morning; I can't even talk."

"*What* don't I want to know, Heather?" Kelly prompted impatiently.

"Oh, stuff. I hear stuff."

"*What stuff, Heather?*"

"Oh, like, I heard his Dad was in jail."

"Jail?"

"Like, Jackson Prison, you know? I mean, we're talking heavy-duty prison. We drove past Jackson Prison one time when we visited my mom's uncle who lives in Jackson, and it's this huge, ugly place and it's just gigantic, Kelly. The prisoners are all dangerous and they have these signs about not picking up hitch-hikers . . . and there's more stuff I heard, too." Heather added accusingly, "You like him, don't you?"

"What?"

"You like Mickey. As in L-I-K-E," Heather spelled it out.

"I don't," Kelly immediately lied. She'd been going to confide in Heather, but now was stopped by the superior tone in her friend's voice, the teasing just below the surface. She knew you were supposed to like only certain boys—the cool ones, the good-looking jocks, the popular guys. If you liked a boy who wasn't popular then you became unpopular, too, because the type of boy you liked determined who you were.

"You do, you do, you do. Hey, don't be crazy, girl, he's not *really* a babe, know what I mean? I heard some more weird things, too."

Kelly closed her eyes. "What weird things, Heather? Tell me what weird things."

"Why're you so anxious?"

"Because I want to know, that's why. Because he's driving past my house and my mom's mad about it. My mom's on my case about it, okay?"

"Oh. Hey, look, all I know is what Michele Greenstein told me. . . ."

"What did Michele say?"

Heather let her voice string out. "Wellllll, you don't want to hear it," she teased. "It's too baaaad."

"Heather Marie Schoenfeld! Dammit!"

"Okay. Michele says he shot a kid once. Shot him with a gun. It was a so-called accident."

At the words, Kelly's head jerked back. "You are such a liar, Heather."

"Is Michele Greenstein lying? Is Amy Hart lying? 'Cause she said it too. And Mike Spacek. Everyone knows . . . everyone but you, silly Kelly. Are you coming to Lakeside today?'' Heather added, her tone of voice so offhand that it was just barely an invitation.

Kelly hesitated. The kids usually went over to Lakeside Mall on Saturdays and hung out in the central concourse, or cruised the stores, then ended up at the movies. But now she didn't know if she wanted to. She felt different today . . . and a little mad at Heather, too. Heather was acting less and less like a best friend.

But she didn't have any other best friend, and there wasn't anything to do around the house today, not with her mom mad at her, and she didn't want to go to the mall alone.

''Sure I'm going,'' she said quickly.

''What're you wearing?''

''Oh, those new leggings and that top I bought—the lavender one with the tie.''

''The one you got at Casual Corner last week?''

''Yeah . . .''

They discussed clothes for a few minutes longer, smoothing over the rift that had suddenly appeared between them. Then Kelly's bedroom door swung open, and Matt appeared. Her little brother was dressed in his favorite Teenage Mutant Ninja Turtles T-shirt. ''I wanta use the phone,'' he complained. ''You *always* hog it, Kelly.''

''Mattie!'' She put her hand over the receiver in annoyance. ''Matt, it's rude to just barge in here. And you've got your shirt on inside out. Can't you dress yourself right?''

He drew himself up. ''I dress good.''

''You dress wrong side out, turkey.''

''I wanta call *Michael*, we wanta play GI Joes today. An' watch *Karate Kid*.''

''Oh, all right, all right,'' Kelly agreed reluctantly. ''Now, go on—go! I've got to talk to Heather for a minute more. Then I'll hang up.''

Obediently Matt retreated. She and Heather arranged the time and place to meet at the mall and finally began to talk about Michele Greenstein's new boyfriend, a senior at Birmingham's Seaholm High School.

But even as she gossiped, the tight feeling in the center of Kelly's chest did not go away. It was because of Mickey, she knew. Mickey, who drove past her house dozens of times in one week. Who was in love with her.

And she loved him back.

That was her secret. But she'd die before she'd ever tell Heather now. Because Mickey was one of those boys you didn't tell anyone about liking—not if you wanted to be popular.

FIVE

Mom . . . I can't do this!" Matt came padding into the kitchen, his small arms in a tangle as he tried to pull off his Ninja T-shirt while he was still walking. "This is the wrong side."

Shay helped her son to put his shirt on right side out. He looked so adorable that she gave him an extra big hug. At least one of her children was still uncomplicated, his problems easily solved.

Matt went on, "An' Kelly's on the *phone* again an' I want to call Michael. Want to see if he can bring over his GI Joes."

"Did you tell her to get off?"

"I did, sure, but she's talking an' talking," Matt complained. " 'Bout boys."

"She's just being a sixteen-year-old girl, honey. They live on the phone."

"They don't live in houses?" Matt cocked his head at her, giggling at his own joke.

Shay got out the cereal for breakfast, her mind on the problem of Kelly and last night. Until the divorce, Kelly had been a sweet girl who did her homework with only minimal complaints, kept her room reasonably neat, and was called by one teacher "a wonderful student to have in my classroom." Now anger and teenaged hormones were turning her daughter into a stranger.

Couldn't Kelly see that Mickey was potentially a big mistake? Who knew what thoughts coursed through the head of a teenaged boy watching a girl do a strip-tease in a window? Mickey was at the age when all boys could think about was sex. Was he a rapist? Was that why he'd been put in a juvenile facility? God, it was possible.

Shay sank down at the table, her temples beginning to pound with a tension headache. She poured herself a bowl of Kellogg's Mueslix and sat staring at it. She was going to have to clear this up with her daughter, no matter how much effort it took.

Tact, she thought. *I'll be tactful. But firm.*

Twenty minutes later Matt had gulped down his breakfast and was on the phone with his friend Michael, arranging for the other boy to come over to play. Shay walked through the laundry area to the breezeway that had been cut through to her studio.

God, she loved this room. To her it was beautiful. This morning, the eastern side was flooded with sunlight the color of Coor's beer. In the pale beams floated tiny particles of plaster dust.

From the small closet where she kept her work clothes, Shay took down her favorite pair of loose, farmer-type jeans with suspender straps. They were so streaked with the residue of her work that they were almost an art object in themselves.

She pulled off her clean, stone-washed jeans and,

hanging them on the hook where her work pants had hung, put on the grubby ones. Her clean shirt was traded for an old, holey T-shirt that said DETROIT GRAND PRIX, 1988. Shay slipped on an ancient pair of Reeboks crusted with plaster residue and spilled wax. Sometimes she tied her hair up in a scarf, but today she wouldn't be working with anything dusty.

Still thinking about Kelly, and Mickey McGee, she walked over to the south wall, where she'd installed a stereo system, and slid in several CDs, pushing random play. The rippling, new-age music of Enya's *Watermark* album filled the room.

Beginning to feel better, Shay moved about the studio, getting out her tools for the day's work—needle-nosed pliers, a roll of chickenwire mesh, a hacksaw, and a length of plumbing pipe. She planned to make an armature, a wire-mesh shape that would be used to form a central support for the Entech project. She'd already done several "sketches" in wax, and now it was time to translate these to a larger work.

Shay cut a section of chicken wire and rolled it into a wide tube, examining the result critically from several angles. Had she cut the piece big enough?

"Mom—Mom—" Kelly burst into the studio. "I need the car keys, and my allowance. Please, please?"

Shay looked up and felt her heart drop. Kelly looked stunning. She was made up like a cover model, violet eye shadow feathered over her eyes, her blush professionally blended. She wore tight lavender pants and a baggy violet-colored shirt, decorated with platinum studs, that hugged her hips. It was trendy mall fashion—all the girls wore it—but today Shay's eyes saw the way the skin-tight pants clung to her daughter's curves like paint, leaving nothing to the imagination.

"Don't you think those pants are a little snug?"

A mistake. She saw the expression on her daughter's face shut tight.

"They're not pants; they're leggings." Kelly fidgeted a little, plainly in a hurry to get moving. "Everyone wears these, Mom . . . *everyone*. Please, can I have the car? We're all going over to Lakeside. There's that new Tom Cruise movie."

"Kelly." Shay put down the pliers and approached her daughter. "We really need to talk, honey."

"I haven't done anything," Kelly said defiantly. "I have to *go*, Mom. Heather said she'd meet me in front of Olga's at twelve."

"Then you have two hours." Shay gazed into her daughter's blue eyes, so like her own, but almost immediately Kelly glanced away, breaking the eye contact. "Kelly, I know it's rough, turning sixteen, starting to feel like a woman."

"*Mom . . .*"

"Well, I can remember being your age. I didn't like my body very much, I remember that. I thought my breasts were too large. The boys looked at me and I cringed—"

"Mom . . . *please* . . ."

"—because I wanted the boys to look at me, and yet I didn't. I wanted their attention and yet I was afraid of it, too."

Kelly shrugged, a scowl marring her lovely face. "God!" she exclaimed defiantly. "Do we have to have this mother-daughter thing right now? I mean, if you're going to tell me about the birds and the bees, I already know."

"*Do* you know? Apparently you don't—not if you were upstairs revealing your body to a boy on the street," Shay snapped.

"I didn't do anything bad! I didn't even touch

him—he was far away, Mom; I was in the house and he was outdoors."

"Baby, it's not so much that you—"

"I'm not a *baby!*"

"All right." Shay reached into the depths of herself for patience. "Kelly, you showed off to a stranger. Mickey has spent time in a juvenile facility—he's broken the law. We have no idea what's going on in his mind, what kind of twisted or crazy or illegal ideas he might have—"

"Mickey isn't crazy! Mom, he is not crazy!" Angry tears filled the girl's eyes. "You think *I'm* crazy, don't you, for doing that? You think I'm some kind of whore or something. Don't you?"

"*Kelly,*" Shay gasped, shocked. On the stereo, Enya was singing the intricate rhythms of "Orinoco Flow." It was an eerie, calm counterpoint to the emotional heat of this discussion.

Kelly cried, "Well? Isn't that what you're saying? Just because I took off my shirt. Well, big deal, Mom. Remember those women on that college campus—in Wisconsin or wherever? We saw it on the news that time. Everybody thought they were great. They took off their shirts to protest and nobody called *them* whores."

"I never called you a whore—"

"Well, I'm not one. I haven't done anything. I'm a *virgin*. How do you like that? A stupid, stupid virgin!"

Somehow Kelly had twisted everything Shay had said into an accusation. Shay drew several deep breaths, trying to calm herself and get this discussion back on track.

"Honey, this isn't about being a virgin; it's about—"

"Oh, what do you care anyway," Kelly shouted. "*You* have a boyfriend, don't you? How much do you know about Ben Lyte?"

Shay winced. "That has nothing to do with this. Ben is a respected teacher and a published author, not an unstable seventeen-year-old."

"You're going to marry him, aren't you? Oh, yes, I know you are—I see the way you two get all lovey dovey, and I read that card he sent you. You're going to betray Daddy, and I consider that much, much worse than anything I've done!"

"Kelly. Oh, Kelly."

The adult hate written on her daughter's face struck Shay like a blow in the stomach. That was the real source of her daughter's fury—Shay's going on with her life. The rift between them was even deeper than she'd thought.

"Well? That's what I think it is! Betrayal!" Kelly had started to cry.

Shay was shaking. "In the first place, if you must know, Ben and I haven't even discussed marriage. We aren't sleeping together and I don't know if we're going to. I'm not ready for marriage with anyone. In fact—"

"*Oh, who cares!*" Kelly shouted, turning on her heel and running out of the studio. Car keys jingled as Kelly snatched them off their hook in the laundry room, then slammed the back door. Within seconds, her white Mercury Cougar roared to life. There was the squeal of tires in the driveway.

Shay listened to her daughter peel away, making the familiar car sound like a drag racer. A wave of anger and despair washed over her. She knew she hadn't said any of the right things—not one. But what *were* the right things to say?

Being a mother was so much harder than she'd ever imagined. Why didn't anyone ever tell her that the very act of helping and caring could push your child further away?

* * *

Kelly drove blindly, narrowly missing a small black-and-white spotted dog that had wandered out into the street. Frantically she braked the Cougar, its tires screeching on cement.

An older woman watering some flowers with a garden hose glanced sharply in her direction, and seemed about to stride up to the car and give Kelly a piece of her mind.

Kelly accelerated again, but more cautiously, nausea clenching in the center of her stomach. God, she couldn't believe the things she'd said to her mother . . . But she knew she'd meant them. Especially the part about betraying her father. That was exactly the truth, and her mother refused to look at it.

Her cheeks were wet with tears. Kelly fumbled inside her purse until she found a tissue to wipe them. Life was a fucked-up mess, wasn't it? Who said the teenaged years were supposed to be happy?

At the intersection of Meadowlark and Portsmouth, Kelly was glancing to her right when she heard the pop of a motor and saw Mickey's Harley Davidson pull out of a driveway.

Her heart did a flip-flop. Of course, she'd known Mickey lived on Portsmouth—in an apartment in some old lady's basement, some of the kids said. But Kelly hadn't known which house. Now she saw that it was a gray colonial with fussy tulip beds in front.

She peeked at him in her rearview mirror as he rode up behind her. His helmet's smoke-tinted plastic face shield hid his features and made him look dark and dangerous. The bike, with its heavy, shiny chrome, looked dangerous, too.

She put her foot on the gas and drove to Stony Circle, the entrance to the subdivision. He followed her. Kelly's throat thickened as she felt his eyes behind the mask, boring into her.

She turned right onto Rochester Road and headed south toward M-59, an expressway that would take her to Lakeside Mall in Sterling Heights.

Twenty feet behind her, Mickey followed.

Kelly pushed open the entrance door to the mall, dodging a fat girl lugging a big Hudson's bag. The usual Saturday shopping frenzy had begun. A two-year-old boy wearing a Detroit Pistons T-shirt had chosen the central concourse floor to stage a kicking, screaming tantrum. The smell of pita sandwiches drifted from Olga's, the restaurant where she was supposed to meet Heather.

Kelly peered ahead. A couple stood inside the ropes at the restaurant entrance, waiting for a table. But she didn't see Heather, Amy or Michele.

She frowned, disappointment filling her. Mickey had followed her for about two miles, then he'd lost her in the heavy weekend traffic on M-59.

Maybe, she thought despondently, he hadn't really been following her at all, but simply had been heading in the same direction she was—just pure accident, nothing more.

Twenty minutes passed. Her nerves on edge, she paced the sector of the mall where she was supposed to meet the others. Why weren't they here yet? Maybe they'd decided to meet each other somewhere else and leave her waiting. Glumly, Kelly realized this was a real possibility. Heather had changed. It was as if she thought Kelly was immature and she wanted someone different now in a friend. Someone sophisticated, not a girl who daydreamed about a rebel on a motorcycle.

A boy coming out of the nearby movie theater stared in Kelly's direction, his eyes riveted on the tight leggings she wore. He was a Rick Moranis–type nerd. Kelly flushed and turned the other way. To have a nerd stare at you was almost an insult because it reduced you to his level.

"Hey . . . hey, Kel! That guy's giving you the eye! Wants to pick you up. What a *baaaabe*," someone called, and there was a chorus of derisive giggles.

Kelly jerked around to see Heather, Amy and Michele. They sauntered toward her, all three of them blond, pretty, their hair expertly streaked, painted, crimped, moussed and curled. They wore either spandex or leggings, and Heather's fashionable, baggy shirt was decorated with set-in lace and fabric painting.

"Hi," Kelly said, going up to them.

"Where were you?" Heather demanded.

"Where was *I*?" Kelly stared at her best friend, bewildered. "I was right here. You said Olga's, right?"

Heather giggled. "No, dummy, I said *Casual Corner*, don't you remember? I said meet us in front of Casual Corner."

"No, you said Olga's, Heather. It was Olga's." Kelly spoke quickly, hating herself for the pleading tone in her voice. They'd always met at Olga's. Now suddenly she had it all wrong? No way. But there was nothing she could do.

She fell into step beside them, feeling like an awkward fourth. "I didn't get my allowance yet," she told Heather. "My Mom and I had a big fight."

"So what else is new?"

A housewife pushing a double stroller containing twins was approaching them and there was not enough room for four abreast. Kelly was forced to drop back, again feeling like the outcast.

"Let's go to the video arcade," Amy suggested. "I saw a real babe there last week. I think he's from Utica High."

"Oh, *Utica*," scoffed Heather.

"Well," said Amy, "they can't all go to Walton."

"If you've had a Walton man, you've had the best," Heather intoned, and Amy and Michele repeated it after her two or three times, bending over in fits of laughter.

They started their usual cruising stroll, hitting Ups and Downs, then Winkelman's, ruffling their hands along the racks. Prom dresses were still on sale, although well picked over. This year all the dresses were black, strapless and short, very sophisticated. Heather began boasting about being invited to the Walton prom by Grant Vanderpluge, and it turned out that Amy and Michele also had gotten dates.

Only Kelly had no date to talk about.

Miserably she pretended to examine a dress with a black net flounce on which cheap black sequins had been glued. Did she even belong with these girls any more? They knew all about sex; . . . she didn't. She was unpopular. A loser.

All she had was Mickey—an imaginary boyfriend who held her and kissed her in her mind before she fell asleep at night, holding her tenderly. A boy she had played a game with from her window.

Edging away from the other girls, Kelly moved toward a rack at the front of the store, near the section of carpeting that opened onto the mall concourse. Suddenly she felt an odd sensation in the center of her shoulders.

She turned, and sucked in a startled breath.

His black hair shone glossily in the artificial mall lighting, the sideburns shaved close. He wore his usual black Harley T-shirt, and his jeans were so arrogantly tight that they showed his thigh muscles, even his crotch bulge.

Mickey's eyes widened, staring hotly into hers.

Kelly gasped, caught in his electricity, frightened by his intensity.

Then she realized that his lips were moving, mouthing something to her over the thirty feet of space that separated them. Wild elation filled her. He was finally noticing her! He was talking to her!

But she couldn't grasp what he was saying. Something about "you." She didn't get the rest.

She must have had a questioning look on her face because he repeated the words again. This time Kelly lip-read the meaning.

She reeled backward, shocked to the core. She could only stare at him, the handsome "babe" who looked like Jordan of the New Kids, and who'd just said the most extraordinary thing.

He'd said, *"I'm going to get you."*

What did that mean?

SIX

Shay worked most of the afternoon, taking frequent breaks to check on Matt and Michael, who were "GI Joe-ing" in the family room. Several times she looked up, thinking she heard Mickey's motorcycle, but the motor sounded much smoother and she decided the bike belonged to someone else.

At four o'clock, her friend Noah Ransom dropped over to return a book Shay had lent him.

"Hey, darlin'. You look as if someone dropped the entire North American continent on your head," he remarked cheerfully.

She sighed ruefully. "That bad?"

"If not worse. Come to Dr. Noah, hon', tell him your troubles. If he can't solve 'em, he'll make you feel so well adjusted you won't care. And he'll take out his hourly fee in chocolate chip cookies, which makes him a real bargain."

She uttered her first genuine laugh of the day and

looked at her old friend fondly. Noah Ransom was sixty, divorced, and looked like a Santa's elf wearing stone-washed jeans and high-topped Air Jordans. His fine, soft white hair flowed down to his shoulders, and his eyebrows were quirky tufts of white. He was the kindest man she'd ever known, a former alcoholic who'd given her support during her divorce and kept her going through the worst, blackest days.

"God, Noah, I need you today," she sighed, putting the book back on a shelf. "Do you want some lemonade or something? And I do happen to have some chocolate chip cookies in the freezer."

"A lady of consummate good taste."

She made lemonade and thawed cookies, took some to the boys, and carried the rest on a plate back into her studio. "Let's go out on the deck," she suggested to Noah. "I need a fix of fresh air, I think."

She'd designed the beautiful little redwood deck herself, hiring a builder to carry out her plan. A birch tree grew up through a hole in the center of the deck, which looked out on a small vista of woods and an abstract sculpture she'd done as a student at the U. of M., back when abstract art had been practically a requirement.

"So why the long face?" Noah inquired, selecting two cookies.

She laughed. "You mean you can tell?"

"Does Madonna wear sequins? Does Roseanne eat pizza? Honey, you never were any good at hiding your moods from old Noah."

She didn't want to violate Kelly's privacy by explaining the details of last night's conflict with her daughter. "Oh, it's just the usual teenage troubles, I guess. Kelly's growing up too fast. The hormones are running strong. And she's angry about the divorce."

Noah nodded. "She'll get through it. She's got good

stuff in her. She's yours, isn't she? She'll come out a winner.''

They settled down for one of their long, comfortable talks, gossiping about other artists, who was getting a one-man show, who'd sold to what museum, who was going through a mid-life crisis.

Their talk drifted to a robbery of some consignment art at a Grosse Pointe gallery. "Which is a very strange sign of the times," Noah opined. "The good news is, your usual scumbag ghetto types think art is stealable, hence, valuable. I mean, look at all the potential publicity the artist could get—thieves after *his* work.''

"I suppose . . ." Shay said doubtfully.

"Anyway," Noah added, "I'm not going to mess around any more. I've got $250,000 worth of stuff in my shop and I can't afford to lose it. I went out and bought a gun last week—got the permit and everything's nice and legal.''

"Not a gun, Noah. You didn't buy a gun." Shay stared at her friend, fighting a shiver that started in the pit of her stomach and rippled out to her extremities. When she was fifteen her parents, owners of a party store in Royal Oak, had been murdered by a gunman robbing the store. Since then, she'd had a deep fear and loathing of guns, and an equal dislike of the police, who had responded too late to the call.

"I surely did, sweet one. I hated to, but I finally did it. This is 1993 and people are running scared these days.''

Uneasy, Shay stared into her lemonade glass. "I just don't like to think about you opening yourself up to that kind of violence, Noah. Guns draw violence, you know.''

They debated the topic a while longer, while Shay grew more and more edgy. The mildly sunny, late-April afternoon was already beginning to cool down, and Kelly had been at the mall since morning. She hadn't heard Mickey's motorcycle all afternoon, a fact that Shay found faintly ominous. It was almost as if the boy knew that Kelly wasn't home, therefore wasn't bothering to cruise the house.

As Noah began telling her about his latest project, the sun gradually changed its angle. Suddenly Shay's gaze was caught by a gleam of light from some object resting on the base of the metal sculpture in the backyard.

Curious, Shay got up and walked across the deck, descending the three steps to the grass. She walked over to the sculpture.

Placed on the granite base was an unfired clay figure. Shaped like a naked human form, it carried in its hands its own huge set of penis and testicles. The penis was grotesquely erect, and its grotesquerie extended to the *glans* itself, on which had been depicted a screaming, reptilian mouth complete with teeth.

''Ugh!'' She called to Noah. ''I've just found the strangest thing.'' She picked up the clay statuette and carried it back to the deck. ''Noah? Isn't this incredible? It's even got teeth.''

Noah took the statuette and turned it in his hands, the wrinkles around his eyes crinkling with interest. ''Almost primitive,'' he remarked. ''Angry. With a whole sci-fi feel to it . . . like some weird being who came up from the bowels of the planet to avenge itself on human beings.''

''*Very* funny,'' Shay said. The more she looked at the small, ugly statue, the more alarmed she felt. It was Mickey's work, of course. She recognized that raw, compressed, violent feel that he managed to impart to his materials. Why had he left it here? Was it his strange idea of a joke? Or was there some implied threat in the statuette?

Noah turned the statue over and examined its base. "I don't see any initials here."

"It doesn't matter. I know who made this."

"Oh?" Noah chuckled, hefting the statuette. "Well, whoever it is, I'd say they're pretty ballsy—pardon the bad joke."

"It's a boy named Mickey McGee," Shay explained. "I taught him last year when I did that Artists in the Schools thing. He's been driving past the house on his Harley Davidson, ogling Kelly."

"Mmmm. The plot thickens."

"Don't laugh, Noah! I don't think this is funny. He's obsessed with her; he's driven past this house about a hundred times in the past month." Shay frowned. "And now he's left this. It means he's been walking around here, prowling. . . . I don't like it."

"You can always complain to the police."

"And say what? That he uses the public street? That he left a silly clay statue? No. I've already had a talk with Kelly about him, and—well, certain behaviors of hers are going to change, and then maybe Mickey will leave us alone."

"Well, I wouldn't worry too much," Noah commented. "It's just a prank. You just happened to hit a kid with exceptional talent and a very vivid imagination. Whew!" Noah glanced one more time at the realistically portrayed penis-mouth, then set the sculpture down. "I'm glad I don't have to look at anything like *that* when I go to the john in the morning."

A few minutes later, Noah glanced at his watch and said he had a date and had to leave.

"Oh—" said Shay. "That reminds me. Ben and I have been invited to a book party on May 5—it's a big literary deal. A lot of local authors are going to be there, and I was going to have Kelly sit for me. But now I don't think it's a very good idea. Could you . . . would you . . . ? I'll have microwave popcorn," she offered. "Three or four packages of it. And more cookies."

Noah, she knew, was addicted to popcorn, as well as cookies.

"Would I come over and sit around on your couch gorging on microwave popcorn and chocolate chippies while watching five straight hours of movies and playing with Matt's Legos? You bet I would."

Shay laughed. "Oh, Noah—I don't know what I'd do without you. You're a wonderful friend."

Kelly arrived home just after Noah had left.

"Hi," she said, strolling into the house as if nothing had happened. She was carrying a small sack from All That Glitters, a store that sold inexpensive costume jewelry. "I got some neat earrings, Mom. They dangle all the way to the shoulders. I got them for you."

"For *me*?"

Shay was both surprised and touched. She opened the sack, which was crumpled from being carried around all afternoon, and drew out a pair of inexpensive earrings made of tiny wands of pink plastic that formed a twisted spiral.

"Kelly. Oh, honey." Feeling absurdly pleased, Shay held up the earrings. When worn they would dangle and sway in twisty, flirty patterns. "How did you know I would like these? Oh, you have such great taste, Kel. These are really little pieces of art. A wonderful find."

Kelly flushed with pleasure. "Try them on, Mom."

Shay unscrewed the black onyx studs she usually wore, and screwed on the dangly pink ones. Kelly watched her with an eager expression.

"Oh, these are so pretty, I'm going to wear them to the party next week," she raved, thrilled at Kelly's reaction. Maybe her daughter wanted to be close again. She hated to spoil it by telling Kelly about the sculpture

Mickey had left. But she had to know, Shay believed.

"Honey," she began cautiously. "We had a little gift left on the back lawn; . . . I want you to see it."

"A gift? What gift?"

"Well, it wasn't exactly a nice gift."

Kelly bounced after her, following her through the breezeway to the studio, her body language for once that of an eager, typical teenager.

God, Shay thought, feeling the knot tense in the center of her stomach again. *Let me be tactful in telling her this time; let me not goof it up, please. I love her so much and I'm tired of having her angry all the time. I want my sweet girl back.*

She had left the sculpture on one of her work tables, and now she walked over to the table, retrieved the piece, and silently put it into Kelly's hands.

The girl glanced down at the tiny shape of the man carrying his own genitals. Her eyes took in the details of erect phallus and screaming, teeth-filled mouth. "Ugh! Oh, gross! This is really, really *gross!*" She thrust it away from her.

"It was left outside on the lawn."

"Who left it there?"

Shay drew a breath. "Well . . ."

"You mean . . . you don't think . . . *Mom* . . ." Kelly drew back. "You don't think *Mickey* did this?"

"You're in art class with him, honey, and you've seen his work before. Do *you* think this is Mickey's work?"

The softness had left Kelly's face and her eyes blazed. "He *never* does stuff like that in school. He's not dirty. But you think he *is,* don't you, Mom? You really have it in for Mickey, don't you? Just because he's got a Harley Davidson motorcycle and doesn't dress or act like everyone else, you think he's *soooo* bad."

"Honey, it's not like that—"

"It *is* like that! Some kid leaves a dirty clay thing at our house and you automatically think Mickey did it. Well, Mickey is not like you think, Mom. *You're* the one with the dirty mind, not him."

Kelly thumped the statuette back down on the table top, chipping its base. "This is a very, very stupid statue," she snapped. "I hope you like your earrings. Now I'm going up to my room."

In her room, Kelly threw herself on her bed, her mood so rotten that she didn't even turn on the CD player. She lay on her back, gazing unseeingly at a picture of Joe and Jordan. She had scratched her hand on the clay statuette when she'd slammed it down, and a small bead of red had formed on her right thumb. Absently, she sucked at it.

I'm going to get you, Mickey had promised, and Kelly had interpreted this as meaning he would get her to be his girlfriend. Now he'd left that gross statue. What did it mean?

She stirred restlessly. She had watched his every move in art class all year and she knew the secret things he made when fussy, picky Mrs. Goldman wasn't looking. Once he had made a screaming head that actually gave Kelly the shivers. Mickey's work was very adult, Kelly believed. He was a real artist.

She was a sculptor's daughter, after all, and she'd grown up with art. Kelly knew that real artists went right to the edge. Sometimes they even created things that were a little bit . . . well, gross.

But the big question was, why had she denied it was Mickey to her mother?

Kelly squeezed her eyes shut, already knowing the answer. It was because of the way Mickey kept riding past the house, the way her mom was prejudging him because of that.

Kelly wasn't going to let anyone spoil her love for Mickey, even her own mother. She'd fight for him. And then what would happen? Maybe she'd get so angry she'd threaten to move out. And maybe Shay would tell her, okay, I don't want a daughter that loves some weird, rebellious guy. . . .

Exhausted, Kelly took her thumb out of her mouth, inspecting the cut to see if the bleeding had stopped. It had. She'd also chipped a nail, she noticed.

She sat up and reached for her bedside table, where she kept her collection of nail polishes, and selected the correct shade of deep pink. Carefully she repaired the nail, the small act making her feel better.

When she was finished, she took the little paintbrush and wrote in pink on her dressing table mirror:

K.W. M.M.

That night, Shay prepared for bed, her thoughts uneasy as she put away the earrings Kelly had given her. Before he left, Noah had reassured her that Mickey was probably harmless, and that his sexually oriented sculptures represented the humor of a gifted, possibly eccentric person.

She'd made a face. "Oh, great, just great! My daughter's got a teenaged eccentric after her!"

"Hey, I did a few wild things in my time, too," Noah recalled. "I was nearly kicked out of school for painting a girl's face on the school wall—actually a lot more than her face. I drew her naked, as it happens."

"Oh, Noah . . . but that was a long time ago. Things were different then. And what I really hate is that Kelly has romanticized him. To her he's a boy with a crush, a dashing figure, a romance fantasy. I hate it, Noah! I just don't want her mooning after a boy like that."

"Well, in another week, he'll probably cool down and focus his attentions on some other girl."

Now, undressing, Shay realized that she didn't like the word that Noah had used, "eccentric." "Eccentric" couldn't describe a seventeen-year-old boy who had been in a juvenile facility. What crimes had the boy committed?

Mickey hadn't gotten tired of Kelly in a week. On the contrary, he'd been haunting their house for months now, and his attentions showed no sign of abating.

She set her clock radio, her pulse suddenly beating in her throat. Did he look in their windows? Spy on them? Was Mickey one of those strange "peeping Toms," standing in their yard watching them while he masturbated? The thought chilled and disgusted her.

Damn him, she thought. She decided to talk to Ben about it, see if she could get him to find out what Mickey had really done.

SEVEN

The following Monday, Shay and Ben met for drinks after work at Sassy Sally's, a restaurant located in a shopping mall near Walton High School.

Ben was in an ebullient mood. His agent had just negotiated another book contract for him—this one with St. Martin's Press, for an advance of $135,000. It would be his first hardcover novel, and he'd been promised that this book, *Terror in Black,* had bestseller potential.

"Oh, God, that's so incredible," Shay exclaimed, delighted for him. "Congratulations. . . . I can't believe I'm sitting here with a bestselling author." She had changed out of her work "grubbies" and wore acid-washed jeans and a silk T-shirt she had machine-embroidered with a design of entwined flowers and leaves.

"Don't say it yet. I don't want to jinx myself."

"You're going to be as big as Elmore Leonard,"

Shay predicted. Elmore "Dutch" Leonard would be at the party they planned to attend.

"If only," Ben said, the expression on his face showing just how intensely he wanted this.

"Assuming you do hit it big, what do you plan to do about school? Do you plan to keep on teaching?"

"I can't think about that yet. When the time comes I'll know."

As their appetizer tray arrived, Shay brought up the topic of Mickey, the disturbing sculpture she'd found, and her suspicion that Mickey prowled their property, spying on them. "Could you possibly ferret out his case record and let me know what he did? I mean, why he was in the juvenile facility?"

Ben looked uncomfortable. "I'd do anything for you, Shay, but I don't know if I can do that."

"Why not?"

"It's not that I don't want to. But there's a slight problem in that the case records are closed and I don't have access to them. Dr. Vigoda handles all that, and she's a stickler for legality. The school doesn't want any law suits."

"Can't you get access? This is so frustrating!" she exclaimed.

Ben hesitated. "What would you do with the information if you had it, Shay?"

"Why, I—I'd—"

"You'd stop your daughter from seeing him, right? Well, you can do that anyway. You already know that he isn't the kind of boy you want her to be involved with, so I suggest you just act on that knowledge. Tell her not to talk to him any more."

Shay stared into the depths of her wine spritzer. She felt a sudden upsurge of irritation. "I'd just feel a lot better if I *knew* what he'd done. Then at least I'd know how concerned I should be."

"You mean you want something to scare Kelly with?"

"Well, yes."

Ben frowned. "But if you told her, it'd be all over school in half an hour, Shay, and the boy's reputation, such as it is, would be even further compromised. This particular school rule is one that might have some basis."

Shay sat still for a moment. The happy hour sounds of the restaurant clattered around them. "I know that Mickey has rights. But this is my *daughter*. I just have this uneasy feeling about Mickey McGee and it won't go away. Please."

"Well, I'll talk to Dr. Vigoda," Ben promised.

That day at school, it seemed to Kelly that Mickey was always staring at her. Her locker was in the third-floor "jungle," and twice, as she left the rows of lockers, she spotted him leaning against the wall, watching her.

"Well, it looks as if *you've* got a boyfriend," Heather remarked as they walked to the cafeteria, dodging the throngs of laughing, pushing kids.

"Me?"

"Yeah, you." Heather giggled. "Hey, there he is now. Staring at you again. You're *sooooo* popular, Kelly."

Hurt at the jeering tone, Kelly turned to gaze at her friend. "I . . . I can't help it if he's always looking," she protested.

"You *like* him," Heather accused.

Kelly shook her head, knowing that this was what Heather's rejection was all about—her liking a boy who wasn't sanctioned by the clique of girls.

"I do not," she lied.

"You do so. Ugh, Kelly, he might look cute but he's

a real dork. . . . He's bad news, know what I mean? I heard things. Michele told me stuff . . .''

"Like what stuff?" Kelly asked.

"Oh, like last week he got in a big argument with this girl, Kimberley Pizer, and he pulled a knife on her."

Shocked, Kelly stared at Heather. Kimberley Pizer was in their art class, a stocky girl who talked all the time and was Mrs. Goldman's pet, the one she praised sky-high to the others. She hadn't been to class in a week.

"He didn't," she said numbly.

"Are you deaf? I said a knife. She went home crying and she didn't come back to school, either. She's afraid he's going to cut her titties off. He told her he was going to put her on his shit list."

They had reached the stairway and were forced to go single file behind a group of giggling tenth-grade girls.

"I don't believe you," Kelly whispered. "You're a stupid liar, Heather."

"Then ask Kimberley," Heather threw over her shoulder. "*You're* the stupid one, Kelly. You're immature, that's your trouble. Nobody wants to sit with you any more because you're so immature. You think because he likes you that you're special or something. . . . Well, you're not. You don't even wear the right clothes."

Stung, Kelly gazed down at her Chic jeans and flats embedded with rhinestones.

The knot of girls had pushed ahead of them, laughing uproariously. Heather darted ahead and disappeared into their midst, leaving Kelly flat.

Kelly walked down the hall toward the cafeteria, tears brimming to her eyes. She felt incredibly betrayed. Why had Heather told her such a terrible thing?

To hurt her. To be bitchy. Because she was having sex and Kelly wasn't. Kelly felt sure Mickey had never done such a horrible thing as pull a knife on a girl.

The crowded cafeteria reeked of pizza, chili, french fries and hamburgers, all on that day's menu. Kelly want through the salad line, then found a table with some eleventh-grade girls she knew slightly, uncomfortably aware of Heather, Amy, and Michele seated at a table near the window. Heather was laughing, throwing her head back and shaking her long hair in imitation of Paula Abdul.

Kelly forced herself to chew her taco salad, feeling as if the whole world knew of her rejection.

Then she stiffened. Mickey was sauntering into the room, joining the sandwich line. Several boys edged out of his way. Mickey swaggered ahead of them in line, acting as if he did not notice that a space had been created around him.

Kelly wondered if he was carrying a knife right now.

What kind of a knife was it? What did it look like?

She hated Heather for telling her that . . . for making her think about it. She felt her heartbeat speed up until it pounded chokingly in her throat. Gasping, she put her fork down, unable to finish her salad.

The fourth-hour art class was working on a collage project. At the long tables, students bent over sheets of paper on which they were gluing scraps of paper, cloth, buttons, paint samples, and hole-punched strips torn from computer paper. Laughter and chatter rose into the air—much of it talk about the upcoming prom festivities, which were to take place in ten days.

"Now, class, can we forget about the prom for just one short hour?" Janice Goldman, the teacher, spoke with a perpetual whine. She was about thirty, thin and arty-looking, and wore six bangles on her wrist, and a tie-dyed skirt and blouse outfit that reached below mid-calf. "Now, don't forget—do your gluing *neatly*. Otherwise I'll take it off your grade. Which some of you desperately need if you are going to pass this course. You know who you are. A few of you think you can ace this course just by showing up and being insolent, but I assure you, that is not true."

Kelly bent over her project, a vase of flowers she was making with cloth and antique buttons. Last week she'd been excited, but now who cared about a stupid flower picture? A dumb collage? Across the table was a vacant seat—Kimberley's. The empty chair seemed to mock her.

Since her conversation with Heather on the stairs, a huge, horrid, tight knot had formed in her throat and she couldn't seem to swallow it down.

Out of the corner of her eye, she could just see Mickey, seated in his usual place at the back of the room. He'd sauntered in late, and spent a long time scrubbing his hands at the wall sink. He was not working on a collage but instead was fussing with a piece of clay he'd taken from a storage bin. She felt a sensation of heat on her skin and realized he was staring at her. She glanced away, a hot flush stinging her cheeks.

"*Mr.* McGee," the art teacher snapped. "I see that, as usual, you've decided not to join us in this project."

Mickey mumbled something inaudible.

"Can't you talk, Mr. McGee? Or do you just choose not to?"

Mickey stared at the teacher. "I talk fine, bitch."

Mrs. Goldman made an unconscious physical movement of revulsion. Her voice trembled a little as she said, "Mr. McGee, don't you *dare* talk to me like that or you'll be sitting in the principal's office."

Mickey's glance at her was scornfully disbelieving.

The woman pressed her lips together and moved down the row, bending over the shoulder of a boy seated several spaces away from Mickey. Kelly watched her with a feeling of sad knowledge. Mrs. Goldman was afraid of Mickey. And she wasn't the only one. Heather was afraid of him; . . . it was why she was mad at Kelly, because she didn't understand Mickey and he made her feel uneasy. And that's why the kids made a big space around him in the cafeteria line.

Mickey was different—and people were uneasy if someone was too different.

She was afraid of him, too.

Well, wasn't she?

Wasn't that why he seemed so exciting sometimes that she could hardly catch her breath?

She anchored another button, at the center of a cloth daisy, and pushed down hard on it, waiting for the viscous fluid to dry. Her hands were sticky and tacky, and she decided to get up to wash them.

Standing at the sink, waiting for the water to run cold, her eyes fastened on an object resting on the shelf over the sink. It was the earthen color of hardened, unfired clay.

Herself, naked.

Kelly stood frozen, her eyes riveted on the clay mannequin which had been shaped by clever, diabolical hands into a recognizable figure of herself. Her breasts were sculpted so that her nipples protruded like tiny projectiles, her pubic hair carefully picked out with a sharp point. It was an evil, sarcastic nakedness, Kelly saw, an exaggeration of her body features.

But the nakedness wasn't the worst. No, that wasn't the worst at all. A knife cut had been run through the statuette's stomach. Protruding through the edges of the cut were odd-looking structures which . . .

Kelly gasped, taking an uncertain step backward.

. . . which represented her own intestines, spilling out of the wound.

Someone was standing behind her.

Kelly jumped, uttering a tiny scream.

"Hey," said Jim Beeson, a computer nerd who wore horn-rimmed glasses and had been accepted at the University of Chicago. "Hey, are you done? Because I need to use this sink."

Kelly realized that in about three seconds he'd look up and see the statue, too—and he'd say something, and then all the kids would look at it and laugh. Mrs. Goldman would be furious, and Kelly would be totally humiliated.

"In a minute," she snapped, making a grab for the towel paper holder. She yanked out two sheets at once and reached upward, grasping the statuette in the paper. It was still fairly fresh, she noticed, its texture soft.

"What's that?" Jim wanted to know.

"Oh, just something I left up here—it's just some crap." She wrapped two more layers of towel around the clay mannequin, then put it on the counter top and leaned all her weight on it, squashing it. Gingerly, she dropped the mess in the large garbage can that stood next to the sink.

"Well, take your time," the boy complained.

Mrs. Goldman was glancing their way, her teacher antennae alerted. Kelly walked back to her table and sat down again. She realized that her hands were still sticky—she hadn't washed them.

Her own intestines.

She stared blindly at her half-finished collage. For a brief second she remembered her old daydreams of Mickey, his mouth softly pressing on hers. Then waves of hot and cold rolled over her skin and she thought she was going to be sick. She opened her mouth and tried to suck in air, but none came.

Fearfully she glanced up. Mickey was watching her again. His lips were turned up in a smirk of laughter.

Shaking, Kelly grabbed up her purse and pushed away from the table.

"Kelly?" Mrs. Goldman called.

Ignoring her, Kelly burst into the hallway, turned right, and broke into a half-run, her Reeboks squeaking on the marble flooring. The empty hall smelled of art materials, floor polish, and something foul-smelling and sulphurous that emanated from the Chem Lab.

Kelly felt a sob building in her chest. She pushed it back, hurrying upstairs to the locker jungle, where there was a pay telephone.

The phone apparatus was grimy, battered from thousands of teenaged phone calls, and smeared with pen and pencil marks and wads of ancient gum. Also stuck to it was a pressure-sensitive name tag, on which someone had written "Jim P. Sucks Dick."

Kelly phoned her father's insurance office, and was left on hold for several minutes, listening to elevator music. She tapped her foot impatiently, facing into the phone to hide her tears from anyone entering the locker area.

Finally her father came on the line.

"Daddy," she cried. "Oh, Daddy, this boy in art class—this boy . . ." She stopped, unable to complete the sentence, and started to cry.

Her father cleared his throat. She heard the clink of ice in a glass. "So, you're having a bad day, huh? Well, I don't want my baby to have any bad days."

"Daddy," she said imploringly.

"What is it, baby? Spit it out."

"Are you all right, Daddy?"

" 'Course *I'm* all right; what're you talking about?''
Randy Wyoming's voice became belligerent. "What
are you crying for, baby? Did your mother get on your
case about something? She been mistreating you?''

"Daddy . . . no! I told you . . . it's this boy . . .''

"Boy? My little girl is having boy trouble?''

"I—''

"Well, you tell that young man he doesn't know
how lucky he is to have a girl like you . . . best little girl
in the world. . . . Just like your mother. She's the best
girl in the world, too, except that she's got this idea in
her head, this unforgiveness . . .''

Her father never let go of that idea. Kelly heard high
heels clacking on the marble flooring, echoing against
metal locker surfaces, and knew it was probably Gloria
Adamson, the assistant principal, who patrolled the
halls regularly. She huddled closer to the phone and
lowered her voice. "Daddy . . . I have to tell you something; . . . it's *so* gross . . .''

Randy interrupted, slurring his words slightly,
"Did you talk to her, honey?''

"Who?''

"I said did you talk to *her.*'' He meant her mother,
Kelly realized with a shock. "Did you explain? I just
want to see her, honey—maybe take her up to Mack-
inac Island for a weekend. She's never been there . . .
we've never been there. Would you like to go to Mack-
inac, honey? We'll stay at the Grand Hotel. Have a
grand time. I promise I won't talk about anything emotional, tell her that. Kelly, tell her that I just want to
enjoy her company as a friend, nothing more, I swear
it, baby . . .''

Kelly closed her eyes, trying not to think the word
drunk.

"Kelly Wyoming?'' the assistant principal said,

coming up behind her. "It is Kelly Wyoming, isn't it? What are you doing out of class? Are you all right?"

Kelly looked up wildly. Gloria Adamson was an attractive woman of forty, wearing a beige suit and baby-blue blouse with a little bow tie. Her experienced, searching glance at Kelly took in the tear streaks on her face, the agitated hunch of her shoulders.

"I—I'm all right," Kelly muttered.

"Are you sure? You seem a little upset."

"I . . . I didn't feel well. I felt sick. I was calling my dad. I—it's that time of the month."

Mrs. Adamson nodded. "Is he coming to get you?"

"I . . . no . . ."

"Would you like to come down to my office and lie down?"

"No . . . no. I'd better go back to class," Kelly gasped, and fled.

She walked blindly through the halls, avoiding the main entrance by the office, and left by a side door.

"Kelly? Where are you going?" Coming out of the library was Ben Lyte.

"I'm—getting some art supplies," she lied, hurrying past before her mom's dumb boyfriend could question her further or ask for a hall pass. She felt rocked to the very core by what had happened. She loved Mickey; . . . he loved her. Now this.

She couldn't understand it. What had she ever done to him?

She hurried down the sidewalk, cut across the school lawn, now covered with the cottony heads of thousands of dandelions that had gone to seed. She half-ran toward the street. There was a shopping center across Walton where she and Heather sometimes hung out.

Glancing back at the school, she could see the long

rows of classroom windows, the art room distinctive because of the plants that Mrs. Goldman hung in the windows on macrame ropes. Someone was staring out of the window; . . . she couldn't see who. Her heart leaped. Was it him? Was he watching her?

Walton Village Mall was small but attractively decorated, with a real brick floor coated with many layers of varnish to give it a "village" atmosphere. A cider mill occupied the center of the mall, along with a small puppet theater. The place smelled of the cookie concession cart parked in the concourse, an odor that Kelly usually loved. Today the smell made her feel nauseous.

She darted down the side corridor that led to the ladies' room, and within seconds was crouched over a commode, throwing up.

She finished, shaking, and went to the sink where she rinsed out her mouth, and carefully reapplied her makeup. She didn't feel much better.

Leaving the rest room, she found a phone booth near the security office. A tattered phone book hung by a chain from the phone stand, and after a second she went over to it and looked up the name Pizer. The Pizers, she knew, owned a convenience store in Waterford Township, and Kimberley worked there part-time.

She found two Pizers, one in Walton Hills only a few blocks away. That had to be the number. Shakily, she dialed, doing it quick, before she could change her mind.

"Hello?" Kimberley's familiar voice answered on the second ring. A TV set blared loudly in the background, playing one of the afternoon soaps.

"Kimberley? It's me . . . Kelly."

"Kelly *Wyoming*?" Obviously Kimberley was not expecting a call from her. "Hi," Kimberley added.

Kelly hesitated, her heart pounding. How could she just come right out and say, did Mickey McGee pull a knife on you? She moistened her lips, wishing she hadn't called.

"I wanted to ask, when are you coming back to school. Mrs. Goldman wants to know."

"Oh," Kimberley said after a long pause. "Well, my mom wrote me an excuse and all. . . . I've got mono."

"Mono?"

"Yeah . . . it makes you tired and all, and I have to stay out and get lots of rest. I'm not going back to school at all this year; I'm finished until next fall."

But there was a tremble in Kimberley's voice. Kelly knew she was lying. There was another reason for her being out of school and it wasn't being sick. Her own heart jumped, and she felt another wave of the nausea.

"Mickey asked me to call," she whispered.

There was a startled silence, filled by the sharp sound of Kimberley's indrawn breath. Then Kelly heard a loud clatter as the phone was slammed down in her ear.

She stood holding the phone, hearing the buzz of the dial tone.

It's not anything, she told herself fiercely. Maybe Kimberley just had a crush on Mickey, that's all, a crush like her own, and maybe she thought Kelly was talking about that, just teasing her.

Or course Mickey *hadn't* pulled a knife on Kimberley; it was just Heather's mean lie, Heather's bitchiness. Kelly's best friendship with Heather was over and now all Heather wanted to do was hurt her.

She had succeeded very well. Kelly uttered a choked sob. Her chest hurt from all the love for Mickey that was clogged inside her, trapped there with no place to go. And she could not stop thinking about that awful statuette with the intestines. *Why had he made that statue? Did he hate her that much?*

A young security guard with a mustache exited from the security room, glancing curiously in Kelly's direction. Unescorted kids were not permitted in the mall before three-thirty, Kelly knew. She turned and started down the corridor, toward the main part of the mall.

Then she saw Mickey, leaning against the wall at the end of the service corridor.

Kelly's steps faltered, and she almost turned and ran back toward the ladies' room. Then she stopped. She couldn't show her hurt to him. He'd know then how much he'd gotten to her, and would become worse than ever. He might even—she couldn't imagine what other horrid things Mickey might think to do.

Desperately she brushed past him, fleeing into the mall.

"Hey," he called in a thick, excited voice.

Kelly quickened her steps, wishing she'd never left school. But his legs were longer and he kept up with her. Already a woman carrying a Willow Tree bag was staring at them.

"Hey, pretty girl. Hey, bitch girl. I want you to watch me."

She remembered the statuette. God, did he want her to watch him make another nude statue of her? No way! She *was* immature, she guessed. She wasn't on Mickey's level; she didn't know what to do, how to treat him, what to say or think.

"Hey, Kelly. . . . You're going to watch me," he taunted. The sound of his laughter rang out.

"No!"

The beloved voice so sneering. "I can make you, Kelly. I can make you watch me. I can make you watch everything. Everything I do."

"No . . . please . . . just go away."

"I'll never go away, bitch Kelly, because I saw you, didn't I? I saw what you look like. *I saw what you've got.*"

Kelly had reached the row of exit doors that opened onto the mall parking lot. She ran through. She hated him. He had seen her naked . . . and it was her own fault.

The shame was so overwhelming that she almost threw up again, right there on the pavement.

"*Kelleeee,*" he taunted, pushing after her. "Do you want to ride on my bike?"

"Oh, shit!" she sobbed, running toward her mother's car. "Get away from me, Mickey. . . . *Get away, get away!*"

EIGHT

Mickey stalked away, deeply furious at being spurned. He clenched his fists, squeezing until his fingernails drew blood, anger stabbing him like a welding torch. The bitch! The ugly bitch! Girls did *not* reject Mickey McGee. It just did not happen. *No way, José*.

He was handsome and he knew it. In fact he knew damn well he looked like Jordan and he loved the resemblance. He could have any girl at Walton High School if he chose. He was the who rejected *them*.

He thought about Kimberley Pizer, another Class A bitch, high on his shit list. He'd gone to the art room early one morning last week—his usual habit, the only time he could grab any privacy for his real projects, the ones important to him.

But he hadn't been there five minutes when Kimberley sidled in, early too.

"What're you doing?" she demanded inquisitively.

Mickey had looked up from his work, not bothering

to hide the statuette with the erect, oversized genitals. He hated Kimberley. She was Mrs. Goldman's favorite pet, who possessed far less talent than his own. Mickey despised girls like that, self-righteous cunts who thought their own pee was nectar.

"See?" he said, lifting up the piece of moist clay.

Kim jumped back. "That's *dirty*."

Mickey grinned. "No shit, Sherlock."

"But . . . it's dirty. You shouldn't be doing that here; I'm going to tell Mrs.—"

She didn't get the rest of it out of her mouth.

"You aren't telling no one," Mickey grated, pulling the butterfly knife out of his pocket.

"Please . . ." Her eyes fastened on the twirly, snicking blade as he flashed it in his palm, opening and shutting the blade into the handle. He gave her the full show, just the way Danno, his father, used to do it for him.

"You like this, Kim?"

Her mouth worked. "I . . . please . . ."

"You want to watch me use this? You'd love watching me. I could show you so much, Kim. Maybe I'll use it on you. Maybe I'll cut those big titties off."

"Oh . . . don't. Oh, don't."

Her shock and horror were thrilling. Mickey felt a spurt of joy that began deep in his genitals. "Then don't you tell, Kimberley baby. Don't you say one word or that's just what I'll do. I'll slice your titties right open, how would you like that? . . ."

"Hey, man." The voice behind him startled him, bringing him back to reality with a thump.

Mickey turned. The weasely-looking security man hurried down the utility hallway, approaching Mickey warily. He was only 5'9" and skinny, with a little brush mustache and zits on his chin. But Mickey could see he was getting pumped up, ready to kick ass.

"You causing any trouble here?"

"Me? No way."

"Well, you better cause it somewheres else, hear? We don't allow students in the mall before three-thirty. We enforce that."

"Get fucked," Mickey growled, turning on his heel.

"Hey—"

But Mickey ignored him, stalking through the concourse, pushing past two suburban ladies dressed in sweats. He imagined the asshole security guy cowering away from the butterfly knife, his fingers gushing red as he tried to defend himself. Yeah, he'd slice a few fingers first before getting to the best part.

Then he added Kelly Wyoming to the picture.

She would watch it all, getting more sexually hot by the second, as she stared, transfixed at his skill and daring.

In the parking lot he found the Harley and pulled on his helmet, lowering the black visor over his face. Immediately all sounds became muffled, and the world looked different, giving him the sensation of being hidden and dangerous.

He jockeyed the machine out of the parking space and gave it heavy accelerator. He roared out onto Walton Road, whipping into traffic.

On I-75 he ran into a swarm of bugs, tiny, hard bodies that hit Mickey's face visor and stung the sides of his neck. If he weren't wearing the shield, they would be splatting into his face and teeth.

The expressway was full of trucks, and Mickey played with them, riding the wind draft they created. He opened his lips wide, breathing deep and hard. He could feel the hate in him as he went over his shit list, naming all the names, all the ones who hurt him.

Yeah, he had quite a few people on that list, which he'd scratched on the wall by his bed at home, so he would never forget. Mrs. Goldman was on that list. And bitch Kimberley, as well as several of his former probation officers and counselors.

One of them was the biggest name of all—the one person he hated more than any other.

A semi sucked him along and he almost yelled with the crazy joy of it, the sensation of surfing with the truck—riding it! He was Mickey McGee and when he was on the bike he was king, and every other vehicle existed only for him.

He was supposed to meet DeJuan Mullins at a park in Royal Oak, so he exited at Rochester Road and tooled south, disappointed because surface roads didn't give him that deep thrill of the expressway.

DeJuan was waiting for him, his Yamaha 250 pulled up onto the grass. DeJuan was a tall black boy of eighteen with wide lips and unevenly spaced teeth that seemed to stick out straight from his pink gums. He had a fascination with flame and boasted he had set more than a hundred garages and abandoned houses on fire. He had been Mickey's roommate in the juvie home. Now he worked in an Uncle Ed's Oil Change shop, doing ten-minute oil changes.

"Hey, man," DeJuan greeted him.

"Yo," Mickey said. He parked his Harley next to the Yamaha, proud of the way that the big 1200-cc Harley Davidson dwarfed the other machine. He swung his leg over, pulling up the visor of the helmet but not taking it off.

"What's happenin', man?" DeJuan wanted to know. He eyed Mickey cautiously. Better than anyone, he knew that Mickey carried grudges and made reprisals. He himself had helped Mickey with one such reprisal, a kid at the home who had the foolishness to call Mickey a "white nigger." They had stabbed the guy eight times and forced his bleeding head into a toilet bowl.

"You got the address?"

"Hey, man . . . I ast my brother; he say he can't give out no addresses like that. He say he catch hell if he give out addresses, man. I ast him."

DeJuan's brother, DeWayne, had just landed a cushy job as a parole officer for Oakland County.

"I want the address."

DeJuan took a nervous step backward. "I tol' you . . . I ain't got it."

"I want it, DeJuan, and you said you could get it."

"I can't, man . . . I tol' you. . . . Cost you more than you give me to get that address. I got bills, you know. I get nothin' but a shitty four-fifty an hour. I got to pay my rent out of that. An' I owe seventy-five a month on my—"

Mickey's smile showed his teeth. "I paid you thirty bucks, DeJuan, and now you're not gonna tell me? I call that holding back. Don't you?" He reached into his pocket and pulled out the butterfly knife, clicking it open and shut. "Don't you call that holding back?"

DeJuan's brown skin turned muddy. "I . . . man . . ."

"You have it on you, don't you? You have the fucking address on you and you're holding me up for more money and I don't like it, DeJuan. *I want that address, I want it now, you fuck head, and if you don't give it to me you're going to eat blade.*"

"Man . . . man . . ." DeJuan's thick, pink tongue went out to lick his lips, and he sighed. "Okay, dude. Okay, see, he live right aroun' here, Mickey; . . . he drive a truck. He use another name, see? He live out near Ann Arbor, man. DeWayne does got the address and all. He give it to me. I swear it's the right one. It's out in fuckin' Ypsilanti.''

Mickey took the crumpled, dirty sheet of notebook paper that DeJuan handed him. Hatred and fear boiled up in him as he stared down at DeJuan's wavering, illiterate penmanship. It read Stony Stream Court.

The piece of paper seemed to turn black and white in front of his eyes, glowing until it filled his entire vision. Mickey felt a sick, swooping feeling in the center of his gut.

Things were going to happen . . . big things, out of control things. Yeah, as inevitable as breathing. But he could not let them happen too fast.

''Hey, man. You okay?''

''Shut up!'' Mickey snapped, shoving the precious sheet of paper in his pocket.

''Mickey?'' began DeJuan, his voice full of relief now that the transaction had been accomplished.

Mickey swung his leg over the Harley and kicked it to life. He spun across the grass, kicking dirt in De-Juan's direction. Yeah, he had the address. But it was not time to use it yet.

There was something else he had to do first.

Something he would enjoy doing.

And it had to do with that little shit, Kelly Wyoming, and her snobby mother, Shay. Shay the sculptor.

It was after eleven. Matt was in bed, Kelly in her room, and Shay was exhausted from another long day spent in her studio, redoing the armature, with which she had not been satisfied.

Now she sat at her portable typewriter, hunt-and-pecking a letter to her sister, Marianne, in Wilton, Connecticut, to whom she owed a thank you letter for a birthday sweater sent more than a month ago. Drifts of fragrant night air wafted through the opened patio door, full of the promise of summer. There was a powerfully seductive flavor to it, making her feel restless.

I am making progress with the Entech sculpture, she typed. *I can't believe the amount they are paying me. I feel like an imposter sometimes but I love the feeling. We can really use the money.*

She wrote several more paragraphs, describing the project for her sister, a psychologist with a large practice in wealthy Wilton, who did some painting of her own.

A motorcycle whined far away. Shay sighed, thinking how damn sick and tired she was of Mickey McGee. His persistence was abnormal, she felt, almost mindless. Like some sort of insect that kept trying to crawl up a wall.

She'd even started imagining him peering through the window walls as she worked in her studio. For the first time, she wished she had not been insistent on so many windows. They made her feel vulnerable, isolated from the rest of the house. She should move a phone extension out there, she realized.

In fact, maybe she should take the kids and fly to Connecticut to visit Marianne for a week or so, she thought. Pick her sister's brain about Kelly, and the problem with Mickey, too.

"Mom!" Matt burst into the room, wearing much-washed Garfield pajamas, now too small for him. As usual, the top was on inside out. "Mom . . . I don't like that mo'cycle. I can't sleep."

Shay glanced at her son, whose cheeks were pink with rambunctious nighttime energy. His eyes weren't droopy, but wide awake and alert. If he'd truly been trying to sleep, Shay was Hillary Rodham Clinton.

"Matt! It's after eleven o'clock! Have you been jumping up and down on your bed again?"

"Not much," he admitted.

"Not much?" She suppressed a laugh. "Well, young man, how about if we both go upstairs and I'll tuck you in, all right? And let's get those jammies right side out."

Matt obediently lifted his arms so she could make the switch. "Don't *wanna* sleep yet," her son protested as they climbed the stairs, Shay's arm around him. The thump of Kelly's stereo echoed down the hall.

"Baby, baby, you've turned into such a night owl. You're getting to be a regular night person."

"What's a night person?"

"Well, it's—"

CRASH!

The collision, coming from the direction of Shay's studio, shattered through the house like a bomb, accompanied by the smash of broken glass.

"Mom, Mom, Mom!" Matt began to scream, as they heard the roar of a powerful motorcycle engine, revving away from the house.

Shay's arm had tightened around her son in automatic, protective reflex. Her heart was slamming inside her throat, and she thought she would be sick from the waves of rage that surged through her.

Mickey. The little bastard.

Who else could it be?

He must have ridden his bike right through the doorwall of her studio.

In her bedroom, Kelly had been playing New Kids' *Hangin' Tough* album, letting the sounds blow into her brain and clean out all the worry and unpleasantness. She didn't even have to listen to the lyrics any more— she just needed the sound. It made her feel better. More in control.

She lay on her stomach with her arms draped over

the edge of the mattress, her hands trailing on the floor. With her fingertips she toyed with the beige plush nap of the carpeting.

Since she'd thrown up in the mall she hadn't been able to eat anything. And although she'd rinsed out her mouth dozens of times since arriving home, she imagined she could still faintly taste the acid of her own vomit.

What was she going to do about Mickey McGee? How could she look at him again after what he'd said and done? God! She didn't want to go back to school— no way did she want to do that. She dreaded walking into the art room again, seeing him there, his eyes fastened on her with that burning stare she'd once found so exciting.

Maybe Mickey was . . . mixed-up.

Her mind fastened on the idea. Yes, that was exactly it. He was mixed-up and confused and needed someone like her to help him get through this terrible period in his life. Her heartbeat quickened as the fantasy took root. She could rescue him. Help him to go to Dr. Vigoda at school for counseling.

She would go with him, let him express his feelings, talk to her as much as he wanted. And she would give him all of her love, because everyone said that if a girl loved a boy enough, he could be anything.

A sound interrupted her reverie. She listened. Wasn't that the sound of Mickey's bike in the street?

Then he wasn't mad!

He still cared!

Or he wouldn't be driving past!

She lifted her arms, stretching them out into the air as if to reach for Mickey's hug. It was at that precise moment she heard the crash.

She jumped off the bed and ran toward the window,

just in time to see the motorcycle roar away from the house.

Mickey.

Kelly raced out of her bedroom and took the stairs two at a time. She stopped short at the sight of her mother and Matt who were seated at the bottom of the stairs, Shay's arms tightly wrapped around the weeping six-year-old.

"Mom! Mom! What happened?"

"I think your friend came to call," Shay said tightly. "Drove his damn bike into the studio. Here, take Matt, will you? I'm going to go look."

Kelly felt a wave of anxiety at the thought of being left alone on the stairs. "But Mom—"

"Take him," Shay ordered, and the tone of her voice indicated there would be no back talk.

As Shay left for the breezeway that led to her studio, Kelly took her brother in her arms, feeling the fragility of his small body through the light cotton pajamas. He immediately cuddled up against her, his sobs easing. "It's okay, Matt," she murmured.

Holding him, Kelly felt a rush of sick guilt. Lots of times Matt played in the studio, playing with the clay that Shay kept in a Tupperware container for him. What if he'd been there when Mickey drove his bike through the glass? What if Mickey had hit him?

"He wecked our house," Matt mumbled, reverting to baby talk. "He wecked our stuff."

"It's okay, Mattie. It's okay. He won't come back. I won't let him."

Shay returned, her jaw thrust out dangerously. "A whole window wall gone," she announced. "Glass everywhere, and two of my plaster pieces broken. It'll take a week to clean it all up."

"I want to see," Kelly said.

"No! I don't want you going out there, or Matt either. I don't want either of you getting cut. I'm calling the police." Shay walked across the foyer to the small table where they kept a telephone. Her finger stabbed at the key pad. "Yes . . . yes . . . I'd like to report a—someone drove a motorcycle into my house. That's right . . . please send the police out here."

She gave the address while Kelly held on to Matt, feeling a wave of icy fear. A feeling that something truly awful was about to happen to all of them. . . .

Her mother hung up and returned to the stairs. "Kelly, are you all right? You look so white, you look as if you're about to faint."

"I'm . . . all right."

"You are not all right. Put your head down," Shay commanded. She took Matt back into her own arms, and pushed Kelly's head down to her knees. "There . . . let the blood go to your head. Is that better?"

"I don't know . . . oh, mom . . ."

"What is it, baby?"

For once Kelly didn't mind being called baby. She snuggled closer to Shay, remembering the way Shay had glared at a sixty-five-year-old man who tried to put the make on her one time in Kroger's. Her mom had always protected her and she still would.

"It's—I ran to the window," she gasped. "I saw him. On his bike. He was riding it across the grass. He was, I don't know. He loved it. He loved doing it."

Shay's hand tightened on Kelly's arm. In the distance they could hear a police siren. "Kelly, that damned boy vandalized our house and scared the hell out of all of us. We are going to have to talk about this—really talk."

Kelly lifted her head. "*I* didn't do anything," she said stiffly.

"Oh, honey, of course not. But, Kel . . . somehow his attention has been drawn to us."

Kelly scrambled to her feet. All her close feelings vanished, to be replaced by a hurtful, painful anger. "*I've* drawn it! That's what you mean, isn't it? You think this is my fault!"

"Kelly—"

She wept, "Well, I didn't do anything! Not on purpose! I didn't do anything! You just want to blame me, that's all! You just want to blame me!"

NINE

"So how much damage do you estimate was done here?"

The police officer, whose name tag announced that he was Officer Roger Handing, walked amid the debris of Shay's studio, his feet crunching on broken glass.

"There's the glass door—it was an Anderson window, and that's not cheap. I'd estimate fifteen hundred for that. And the plaster casts over there, I was going to sell them for a thousand each. So with two of them, that's two thousand. And I might have to replace some of the floor tiles—I don't think skid marks will come out. Maybe another two hundred. Maybe thirty-five hundred total. That's a wild guess. I have to call my insurance company. I'm not a professional estimator."

"I know, I know, this is just for my report. I have to put down something for the value."

Handing had the same expressionless, closed-off kind of face that Shay had observed in many policemen. Was it an occupational hazard? The heavy police belt and holster he wore seemed large and menacing. The polished butt of the gun gleamed in the overhead lights of her studio.

Shay removed her eyes from it. Now that the crisis had passed, she felt exhausted. Even her anger at Mickey had dulled, at least for now. It all was beginning to seem almost unreal. Only the evidence of the littered glass shards, the tire marks on her floor, proved he had ridden a motorcycle into her studio.

"So you say your daughter knows this guy?" Handing asked, for the second time.

"Yes, he's in her class at school."

"And he's been harassing you?"

"Yes." She repeated the story of Mickey's rides past their house, telling Handing about the clay statue Mickey had left. The only thing she left out was Kelly's strip act. She couldn't bring herself to bare her daughter's innocent, teenaged vulnerability in front of this man.

"You say you taught him in a class last year?"

"For a week, yes. Through the Michigan Council for the Arts."

"He ever give you the eye, Mrs. Wyoming?"

Shay shook her head. "I believe he has a crush on my daughter. It's her he's interested in, not me. I'm thirty-seven years old, Detective Handing. I'm not a Mrs. Robinson, if that's what you're implying."

He gazed at her with serious brown eyes that saw only crime and mayhem. "Well, usually we can't do much with vandalism cases, but since your daughter did identify him, and since he has a juvenile record, I'll bring him in for questioning. If you sign the complaint, that is. I don't do nothing without a signed complaint."

Shay hesitated. Sign the complaint! That would

make everything formal and official, wouldn't it? But if she refused to press charges, wouldn't that just signal Mickey that she *was* afraid, and provoke him to further excesses? She wanted to avoid that. If he thought she would not contact the police, he'd feel free to do just as he pleased.

"Yes, I'll sign the complaint," she said.

After the police car left, Shay went upstairs to check on Matt, who'd gone to bed. She found him curled into a small, fetal ball, hands tucked between his thighs. The lamp in his room blazed. She brushed back her son's fair hair and adjusted the covers, deciding to leave his lights on for once. He'd had enough for one night, and she didn't want him to wake up screaming.

She walked down the hallway to Kelly's room and knocked on her daughter's door.

"Kelly? Kel? Are you in bed yet?"

"I'm okay," came her daughter's muffled reply.

"Can I come in?"

Grudgingly, her daughter said yes. Shay pushed open the door and went in. In the dim glow cast by a frog night-light left over from when she had been ten, Kelly sat on her bed. Her arms were wrapped around her knees, her nightshirt reflecting white. Shadows picked out the flawless lines of her face, giving her face a pure beauty.

"You are a very lovely girl," Shay remarked, sitting down on the mattress.

"I'm *not*. I caused this." Kelly turned toward the wall, refusing to look in Shay's direction. It was obvious she'd been crying.

Shay felt a squeeze of such powerful mother-love for her child that it almost rocked her backward. She tested herself for the right words, terrified she would say the wrong thing again. God, she needed lessons in tact and the wisdom of Buddha to deal with the prickliness and vulnerability of a teenaged personality.

"Kelly, this isn't your fault. I never meant to imply that it was. You haven't done anything wrong."

"I *did* do something wrong. You know I did! I . . . in front of the window," Kelly whispered miserably. "And he—Mickey made—" She stopped, cutting off whatever else she had been going to say.

"But you didn't mean any harm, honey. We all feel spring in the air and sometimes it makes us do crazy things. Anyway"—Shay threw caution to the winds—"I don't care what you did. I don't care, dammit! I love you, and you come first. He had no right to scare us like that."

"But I . . . I . . . I let him look . . ." Kelly repeated. "I acted like a cheap trick. Now he's punishing us. Now he's mad."

"Cheap—oh, Kelly, not you, you are not cheap! You could never be cheap." Shay slid her arms around her daughter's lissom young shoulders. She hugged her tightly, swaying back and forth with her, just as she'd done when Kelly was seven.

"Mom," Kelly muttered, but she did not pull away, seeming to draw sustenance from Shay's touch.

"If anyone ever hurt you . . . God . . . I think I'd kill him," Shay exclaimed. "I would. I'd kill him, and I wouldn't think twice about it. Because you're my little girl; . . . you'll always be my little girl. . . ."

She rocked Kelly in her arms, murmuring to her until she felt her daughter's ragged breathing grow slower and more even. Finally, she pulled the covers up over the girl. "Try to get some sleep, honey. I'm going to call Aunt Marianne and we'll go and visit her for a couple of days, would you like that? I'd been thinking about it anyway and now is a good time to go."

''What about school?''

''I'll handle school. You just go to sleep, Kel. Everything will look better in the morning.''

Shay went downstairs, still keyed up. Her nerves felt raw. Marianne's house had been robbed several times, and she had told Shay that it felt like being raped—a personal violation. Now Shay knew what her sister had meant. That crash had done more than just destroy some glass; it had destroyed their peace of mind. Mickey had frightened both of her children and Shay felt a hard, cold anger at him for doing that.

She went around and double-checked all the locks.

The phone rang and she snatched it up, thinking it might be the police. Instead she heard the tinny, jangled sound of heavy metal rock music. Her anonymous caller.

''Mickey?'' she snapped into the receiver. ''Is that you?''

Only the jerky, dissonant bass beat and clanging guitars could be heard along the phone wire. Was he hanging onto the receiver, laughing at her? Laughing at all the damage he had done?

''Mickey? Mickey McGee? Dammit!'' she shouted. ''Don't you ever drive past my house again! Don't you ever! You and that damn bike! Do you hear me?''

The dial tone buzzed in her ear.

Shay lowered the receiver, shaking. She stood breathing deeply, getting her emotions under control. She knew that her real fear went a lot deeper than just some vandalism. Didn't it really go back twenty-five years into her past, when her parents had been shot in that party store robbery? Since then she'd despised violence and feared its randomness. No one was really safe from it. See how it had found them again, just when they had all begun to feel safe and protected, just when they'd tried to begin a new life again.

But Mickey was only seventeen years old, Shay reminded herself. Only a year older than Kelly. She forced air out of her lungs in slow, deep, even breaths. He was infatuated with Kelly, and surely that was understandable. It *was* spring, and those warm breezes did have an aphrodisiacal effect. Even adults felt them, so why not Mickey?

The phone rang and reluctantly she reached for it. If it was the anonymous caller again—

But it was Ben. He was a night owl, often working at his computer until 3:00 A.M., and she'd given him permission to phone her at a late hour.

"How about taking a little break?" he asked cheerfully. "Why don't we go out to Denny's and grab a cup of coffee and a strawberry sundae? I've been on a roll— I've written fifteen pages in three hours, can you believe it? I'm hot tonight. Cranking out the gore and mayhem."

"Ben," she said, her voice cracking tiredly.

"Whoa. You sound terrible, Shay. Is everything all right?"

"Oh, yes . . . now. We had a little excitement here, that's all. Oh, we're all right, it was only a little property damage, but I did call the police."

Ben's voice rose. "The police?"

"About thirty-five hundred dollars worth of damage, I'd say. In fact, I'm about to go into my studio right now and try to clean up the worst of the mess."

"I'll be right over."

"Right now? Oh, Ben . . ." But she cut off her protest. She *would* be glad to have another adult in the house tonight. He could sleep in the guest room—she always kept the bed made up.

Waiting for Ben to arrive, she went into the studio

and rummaged in the storage room until she'd found several large cardboard boxes. She started to break them down and staple-gun them together, making a temporary protection for the broken doorwall. It would not keep out any serious intruder, but would at least provide a barrier against raccoons and insects.

The doorbell interrupted her work. She put down the staple gun, and went through the house to the front door.

"Shay . . . are you all right?" Ben strode anxiously into her foyer. He was wearing a T-shirt that said ILLITERACY IN MICHIGAN IS NOT FICTION. His dark hair looked tousled and rumpled, and he needed a shave. She felt absurdly glad to see him.

"I'm fine," she said, stopping herself from going into his arms, instead giving him a soft, light kiss. "We're tough folks here—we're survivors."

"Survivors, huh? What did you have to survive?"

She took him on a tour of the damage. His reaction was more shocked than she'd expected, each new evidence of damage seeming to strike him as a personal blow.

"The little bastard," he kept exclaiming. "The little fucking bastard."

"It's more annoying than anything else," she asserted, as Ben was examining one of the broken plaster works, a strong female torso whose model had been Judy Marinelli, the woman who came in once a month to clean. "I can repair that one. But it's going to be a lot of hassle, with the insurance and all."

Ben looked at the deep fissure in the treated plaster, then at her. "Shay, I don't like this at all. I don't like it one bit."

She felt her blood pressure rise a few levels as she said, "Well, neither do I. But it happened and I'm going to clean up my studio and that will be the end of it. Oh, and I think I'll visit Marianne for a couple of days. Connecticut is so pretty at this time of year. Marianne says the dogwood is beautiful. And we can drive over to Mystic Seaport.''

Ben picked up a section of cardboard and the staple gun, and shot a staple into the cardboard with a loud report.

"You mean take some time off to let Mickey cool down?''

''If you put it that way, yes.''

''An excellent idea. I hope he does cool off. I hope that's the end of it. But, honey . . . you know I make my living writing about crime . . . you know I've done a lot of research into killers—''

''Killers? Mickey is *not* a killer!'' she snapped, jerking her head up. ''God, I can't believe you just said that.''

''Honey. Oh, honey.'' Ben put down the staple gun and slid his arms around her waist. He pulled her forward, so that their legs were braced together, their bodies touching. ''I know I'm thinking on the negative side. I've gone along in too many squad cars; I've written too many scary novels and I know it. But this rips out my gut. I love you, Shay. I love you. That's the bottom line.''

Shay stood rigid, the words slipping into her mind like silver mercury.

I love you. Ben hadn't said that before, although she'd begun to suspect he had such feelings for her. God, of all times for him to say it, when she was recuperating from the emotional trauma of an act of vandalism.

She wasn't prepared. She didn't know if she loved him . . . maybe she did. Maybe she cared a dangerous lot, and perhaps she was very frightened of that caring. Probably that was why she'd spent so much energy pushing him away and making sure that he did not get too close.

"Did you hear me?" Ben whispered. "I know you're not ready to hear this. I know that I'm just confusing you by telling you of my love, but I can't hold it back any longer."

"Ben," she whispered, panicking.

"I haven't loved a woman in five years, not since my wife died. You're such a beautiful woman, Shay— on the outside, and on the inside, too. You're so strong, I love that strength in you. Do you think you can ever love me back?"

"I . . . oh, God . . ." she groaned. "Oh, Ben. My marriage took so much out of me. I'm still recuperating from it. I know I've been keeping you at arm's length, but I'm afraid. I admit it. And I don't know how long it'll take for that fear to go away."

"I don't care how long it takes."

"What?"

"I said I don't care how long it takes. Three months, a year, even longer. I'll wait. I love you, Shay. Life doesn't hold any certainties—we both know that. But I know one thing, it would be a hell of a lot poorer without love. And I have so much love."

Ben scooped her close, pressing his mouth on hers, his tongue nudging her lips apart. Shay hesitated, then gave herself up to the kiss, responding with a strength of passion she had not felt before. The moment seemed to stretch on forever, exquisitely clear. She could hear her own thickened breathing, and realized that her heart was pounding almost as fast as it had when Mickey rode his bike into the doorwall.

Except that one thing Ben said was wrong.

There *was* love in the world, yes, but there was also hate. She, Kelly, and Matt had experienced that to-night—and she knew they would never forget it.

* * *

Mickey McGee straddled a wooden chair in front of a battered desk littered with arrest report forms, flyers, memos, and Styrofoam plastic cups. His eyes were closed to slits, and his jaw muscles grated tight. He refused to look at the police officer in front of him, even when the man spoke to him sharply several times.

"Mickey! You've been hassling those people for a year now, haven't you? Riding past their house every day, four and five times a day sometimes. Hey, man, we know all about it. They've identified you and your bike."

Mickey was sullenly silent.

"You have the hots for Kelly Wyoming, huh?"

He opened his eyes and aimed a killer glare at Officer Roger Handing.

"Yeah, you have the hots for her all right. But you picked a funny way of showing it."

"Hey, man . . . I wasn't within three blocks of their place." Mickey shrugged.

"Three blocks, shit. The girl I.D.'d you, Mickey."

Mickey felt an acid splash of fury. The bitch! he thought. Couldn't keep her mouth shut. Couldn't take him having a little fun. A picture of blond Kelly Wyoming came into his mind. He was pushing the tip of the butterfly knife into her side, just far enough to make blood come. That was how he would control her. If and when, he thought.

"She went to the window and looked out. She I.D.'d you, all right. Hey, boy, you're still on probation. We charge you with this, you get slapped right back into juvenile."

Mickey's breathing quickened. He ground his jaw muscles tight. "Hey, she's lying, man."

"We got bike tracks. Tire tracks from a Harley Davidson. We can use those to nail you, kid. So don't give me any of your lies. But, hey, maybe we could make things lighter on you, know what I mean?''

The asshole wanted to bargain. This was getting interesting. Mickey tightened his mouth and looked directly at Handing.

''How so, man?''

''You seen your dad lately?''

Mickey was silent.

''Hey, kid, I'm talking to you. . . . You seen your dad lately?''

More silence. The anger blistered in Mickey, tinged with other deeper feelings that ached like fever.

''We kind of lost track of him, know what I mean? We have an address for him, but it ain't the right address. You seen him lately?''

Mickey looked down at the desk top, where someone had jaggedly carved JUSTICE FUCKS into the wooden surface. His heart was pumping hard. ''I ain't seen him, and if I did I wouldn't tell you,'' he whispered. ''He's an asshole—but I don't rat on my father.''

Handing grinned and reached for Mickey's shirt sleeve, yanking the cloth upward on his arm. Mickey's forearm stretched out across the table, dotted with small, round, shiny white scars.

''Hey, kid. What are those, eh?''

Mickey scowled.

''Cigarette burns,'' Handing answered for him. ''Ciggie burns from your old man. I saw 'em when we fingerprinted you.''

''Fuck you,'' Mickey snarled, his voice rising.

''No, kid. Fuck *you*. That old man of yours, he's some case, eh? I heard all about him. Biggest thing that happened in Oakland County that year. Motherfucker holding his wife and kid hostage. Nearly killing the wife—torturing the little kid—hey, the asshole nearly killed you, kid. You were half dead when they finally took you to the hospital. Then Danno did a nice long tour over in Jackson—''

''*Shut up.*'' Mickey jumped to his feet, throwing back the chair with a clatter. He crouched like an animal at bay, breathing heavily. An officer passing in the hallway outside paused to glance curiously through the open door.

''Calm down—''

''*My father didn't do nothing! Not like that! So you just shut up, dick-face, and leave me alone. Because I'm not telling you nothing! I'm not telling you about nothing! NOTHING!*''

Within seconds the man in the hall was in the room, and the two cops had handcuffed Mickey to the chair. He struggled, cursing. ''*Assholes! Assholes! Dick-faces!*'' But as soon as the men left the room, Mickey slumped against the hard seat back, blinking away the betrayal of wetness from his eyes.

Fuck it! Fuck all of them!

Half an hour later his mother arrived, a trim woman with auburn hair nicely curled, dressed in pleated blue twill slacks and a cotton print blouse, with fashionable flat-heeled shoes. But nothing could obviate the puckered knife scars that disfigured Beverly McGee's face and neck, and the five-times-broken nose that looked lumpy and pug-ugly. Mickey looked up sullenly as she entered the cubicle.

''Mickey. Oh, God, Mickey,'' his mother said, walking into the room and stopping short at the sight of the handcuffs. ''They told me you got violent . . . oh, Mickey.''

''*Oh, Mickey,*'' he mimicked angrily.

''Mickey, why? Why?''

''*Mickey, why? Why?*''

''What am I going to do with you?'' Beverly looked

around the small room nervously. "I've been trying so hard to make a good life. Do you think I like working ten hours a day and then going to class at night and on weekends? And now you do this."

Her familiar, nagging tone clawed at Mickey. In his head, he heard her other voice, from years ago. *Don't kill us, Danno . . . don't hurt him, oh, please, Danno . . . I'm begging you, I'm begging . . . I'll do anything, Danno . . . here, I'll show you . . .*

"Bullshit, bullshit, bullshit," Mickey muttered, jerking his hands until the metal cut into his wrists.

"They shouldn't have put you here like this. I'm going to go find someone. . . . Oh, God," his mother fretted. "Mickey, all I want is for us to be happy. When I get through with this course they have job placement—"

Mickey didn't bother to listen. He let the hatred crawl up out of the center of him. It was growing larger and more powerful with every passing hour, and it centered on his shit list, that list of people who'd become his enemies, with the one name in big, big print at the top.

When he let his fury go, it would be like nothing the world had ever seen before. It would sweep everything before it like a tornado. He would be the most powerful person, the king.

Yeah, the king.

TEN

Marianne's large, quad-level home was set in the midst of a pretty Connecticut wood through which wandered a small brook and a tumbledown stone fence that dated back to the 1790s. Flowering dogwoods created patches of white blossoms, and wrens and juncos had gathered at a bird feeder.

Marianne and Shay sat on Marianne's flagstone patio, nursing glasses of Soave. From the side of the house came shouts and screeches as Kelly and Matt played a wild game of badminton.

Shay put down the pair of binoculars she'd been using to scan the woods for wildlife.

"It's *so* lovely here," she sighed. "These woods almost breathe peace. Oh! There's a woodpecker! Listen!" She laughed with pleasure as a hollow rat-tat-tat sound reverberated through the trees.

"I call him Pecker," Marianne said, smiling. "He's out here every day."

Blond with blue eyes like Shay's, she was two years older than Shay, and weighed about forty pounds more, weight that she carried easily. Her large counseling practice in wealthy Wilton, plus teaching, earned her more than two hundred thousand dollars a year.

"I'm sorry to have arrived here on such short notice. I mean, dumping three people on you at the last minute."

"Shay, you know you don't have to apologize. I love seeing the kids and I love seeing you . . . and there's something wrong, isn't there? That's why you flew in here at midnight last night. Something's bothering you."

Shay toyed with the plaid strap of the binoculars. "Oh, it's a lot of things. Kelly, especially. She's pulling away from me so much. And now we've had some vandalism by a boy who seems to have a crush on her."

"Would you like to talk?"

Shay sighed and gave herself up to the relief of pouring it all out. This time she held nothing back, and the recital took more than forty minutes, prompted by Marianne's comments and careful, nonjudgmental questions.

"Well," her sister finally remarked. "This young man does seem to be creative; maybe that's good. But the obsession part worries me. And that clay sculpture shows deep-seated anger."

"But he's only seventeen!" Shay said, almost pleading.

"Seventeen is a volatile age, and some of these young men with obsessions can be dangerous. They brood, they fantasize. Think of John Hinckley. Not that Mickey is probably anything like that," Marianne added hastily, as Shay recoiled.

"God!" Shay burst out. "First Ben, and now you.

Oh, Marianne—I don't want to think so negatively. I just don't want him hanging around the edge of our lives. How do I get him to go away?"

"If I were you, I would change my phone number—that would be a good start. Just in case your anonymous caller is Mickey, that will stop that. School will be out in a few weeks, and that should cool things off, too, when he can't see Kelly every day. One more thing—I would think about sending Kelly away this summer. Maybe to a tennis camp, or a dude ranch—something that will take her out of town for a couple of months."

Shay bit her lip. "A couple of months? That's so expensive. And I'm not sure Randy can help. He's enlarged his agency and that's cost a lot."

"I'll pay for it."

"I can't let you do that."

Marianne set down her wine glass. "I want to do it, Shay. I have plenty of money, I'm single, I haven't got any kids to spend it on—and you are the main beneficiary in my will anyway. Money is just money and if it will help ease your anxiety in some way, then I want to spend it."

Shay slumped back in her canvas deck chair, feeling the temporary relief of being here, safe, of basking in her sister's care and concern.

"All right, I accept. But she's growing away from me, Marianne. I'm afraid I'm going to totally lose her. I don't know how to talk to her any more. The more I talk, the more she withdraws. The more she withdraws, the harder I try to reach her, and the farther away she gets." Shay's laugh was close to tears.

"You mean, you're overfunctioning, and she's underfunctioning. The dance of anger, Harriet Lerner calls it."

"That's what it feels like."

"Once a cycle gets started, each person feeds into it. It becomes a never-ending circle."

"So where does it stop?"

"When one of you breaks the cycle and becomes responsible only for yourself, and not for the other person. I have Harriet's book; it's the best discussion of anger I've ever found. I'll go in the house and get it."

While Marianne was gone, Shay sat on the deck, listening to the sounds of her children calling to each other, Kelly laughing as she chased Matt's serve. Here in the tranquility of the Connecticut woods, everything seemed simple and solvable. You read a book, you learned how to relate in a different manner—you healed your family's wounds.

She frowned, remembering what Marianne had said about John Hinckley. But the chances of Mickey being like that were statistically very small, she assured herself quickly. After all, how many John Hinckleys were there?

A fat, furry gray squirrel approached Marianne's bird feeder. As the birds fluttered off, the animal ran up the feeder and crouched greedily over the cache of seeds. The normality of the cute animal brought Shay's ruminations to a halt.

For God's sake, she told herself, reaching for the binoculars again. *Will you stop imagining the worst?*

Mickey was just a boy, after all, a talented boy. With all that artistic ability, surely there had to be some good in him.

The 7:20 P.M. flight from Kennedy had been on time, and the fifty minute drive from Metro Airport only moderately delayed by construction. Kelly, in the front seat, was telling Shay the plot of a movie she'd seen on cable at Marianne's. Matt, wedged next to their carry-on luggage in the back seat, happily played with a Transformer toy. It had been a good visit.

Shay turned her Cougar into Pebblebrook subdivision where they lived. She had the car windows cracked open, and the night air tasted gloriously of damp earth, new leaves, and lilacs.

She had to admit, she hated to be away from home for very long and always missed her studio. So much of her real self resided among her clay and plaster, and without her art she felt sometimes a little stranded.

A large, pale moth fluttered into the car headlights.

"Watch out, you're going to cream that bug," Kelly said. But it was too late. "Oh, ugh . . . gross! All over the car."

"Splat," cried Matt happily. "Sploosh! Splat! Splunk!"

"Be kind to insects and at least mourn their passing," Shay said, enjoying their good humor. "Maybe you can wash the car tomorrow," she suggested to Matt.

"Me? With the hose? Squirting it all over the car? Oh, boy!" the six-year-old exclaimed. "Will you pay me?"

"How much do you charge?"

"A hundred dollars."

"A hundred dollars? How about a hundred pennies? Would you settle for that?"

"Sure," the small boy agreed.

"Dork!" Kelly cried. "That's only a dollar, you dorky kid." The girl added as they turned down Meadowlark Lane, "Don't you think our house looks different?"

"What?"

"The lights are different."

Shay felt her pulse rate speed up as she gazed at their house. When they left, she'd put three lamps on

timers, but now only one of them seemed to be working. She noticed that the timer in her studio was one of
the ones that had malfunctioned.

"Well, maybe a couple of the bulbs blew. Or I didn't
set the timers right."

She drove into the driveway and flicked the garage
opener. The trip had been wonderful but now they were
back to reality again. She wondered if she had acciden-
tally goofed up the complicated timers, which could
easily be set on A.M. instead of P.M.

She switched off the motor and opened the car door
on her side.

"I'm hungry," Matt complained.

"Okay . . . Kelly, will you fix Matt something in the
microwave?"

"Microwave milkshake! Microwave milkshake!"
Matt cried.

"We don't have any. You pigged them all up before
we left," Kelly said scathingly.

Shay unlocked the back door, and Matt scampered
past her as soon as the door was open, racing to the
freezer to see what microwavable goodies he could
find.

"Elfin Loaves!" he cried. "I found Elfin Loaves!"

Did the house smell strange, faintly "off," or was it
just the odor of a house left empty for several days?

"Stay here with him, Kelly."

Shay walked through the dining room into the living room, noting that everything was in place as she
had left it, except that the large, spice jar lamp that she
had put on timer was no longer lit. She checked the
bulb, discovering that it was, in fact, burned out—a
fact that did not fill her with as much relief as she could
have wished. There was a foul taste to the air . . . a
feeling.

She circled the living room again, then returned to

the kitchen-laundry area, where the breezeway led to her studio. The smell grew slightly stronger as she walked down the passage. It smelled like feces, she realized.

Feces.

She reached the studio, which lay in darkness. Her hair had begun to prickle, rising slightly on her scalp. Fumbling to her right, she switched on the overhead fluorescent lights.

She stepped back, gasping.

The studio had been trashed. The doorwall, repaired by Hills Glass Service before they left, was smashed in again. Tools lay in mad heaps. Her mini-refrigerator lay wide open on its side, pop cans scattered. Her twelve-inch TV set had a broken screen. The armature she had been working on with such painstaking care had been smashed, all of her wax sketches for the Entech commission crushed into shapeless blobs.

Three months' work gone—and there was no way she could duplicate those wax pieces again, not exactly the way they had been.

Fighting shock, she realized that the smell of feces came from the surface of her largest work table. Near it lay another small clay sculpture, Mickey's calling card.

Shay picked up the clay piece, staring at it with disbelief. It had been shaped in the form of a penis and testicles (was the boy fixated on male genitals?), and the *glans* again had been given a snakelike, screaming mouth. But this sculpture contained something new. Speared through the long, bulging, erect penis like a miniature javelin was one of Shay's Exacto knives.

"Mom?" came Kelly's voice from the breezeway.

Shay shook herself. "Stay back!" she cried. "Don't come in here."

"But Matt says—"

"I don't care what Matt says, I don't want you in here!"

The girl appeared in the doorway of the studio and stood staring around with horror. "Mom! Your big commission has been wrecked! Your beautiful sculpture!"

Your beautiful sculpture. Kelly almost never complimented Shay's work, and under ordinary circumstances Shay would have felt warmed and pleased by the comment. Now all she could think was that she didn't want Kelly looking too closely at this terrible mess, with its implications of sexuality and deep-seated anger.

But Kelly had already seen the sculpture. "Mom?" Her daughter's voice was high. "W-what's that?"

"A little token of Mickey's esteem," Shay said. "Don't look at it."

"I want to look. It's . . . *it's got a knife through it. Just like—*" Kelly stopped.

"Just like what?"

"Just like before," Kelly burst out. "He made this horrible statue of me. He did it in the art room, Mom, and it was so horrible. It was me without any clothes and there was a knife cut in my stomach and all my—my insides were hanging out."

Shay felt a block of ice freeze her stomach. She turned to her daughter. "Why didn't you tell me?"

"I . . . I couldn't . . . I was afraid . . . I didn't want you to know."

"Oh, Kelly," was all Shay could say.

She took her daughter's arm and steered her back through the breezeway toward the kitchen. She felt sickened by the terror campaign that Mickey had waged on her daughter. No wonder Kelly had been so moody and difficult. Why hadn't she told her this ear-lier?

But what could she have done, other than what she was doing now? Shay asked herself.

"Mom?" Kelly asked anxiously. "What are we going to do? Why won't he leave us alone? Mom . . . Mom . . ." She started to cry. "I . . . I thought he was cute. He l-looks like Jordan. He looks so c-cute . . ."

"He isn't cute. He's far from cute. *Don't* cry over this," Shay said. "He's just trying to scare us and I won't have it. Don't let him get to you, Kelly. I'm going to call the police."

"Again?" Kelly wailed.

Matt, standing by the microwave, was staring at them wide-eyed.

"Yes, again," Shay said grimly.

"Oh, God! Oh, shit!" her daughter cried. "I hate him! I just hate him so much!" She turned and stum-bled toward the kitchen door. "I'm going up to my room."

This police interview was much like the first, except a different officer responded to the call. Shay was very calm, her voice steady as she went over the entire scenario, showing him the sculpture. He seemed men-tally to shrug, impressed only by the Exacto knife.

"This boy is dangerous," Shay insisted. "And he—he defecated on the table." The word sounded awk-ward and silly.

"Those guys do funny things," the officer told her. "I've seen that before, burglars go into a house and do their business right in the middle of the living room carpet. You say you think it's this McGee kid?"

"This is his work," she said, gesturing at the sculp-ture.

"You recognize his work?"

"I'm a sculptor. I taught him in art class; I've seen the kind of things he does. I mean, not everyone makes a penis and testicles, now do they?" She flushed. "Look, if you want more proof, can't you find fingerprints in the clay? Fingerprints on the doors?"

"Yeah, we can try, but generally juvenile vandals aren't caught unless there are eyewitnesses or someone confesses."

She nodded. She'd guessed as much. Only on TV detective dramas were perpetrators caught and brought dramatically to justice. In real life, matters slid on, and nothing much was ever done, especially if the crime consisted only of property damage.

"Well, can I at least get a squad car assigned to drive past here and make sure everything is all right? If that would do any good at all?"

"Sure, lady. I appreciate how he's scared you. We'll do the best we can. We'll patrol the place, but maybe you should get a security service, know what I mean? One of those services that gives you window and door alarms, and a panic button. It'd cost you, but a lot of people are getting that now, and they swear by it."

"I'll consider it," she said in a clipped voice, walking the man to the door. It was naive, she decided, to depend on the police to assist her. By their standards, the crime just wasn't impressive enough.

At the door she told the man, "I'm not signing a complaint this time."

"Okay, lady. Whatever you want."

"He took revenge on me because I complained before. I don't want him coming back here again; I want him out of our lives."

"I'm sorry," Kelly wailed, lying face down on her bed. "I didn't mean for this to happen. I didn't! I didn't cause it!"

"I know you didn't, honey. I don't want you to feel as if I'm accusing you, because I'm not. It's just that some young men become obsessed with girls, and I think that's what's happened with Mickey." Shay drew a deep breath. "Now, we're going to have to make a few changes in our lives if we're going to deal with this."

"What kind of changes?" Kelly inquired suspiciously.

"For one thing, we're changing our phone number."

"Oh, *no*," her daughter wailed. "How will my friends call me?"

"You'll give them the new number—but ask them not to give it out," Shay added. "I'm also going to be looking into some sort of a summer camp for you, too, something fun, something you'd really enjoy. Aunt Marianne is paying for it. And, Kel . . ." She hesitated. "I want to keep you out of school for the rest of the year."

"Out of school?" Kelly sat bolt upright, her cheeks still damp from crying. "Out of *school*?"

"I think it would be best. If Mickey doesn't see you around every day, maybe he'll start thinking about other things."

"I don't want to miss school! Mom, I can't!"

"It's just a few weeks, Kelly. You're a good solid B student, you can handle it, and you can bring home some work. I'll talk to your teachers."

"I don't want you to talk to them. I don't want to be taken out of school. That's what happened to Kimberley, and it sucks! I don't want to leave my *friends*," Kelly added miserably. "Besides, I'm on the school paper and I want to be editor next year and if I don't go to school, they'll pick someone else."

The expression on her daughter's face was so

stricken that Shay felt a stab of sympathy. "Honey . . ."

"And, Heather and I, well, we had a little fight. She—she's not talking to me much, and I can't just drop out of school and go away, Mom, because if I do, she'll forget all about me and I'll never be her friend again."

"I'm sure if you explain to her—"

Kelly burst out, "No! I can't explain to her! I can't! She just won't listen. She's so different now, Mom; she's got boyfriends and I think she has sex, too. She thinks I'm a stupid baby because I'm a virgin."

Her daughter spat out the word as if *virgin* were an epithet.

Shay bit her lip. "Baby, we can still invite Heather over and we'll do some things together. We'll go to Greenfield Village or something—"

"Greenfield *Village*!" Kelly gave a loud snort that turned into a cry of despair. "Oh, nobody goes to Greenfield *Village*! Heather won't want to do that. She likes *boys*, Mom. Babes! Cute guys! Oh, God! You're going to ruin my whole summer. Sending me off to some horrible camp! I want to finish the school year," Kelly pleaded. "*Please.* I'll stay out of art class, I'll drop that. Okay? And—and Ben Lyte will be at school, won't he? He'll be there every day and he can keep an eye on me. Okay, Mom? Okay?"

At the intensity of her daughter's pleading, Shay wavered. "I don't know. . . . I thought you didn't like Ben."

"Oh, he's okay. I just don't want to stay out of school, all right? My whole *life* is at school. Can't you understand? I can't just *drop out of it.*"

Shay nodded reluctantly. She understood the strong need of a teenaged girl for her peers. She also knew the rift between herself and her daughter wasn't final yet; it could still be repaired. But if she cut Kelly off from her friends, the chasm would grow deeper and she might never be able to cross it.

"I'll drive you to school," she began, capitulating.

"*No!* I'll ride with Amy," Kelly insisted. Amy Hart lived four houses down.

"And you won't be by yourself at any time, Kelly? I don't want you going *anywhere* by yourself. It's important."

"I *know* it's important. I *know* all that, Mom. I read the papers, too; I know all about stuff like that. I'll be careful, I promise. I'll never be alone for one single minute."

Shay again nodded, reassuring herself that there were only two more days until the weekend anyway. And Ben *would* be at school, and she would make sure that he kept a very close watch on Kelly. Maybe she would even telephone several of Kelly's teachers, and ask them to keep an eye on her, too.

She went downstairs, troubled by the decisions she had been forced to make. She phoned Ben with the news of the break-in. He was shocked and troubled, but agreed to keep an eye on Kelly for her.

"No problem," he assured Shay. "I'm not too far down the hall from where her locker is. Anyway, we do have school security, and the assistant principal patrols the halls regularly. This isn't a ghetto high school, and I think it's highly unlikely anything will happen in the school itself, and if you make sure she's always with someone, it should be all right."

Shay cleared her throat. "I did want to ask you, did you ever get a look at Mickey's juvenile records?"

"Oh, boy." Ben sighed. "You ask tough things, don't you?"

"What's wrong? You couldn't get the files?"

"I forgot to tell you. Dr. Vigoda was out with some

minor surgery, and then she attended a seminar in Lansing. I've been trying to get in touch with her but she hasn't returned my calls.''

''Lovely.'' Shay sighed.

''Honey,'' Ben said softly. ''I worry about you. Especially tonight. I want to be with you. Would you like me to come over tonight?''

Usually she was independent, but tonight the shadows cast by the hall lamp seemed exceptionally dark, and the wind had picked up outdoors, batting branches against the aluminum siding with a screechy, scraping sound. ''Would you? Would you stay? In the guest room,'' she added hastily.

''Ten minutes,'' he promised.

Shay hung up, feeling slightly better now that she knew Ben was coming over. After checking all the door locks yet one more time, she wandered back into her studio again, drawn by some compulsion she couldn't quite explain.

The studio looked ravaged, as if some wild animal had run amok through it. For the first time she noticed other, viscous white marks on one of the sculptures. *Semen*.

Oh, God, she couldn't believe this. What kind of a person would vandalize someone else's space, defecate and masturbate in it?

Why had Mickey chosen *her* studio? Was he jealous of her? She began to wonder how dangerous he was, and if he would confine his anger only to objects.

A Tupperware bowl of clay she had prepared for Matt to play with had tumbled onto the floor, and on impulse she picked it up and carried it back through the breezeway into the kitchen.

She cleared some issues of the *Detroit News* off her kitchen table and sat down, taking the clay out of its container. She hefted its moist mass in her hands, feeling the pull of its energy into her fingers. She had always loved the blankness of material, the sense that it was waiting for the structure she would give it.

She began shaping the clay, working swiftly. Caught in a quick heat of creation, her hands seemed to work independently of her mind. After a few minutes a small head and shoulders bust began to form.

She didn't have the shape quite right. . . . Feverishly her hands worked the shoulders, her thumbs gouging in eye sockets and the jut of brows. Then she stopped and began pawing in a kitchen drawer, searching for a butter knife to use as a modeling tool.

Ten minutes later Mickey McGee's face looked up at her.

Handsome, tormented, and savagely alive.

ELEVEN

Mickey had been dreaming about Shay Wyoming. Her head was a flesh-colored sculpture, sitting on the shelf over the sink in the art room. The mouth of the head moved as she cried out, *"Let me watch, let me watch, let me watch."*

Then her voice became Kelly's. *"I want to see you kill him!"* bitch Kelly's voice begged. *"I get off on it. You make me want to come and come and come."*

His mother's alarm clock blatted in the next room, scattering the dream. After a few drowsy moments, he heard the rattle of the noisy shower the old lady had installed in the basement bathroom. The water pipes made groaning noises, vibrating against the wall.

He opened his eyes with a snap. All his thoughts came rushing in again, hot and hard. Last night. The feeling of *smashing*, the sexual excitement building until he'd finally ejaculated, again and again.

He blinked away the sleep, gazing around at the

tiny room crowded with his stuff: clay things he had made, and pads of paper he'd stolen from school, filled with sketches and scribblings. The scratches he'd made on the wall, his shit list.

"Mickey?" called his mother.

"Yeah, yeah, yeah," he snarled, throwing aside the soiled sheet and getting out of bed. He wasn't in the mood to shower today. He grabbed his clothes from where he'd thrown them, pulling on the same Jockeys and jeans he'd worn the previous day. There was a dark red stain on the jeans from where he had bled after cutting himself while throwing around Shay Wyoming's shitty sculptures.

"Mickey, I want to talk to you," Beverly said.

"Yeah, yeah."

"Don't give me that!" she snapped. "I'm still your mother, Mickey, whether you like it or not. Mickey . . . Mrs. Goldman, the art teacher, has called here a couple of times. She wants you and me to go into her office and talk."

"I'm not going. She's a bitch. What's she want to talk to me for? I haven't done anything." He decided to wear a clean T-shirt and rummaged through the cardboard dresser that served as a repository for his clothes until he found an old, black "Harley Hog" number that featured a screaming eagle on it.

"She says you disrupt her class," his mother said through the door.

"I don't do nothing."

"She says you do, Mickey. She says you did something to Kimberley Pizer. She says you scared her bad, Mickey."

Mickey yanked the T-shirt down, giving a tug at the crotch of his jeans, and burst out of the door.

His mother was standing in the cluttered basement area they called their living room. Squares of old shag carpet samples covered the floor. There was one sagging couch, two beige K-Mart floor cushions, and a twenty-inch TV set on a rickety stand. Rows of cardboard boxes and books were stacked near the wall. Dressed for her class, Beverly stood near the couch, fastening a pair of earrings in her ears.

Thin morning light cast shadows along his mother's lumpy nose and scarred neck, making her look old. There was an angry set to her jawline that Mickey recognized. Since she started her therapy, he'd been seeing it more and more often.

"Aw, I didn't do nothing," he told her, sauntering to the end of the room, where a yellow refrigerator and an avocado-green stove, the old lady's castoffs, provided a kitchen for them. Overhead he heard the creak of floorboards as their landlady, Mrs. Butera, walked into her own kitchen, which was directly above.

"We got any food, Ma? You buy any doughnuts?"

"On top of the refrigerator," Beverly said wearily. "Mickey . . ."

He strutted over to the refrigerator and flipped down the package of Pepperidge Farm doughnuts, taking out a handful and shoving them into his mouth. As he took big mouthfuls, bits of powdered sugar fell to the floor.

"Are you going to clean that up?" his mother snapped. "Mickey, I don't like the way you've been acting with those police questionings and all. You've been going in and out of here like this is a damned hotel."

"A welfare hotel," he sneered.

"You be quiet. You listen to me for a change." Beverly's voice deepened as she crossed to the kitchen. "Sometimes you act so much like *him*, Mickey. It scares me. Do you know that you act like him? Is that what you want? To be like that bastard who nearly killed me? And nearly killed you, too? You're turning *into* him, Mickey, and my therapist says—''

At the mention of the hated word *therapist,* something white-hot flashed in him.

''*Shut up,*'' Mickey snarled, reaching her before the next word could leave her mouth. He shoved Beverly against the refrigerator. She uttered a cry of angry surprise.

''Mickey! Let's talk about this! M—''

''Bitch!'' he snapped.

He shoved her again. It felt good, easing some of the hate in him. Yeah, he really hated that new, confident tone in her voice. Fucking therapists, messing up his mother. Almost without him telling it to, his hand dropped to the right pocket of his jeans. It came up with the butterfly knife in his palm.

Deftly he clicked the blade open, first from one side, then the other, making the formation of a butterfly's wings. Beverly watched the movements of the knife with wide open, shiny eyes. She knew butterfly knives—Danno had owned one.

''God, you are stone *ugly,*'' Mickey drawled. He continued the show with the knife, flashing it in and out of his palm. ''So ugly, man . . . he should have finished the job, huh? That's what he should have done. Then I wouldn't have to listen to your shit, huh? Because I'm tired of your shit. You hear me? I'm tired of it.''

''Mickey,'' she begged. ''Mickey. Put that knife away.''

''Why should I?''

''I *have* to go to class,'' Beverly gasped.

''Hey, okay,'' he said, reluctantly folding the knife and returning it to his pocket. ''But let me tell you this, old lady. Let me tell you something that's gonna make you wet your drawers. *I know where he is.*''

If, before, Beverly's face had been a pasty gray, now it was bleached white of all possible color. Her eyes looked huge and bruised, and her lumpy lips were bloodless. "What did you say?"

"I got the address," Mickey boasted. "I got people I know and they talked to other people, hear what I'm saying? I found him. He can change his name but he can't hide from me, because I'm king."

For an instant she sagged. *"Mickey. Oh, my God. You aren't going to tell him where we are."*

"I'll do what I want."

"Oh, Mickey. Oh, Jesus."

"I'll do what I want," he repeated sullenly.

Beverly's bruised-looking eyes focused on him, and suddenly her attitude changed. Her mouth hardened, as if her fear of him had abruptly vanished. She stepped away from the refrigerator, and walked over to an old pine dresser that Mrs. Butera had placed in the kitchen for their use. She stooped down, and pulled out a long object from underneath the dresser.

Mickey stared at it, gawking. It was a twelve-gauge pump shotgun.

"Where'd you get that?" he blurted.

Beverly lifted the shotgun and pointed it straight at Mickey. She pumped it, sliding the action forward, then back with a loud, clicking sound. She pointed it at him, her eyes as steely as the barrel of the shotgun.

"You think you can intimidate me, don't you? You and your father. . . . Well, you've abused me often enough, Mickey, but you are never going to do it again. I've had it. I'm through being your victim."

Afraid, Mickey edged a little to his left. She followed him with the barrel. This was incredible, he thought. He felt a pounding sensation in his chest. She was acting like she might really shoot him.

"Oh, don't get that look on your face," his mother

snapped. "I'm never going to be abused again. *Never, Mickey, do you understand that?"*

"Hey, hey, hey . . ." he began placatingly, but he couldn't hide the note of fear in his voice.

"I want you out of here, Mickey . . . right now, today. Wipe that damn powdered sugar off your face and get out of here and don't come back."

"I live here," he said stupidly.

"No, you don't. You don't live here any more. I've had it with you. Now get the fuck out!" Beverly snapped. *"Now,* Mickey, now! Because my hand is shaking and I just might pull this trigger."

He waited a few seconds, his heart pounding. When he swallowed he heard a loud click of the tissues at the back of his throat.

"Okay," he muttered. "Okay. But—"

"Don't come back!" she screamed.

He went.

Mickey stormed out of the house, rocked by Beverly's rejection, her scream etched in his brain. She didn't mean it, of course—or did she? Part of him knew very well that she did. She hated his father and now she hated him, and it was all his dad's fault.

He hated Danno McGee with such a passion that it sickened him.

He stomped out to the garage, where the old lady let him keep the Harley, and once inside the safety of its walls, amid the clutter of a rusted old Toro lawnmower and snowblower, and various small tools, he gave way to tears.

He leaned against the garage door, nearly gagging with the sobs that tore out of him. He smacked himself across the cheeks with both fists, pounding his own flesh, digging at his skin with his fingernails, until the traitorous tears abated.

Only babies cried!

What kind of a jerk was he? He loathed himself for his weakness . . . one more thing for which he would make someone pay.

Ten minutes later he was on the Harley, roaring toward school. There was a wet morning mist in the air, rising up from the grass, and a dog's bark sounded, thin and haunting. He throttled the bike up, skidding around a pothole on loose gravel and nearly laying the cycle on its side. He didn't give a fuck.

He'd stay out tonight, he decided. In fact, he'd stay away for four or five days, scare her a little. Then he'd go home and she'd take him back.

If she didn't, well, she couldn't walk around holding a shotgun all the time, now, could she? He decided he would make her pay. She'd go on his shit list, too. He'd put a few more marks on that pug-ugly face of hers and then they'd see whether she ever pulled another gun on him.

Feeling better, he parked in the lot at school in his usual spot, up on the grass. He swung his leg off the motorcycle and sauntered into the building, adding a hip-swinging, macho swagger to his walk.

In the school lobby, a couple of girls had arrived early, dropped off by mothers on the way to work. Their bookbags resting on the floor, they sat on a low window ledge that looked into a small atrium, gossiping about boys. One looked up, saw Mickey, and began to giggle.

Mickey swung around and glared at her. He thought of knives, and blood, and screaming. The girl stopped laughing at once. As if sensing his malevolence, the two tenth-graders got up from their perch and hurried away down the hall.

Mickey went straight to the art room, the one place

in school he liked, where he could find some solace. The *thing* building in him had somehow shifted and grown bigger. He felt it filling his entire chest cavity, almost big enough to pop out through his eyes and mouth.

The doughnuts he'd crammed down came up in a sour burp, and he tasted his own hot fluids.

He could hardly wait to get to the art room. He would get out the clay, make something, a sculpture of his father. Yeah, or maybe another statue of that bitch Kelly Wyoming. Use it to scare her a little more. He knew he would feel a lot better after he had done this, a lot more in control, and some of the rawness inside him would recede.

He laughed bitterly to himself. Other guys his age smoked cigarettes or marijuana, or they drank beer— he used clay.

However, he found the art room door locked. He stood staring at its blank wooden door, on which had been tacked a poster that showed an orchard painting by Van Gogh. He felt a wave of disappointment so intense that he couldn't breathe.

That dirty bitch Mrs. Goldman had done it!

She knew he liked to come in early in the mornings, so she'd locked the damn room so he couldn't get in.

Fury seared through him, an acetylene torch burning his gut. He didn't know what to do. He'd come to school early just to go to the art room, he'd had no other purpose in mind, and he had no friends to hang out with here, nothing to do except be in the art room. Hatred flamed through his head, almost knocking him backward.

This was *his* place. It was where he belonged and she had locked him out of it.

"Mr. McGee, is there something wrong?" He heard

a voice behind him. Angrily he turned. It was Janice Goldman herself, wearing another of her dumb art-teacher outfits, this one an Indian *sari*, augmented by handmade pottery earrings. On her feet she wore red leather boots. Mickey loathed her. Why would anyone deliberately try to look so ugly?

"I have to get in," he said.

"Well, I'm sorry, but we have a new policy that students are not allowed in the art room until five minutes before class," she snapped. "Students are not permitted to use the room except when their own class meets."

She wasn't sorry at all. In fact, he disgusted her—he could tell by the way she stood, and even by a sour smell that came from her. Something boiled in Mickey.

"It's because of me," he accused. "Isn't it? You don't want me in here." He glared at her, letting his hate show. The teacher shifted uneasily, one hand going to touch the tan ceramic beads of her necklace. He could smell her fear.

He was glad. He wanted to frighten her. He wanted to scare the living shit out of her. He would love to take his butterfly knife and carve a hole right in that pulsating, smooth throat of hers. He would love to make the blood gush out of her, and then see what she would say about closing the art room.

From the middle of his murderous red haze, he heard her voice yammering. "It's a new policy that we formulated last week in staff meeting, and Mrs. Adamson asked me to start implementing it today. It's because of insurance reasons, Mickey; it has nothing to do with—"

"Bull*shit*," Mickey snapped.

His hand went to his pocket, but then he saw Ben Lyte walking down the hallway with Ardell Mantrig, the chemistry teacher. He withdrew his hand from his pocket.

"Young man, we do not use that kind of language to a teacher," Janice Goldman scolded. She waved to the two male teachers, as if to ask for help, but they had just turned the corner toward the auditorium and did not see her. "I'm going to report you to Mrs. Adamson," she announced. "I've had enough of you. I'm finished with you. Yes, I am."

"No, you aren't," he told her, seeing a death's head in his mind, her naked bloody skull. "You aren't finished with me yet at all."

TWELVE

Shay spent the remainder of the week calling various summer camps to get their catalogs and cleaning up her studio. She assured herself that the catastrophe might even be a blessing for her Entech project. She now had a chance to rethink her original thoughts, and come up with something even better.

As for Mickey, Ben believed the seventeen-year-old probably would drop out of school by next fall. With a low-D average, he was not likely to sustain the interest. So that meant they only had a few more weeks of school to live through.

At six o'clock Saturday evening, she went upstairs to shower and dress for the writer's party. She really wasn't in the mood to leave her children and go out to a party, but Ben had been counting on her, and she felt she could not back out now.

''Mom, you look *pretty*,'' was Matt's shy assessment as she emerged from her walk-in closet, wearing a thigh-length, beaded white silk dress that rustled sensuously. In her ears she had fastened the dangling pink earrings that Kelly had given her, and on her finger she wore a diamond cocktail ring that had belonged to her mother.

"Do you like it, honey?" She twirled for her son's inspection, at last feeling her spirits begin to rise.

"Mom, is Noah here yet? When is Noah coming? Is Noah going to let us watch the VCR? Is he going to show me that string thing?"

"You mean cat's cradle?"

"Do cats have cradles?" Matt persisted as Shay went down the hall to Kelly's room.

"The way Noah tells it, they do. Kelly?" She knocked on her daughter's door, from which issued the strains of, for a change, a new Jon Bon Jovi album. "Honey, Noah's due here any minute, and I've put the videos I rented on top of the TV set. I want you to spend some time with Noah and Matt, and not just hole up here in your room. Noah really likes you, honey, and I don't want you to hurt his feelings."

"I won't hurt his feelings," came her daughter's voice from behind the door.

"Well, please, be on your best behavior tonight, all right? And I've told him to order pizza for dinner. You can get two separate pizzas, one for you and Noah, and one with just cheese for Matt."

"Okay, okay, okay," her daughter said. But the tone came out cheerfully. Actually, both children liked Noah very much, and she felt lucky he'd consented to stay with them.

Five minutes later, Noah arrived in a flurry of jokes and laughter, bringing with him a plastic grocery bag stuffed with some chocolate chunk cookies he had made. He was dressed in his usual faded jeans, wearing a Bart Simpson T-shirt, his white beard freshly shampooed.

"Oh, cookies!" Matt squealed, running over to dig in the bag. "Oooooh, can I have one now?"

"Not until after the pizza, my boy. We have to get in our good pizza nutrients before we can take in the nutrients of finest quality chocolate. Ah, I see that your mother has left packages of microwave popcorn on the kitchen counter. Tonight is indeed going to be one of culinary joy."

"Culinary boy," repeated Matt, grinning wickedly.

"No, culinary *joy*, my son. That means we're gonna have a blast eating ourselves sick."

The sound of the doorbell penetrated her son's happy squeals and Shay went to the door to let Ben in. He was freshly shaven, resplendent in a new evening jacket with a black-dotted silk cummerbund and tie. It accented his dark good looks, and she knew she would not be the only woman tonight whose heart fluttered at the sight of Ben.

"Oh," she murmured. "Oh, you're splendid, Ben. You look like an ad for Cutty Sark."

"And you're L'Oréal, my love," he told her, giving her a small, courtly bow and a dazzling smile. "You're worth it."

As Shay gave Noah detailed instructions, she felt another spasm of misgiving.

"You'll be careful, won't you, Noah?" she asked her friend.

"Damn sure I will be."

"The police have promised that they'll patrol the house, and I've seen the cars two or three times today, so I just want you to know they're out there."

"Consider me told. Go on, now, get out of here," Noah added. "Go on and mingle among the famous.

We're going to eat ourselves blind, and we won't even miss you.''

The dinner party was being held at the Bloomfield Hills home of Eileen Dallwood, the current president of the Detroit Women Writers, a writers' group that had established itself in 1900 and was now nearing its ninety-third birthday. One of its members was Judith Guest, author of *Ordinary People*. Eileen herself wrote historical romances for Harlequin. With her size-six figure, cloud of russet hair, and huge melting blue eyes, she looked like a reader's fantasy. Her pale blue beaded dress sparkled.

''So *glad* you could come,'' she said, embracing first Shay, then Ben. ''Oh, Shay, that dress is marvelous, just smashing. And, Ben, I hear you've just sold a new hardcover book. Can you tell us what it's about, or is that a secret? I know how you mystery writers love secrets.''

Ben laughed, won over, and began telling Eileen the title of his book and a sentence or two about the plot, which was, Shay knew, all that he ever revealed.

A hubbub of party noise drifted from the other room, punctuated with laughter. Eileen led them through the large foyer to a series of long, beautifully decorated rooms hung with good art. Guests clustered around an oak wet bar, or grouped around the two guests of honor, Elmore ''Dutch'' Leonard and Loren Estleman. Shay had never met Leonard but recognized him from his book jackets.

Estleman, wide-built, dark, and seemingly saturnine with his heavy black mustache, was in the middle of telling a story that, judged by the reactions of the group, was very witty.

''Uh, oh,'' Ben said, his smile stiffening just slightly. ''I've met him twice, but I hope he remembers me.''

"How could anyone forget you?" Shay said, giving Ben a sympathetic smile.

"Easy, my dear, easy. A broken down old English teacher like myself . . . we're a dime a dozen." But by Ben's grin she could tell he didn't mean it, and as he steered her across the room toward Loren Estleman, she had another swift thought about Noah and the kids.

Would they be all right? Noah was resourceful, she thought, again feeling that oddly urgent doubt. But he was also sixty years old.

"I want cat's cradle! I want cat's cradle!" Matt begged, jumping up and down on the couch. "Meow! Meow!"

"Do you have string?" Noah questioned, winking.

"Oh . . . string." Matt's downcast face was so disappointed-looking that Noah relented and pulled a ball of yo-yo string out of his pocket. He loved both of Shay's children, of course, but ebullient Matt was his favorite.

"See? All the string we need. But first let's call and order the pizza. What do you like on yours? And run up and ask your beautiful sister what she wants."

"Cheese! Cheese! Cheese!"

"I think Kelly wants a little more than just cheese, Matt. Run upstairs and ask, and then we'll do cat's cradle, then all these great videos. What an evening," Noah said, smiling kindly.

As the child scampered upstairs, he walked across the family room, switching on the table lamps, although it was still light outside. But somehow the room seemed gloomy, and he was glad to have the circles of light to add a touch of extra coziness.

The truth was, he hadn't been looking forward to tonight.

He heard the voices of the two youngsters in the

upstairs hallway, engaged in a heated discussion about pepperoni. Sinking onto the couch, Noah expelled his breath in a lengthy sigh.

A police car driving past the house. Well, well. He wished that the gun he had ordered was ready to be picked up, but he was still waiting for the permit to come through. Again Noah sighed. Hey, if anything happened he would just dial 911. Anyway, what was likely to happen?

The worst that could happen was more vandalism, and Noah seriously doubted that the boy, Mickey, or Mikey, or whatever his name was, would dare to break into Shay's studio again with the house lit up like a Christmas tree and yard lights blazing. Vandals didn't like lights; that was one thing Noah felt sure of.

He got out the string, cut a length with his penknife, and knotted the ends of the piece together, forming a long loop. He had several new cat's cradle figures to show Matt.

Ben was deeply involved in a discussion with Estleman and a woman named Sarah Wolf, who had written a book called *The Harbinger Effect*. Shay was glad that he'd found some kindred souls to talk to. She knew he hungered for other writers and could cheerfully talk about agents, contracts, and serial killers all night.

She wandered toward the hors d'oeuvre table, where a huge bowl of shrimp had just been replaced by a maid in a black uniform and white apron. She browsed the table, filling her plate from a selection of seafood appetizers and adding a tiny slice of what looked like broccoli quiche.

"Shay? Shay Wyoming, is that you?" The voice behind her sounded familiar, and Shay turned to see Margie Hennerle. She and Randy had occasionally played bridge with the Hennerles. Grant Hennerle had a law practice in town, and dallied with writing short stories, considering himself literary.

"Hi, Margie," Shay said, forcing a smile.

"How *are* you, Shay?" Margie was one of those lizard-skin blonds who spend every summer from May to September baking in the sun.

"Never better."

"And how's Randy? We haven't seen either of you in *months*, or is it years? We're going to have to get together, aren't we?" But Margie's eyes sparkled with a wicked light, and Shay realized that she had seen her on Ben's arm.

"We're divorced, Margie, as you might have heard. It was final eight months ago. I'm here with Ben Lyte, the mystery writer."

"Oh. . . . I see . . . ! Well, well. He *is* good looking, isn't he, especially in a tux. Poor old Randy. I imagine his heart is just broken. In fact, I know it is. How are your kids taking it? Do you want to talk about it, honey? I'm always available to talk."

I'll bet, Shay thought angrily. She knew the remark about Randy's heart being broken meant that Margie had heard the sad story—his version—via the grapevine already. She knew the Hennerles had really been Randy's friends anyway, not hers.

"I guess not, Margie," she said coolly. "I'm feeling better every day. Oh, I think I see Eileen waving to me from over by the bar . . . excuse me."

"Oh, Shay . . ."

"Yes?"

"Randy asked me if I saw you here tonight, to tell you that he really wants to talk to you, just for an hour. If you could only listen to him—"

"I don't want to hear any messages from my ex-husband," Shay snapped, turning so swiftly that a jumbo shrimp nearly slid off her plate. She threaded her way across the room, her heart pounding. How dare Randy send a silly gossip like Margie over to do his pleading for him? He had no shame, did he? He would use Kelly, anyone.

Her heart was pounding fast with irritation, and she decided to find a telephone and call home, just to see how the kids were doing. A maid told her where to find one.

In a room that contained an IBM computer with color monitor, and framed book covers with titles like *Big, Golden Sky* and *Cheyenne Sunrise,* Shay dialed her own phone number.

"H'lo?" Matt's voice answered her first ring. He sounded muffled and smacky, as if he were in the midst of chewing something. In the background Shay could hear the TV set, and Kelly's sudden squeal of laughter.

"Matt? Is Noah there? Is everything all right?"

It was all right, she knew.

"Everything's great. We got pizza and I had *four* pieces," the little boy boasted.

Gripping the phone, Shay nearly sagged from the strength of her relief. Oh, God . . . she loved her children so much. She really did. She wished she could leave the party and go home right now, and sit on the couch between them, drinking in the sweet wine of their laughter.

On the screen Darryl Hannah was lying in a bathtub as a mermaid, her tail flippers spread and protruding upward from the water. Noah had been watching this with interest, thinking that mermaids and mermen might make a good theme for some of his work. Except that Darryl Hannah was entirely too thin, he thought. His mermaids would be hefty, voluptuous, and they would have gills with which to breathe, perhaps some kind of frilled apparatus placed in their flowing hair.

A wind knocked at a branch outside the house, batting it against the siding. Little puffs and gusts seemed to penetrate into the family room, turning it chilly.

So far everything seemed peaceful. Matt was snuggled up next to Noah on the couch and Kelly lay sprawled on the floor, leafing through a copy of *Teen Beat* while keeping one eye on the screen. He hadn't heard any motorcycle—not even once, Noah told himself with relief.

He glanced at his watch. It was ten-thirty. Only an hour and a half left to go. Shay had said she and Ben would be back around midnight.

"I'm going to swim underwater," Matt was chattering. "I want to be an underwater boy."

"That's scuba diving," Kelly said condescendingly. "You're too little to scuba dive, Matt."

"I'm not! I'm not too little! I can too do it! I can!"

"Hush," Noah intervened. "Watch the movie."

Rmmmmr. Rmmmmr.

At the sound of the motorcycle whine, Noah stiffened. Kelly froze, too, her body language reminding him of a deer caught in car headlights. Only Matt seemed absorbed in the program, not noticing.

The engine roar grew louder, passing directly in front of the house. Was it Noah's imagination, or did the driver give it an extra oomph of gas just as he whizzed past?

Your friend? Noah was about to ask Kelly, but when he saw the girl's face he decided not to. Anyway, the bike *had* gone right on by without stopping, so it was all right.

"I'm *bored* with this video," Kelly suddenly cried,

her voice high and plaintive. "*I* wanted to watch Mad Max."

"That's for after Matt falls asleep."

"Oh, he never falls asleep. He fights it and fights it. I'll never get to watch anything *I* want to watch. He's such a ridiculous baby," Kelly exclaimed in disgust, but she settled down again on the floor, gazing at the screen with resignation.

Noah sat for a half hour longer, part of him concentrating on the movie, and part listening for a repeat of the motorcycle sounds. Shit, he was turning into a regular old lady, listening for every tiny noise. Finally he got up to stretch his legs and use the bathroom.

The powder room was down the hall and to the left. Noah always enjoyed seeing it. Intended only for family use, it had been decorated by Shay in one of her whimsical moods. The entire wallpaper was a collage made of clippings from magazines that showed eyes. Smiling eyes, sexy eyes, crossed eyes, Mickey Mouse eyes, Bette Davis eyes, dog eyes, and cat eyes. Both children had helped find the clippings, Noah knew.

He stood in front of the toilet, releasing the stream of his urine before an audience of a thousand eyes. What a complex and interesting woman Shay was, he thought. She'd been codependent in an alcoholic marriage for years, but somehow had found the guts to move past it. Some people might call her tough. Noah called her strong.

God, he hoped things went well for her with this Ben person. If she could only loosen up enough to allow him into her life. He zipped up and went to the sink to wash. But did unions of two creative types usually work out? Noah knew from his own experience that artistic personalities could clash cataclysmically. His ex-wife, Jen, had been a writer. He'd had one girlfriend who was a painter, another who was a poet. A few sculptors thrown in for good measure. Wildly passionate, all of them.

He felt a sudden, strong spasm of love for them, the women who had filled his life.

Then he saw a flash of something in the mirror.

Eyes that were not paper eyes at all but real.

"My G—" he began.

Before he could turn, an arm snaked around his neck. His head was wrenched backward with such force that he nearly fell.

"*Uhhh . . . uhhh.*" Noah struggled to cry out, but the blade flashed in front of him, digging into the skin of his neck. There was a tearing, agonizing pain and then Noah's knees buckled. He clapped his hands to his neck as he went down, cupping the gush of red that jetted out from between his fingers.

As he hit the floor, he saw black motorcycle boots decorated with a stainless steel chain bracelet that looped around the ankles, and sharply pointed steel toe caps, etched in a scroll design. He saw the flash of steel and felt an indescribable pain in his stomach.

Noah cried out again, but all that emerged was a thick, bubbly gargle.

The red. All the red. Incredible. He was strangling now, choking on his own blood.

"I'll make her watch next time," said a voice, but all Noah heard were sounds, and their meaning was lost to him. He swam through clouds of red and then he was standing outside himself, gazing down at his own corpse. He looked like a pile of bloody rags. His mouth lolled open, filled with blood, and red matted his beard.

With an almost thoughtful motion, Mickey lifted the knife tip and skewered it into Noah's left eye socket. Noah didn't feel it at all.

THIRTEEN

The video had ended and Noah still hadn't returned from the bathroom. Kelly stirred restlessly, tossing *Teen Beat* away. It hadn't had any good articles anyway, except for the one about the B-52's.

What a *boring* night. Except that in a deeper way it wasn't boring at all, because there was a funniness about it . . . not *ha ha* funny, but dangerous funny.

She'd seen the way Noah's face went all alert when the motorcycle drove past the house. Yeah, Noah was tense, she'd felt it from the minute he'd first walked into the door, talking too much and making silly jokes and waving a bag of cookies around.

Having a grown man come to babysit for them—well, Kelly knew Noah wasn't really babysitting. He was *bodyguarding*.

All night long, she'd been trying not to think about Mickey.

A tree branch slid against the house right outside

the family room. The noise it made sounded like Halloween. Off in the distance Kelly heard a rumble she thought might be thunder. She hoped it didn't start to rain until her mother and Ben got home.

Where was Noah anyway? It had been nearly twenty minutes. Had he fallen in? Or did old people just take longer? Sixty seemed very ancient, and Kelly knew for a fact that Noah had worked several Christmases as Santa Claus, which made him seem older still.

The credits were rolling by. Kelly reached for the remote and started to rewind the tape, annoyed with Noah for taking so long. It would be rude to start another movie until they asked him what he wanted to watch.

The little red arrow ran backward as the tape spun. When it was finished Kelly put the video back in its blue plastic box, replacing it in the stack of movies her mother had rented. They still had *Honey, I Shrunk the Kids* and *The Bear*, plus *Mad Max Beyond Thunderdome*.

"What are we gonna watch next?" Matt piped up. "Are we gonna watch *Honey, I Shrunk the Kids?* I seen that ten times. I wanna see it again. I wanna see the friendly ant."

"Not if I can help it. I don't want to watch any more baby movies. Noah?" Kelly called, getting up and starting down the hallway.

It was odd how quiet the house sounded once she left the family room . . . yet it was not completely still. There was a feeling to the air as if someone were nearby, breathing. Not Noah, but someone else. Kelly almost stopped walking. Then, with an effort, she got control of herself again.

This whole night was creepy, she thought.

The bathroom door was half ajar, the light still on. A smell drifted from the room—coppery, dark. Maybe

Noah had gotten sick. Maybe that was what had taken him so long. Kelly paused, hearing the TV set go on in the other room as Matt took matters into his own hands and inserted *Honey, I Shrunk the Kids* into the VCR.

"Noah?" she called politely.

There was silence.

"Noah?"

Kelly stood very still. She couldn't hear any water sounds, no flushing, no shifting of feet. There was nothing but the inhale and exhale of someone breathing. Was Noah standing on the other side of the door, trying to tease her? If so, she didn't like it.

"Noah!" she cried angrily. "I don't like being teased. This is dumb. Come on out so we can watch the movie."

Kelly saw the door swing inward about an inch.

Her mouth tasted suddenly very dry. "Noah! We're playing *Honey, I Shrunk the Kids*. Don't you want to watch?"

The door swung inward another six inches, and now Kelly saw a puddle of bright red on the floor, as if Matt had spilled some of his watercolor paints.

But Matt hadn't been painting today.

In fact, he hadn't painted at all lately. His paints were dried up.

Kelly's throat worked convulsively. Now that she looked more closely at the red, it seemed to be thicker than regular paint, more like ketchup, or bl—

The door swung all the way open.

Mickey McGee stood wedged against the sink, his forelock of dark hair falling untidily into his eyes. Blood was smeared on his black Harley Davidson T-shirt. At his feet lay the body of Noah Ransom. A dark mouth grinned at Noah's throat, and red soaked his Santa Claus beard. His left eye was swimming in blood, too.

Kelly took a tottering step backward. A scream rose inside her, but it couldn't get past her dry, terrified mouth. Where had Mickey come from? How had he gotten inside the house?

"Hello, Shay," he drawled. "You missed the fun. You missed seeing me."

She stared at him dumbly. He had called her Shay, not Kelly.

"I said *hello*, bitch! You better answer me, or I'll cut you up, too."

Mickey lunged forward and grabbed Kelly's arm. He spun her toward him and pulled her inside the bathroom, jamming her up against the wall opposite the toilet. The floor was slippery with blood. More was on Mickey's jeans and boots.

Kelly looked down at Noah's grisly face with its slit throat that revealed wet, stringy veins and tendons. *A dead Santa Claus,* she thought wildly, and started to vomit.

"Shit, shit, shit," Mickey exclaimed.

Gripping the sink, Kelly heaved and retched, bringing up considerable quantities of pizza, pepperoni, cookies, and other things she had eaten throughout the day.

"Man, man," Mickey kept saying. "Do you have to do that?"

Kelly was sobbing as she vomited, too miserable and frightened even to notice the knife blade that was pointed into her side. But then, as her stomach was cramping into a dry retch, she did notice it. The pain was like being stuck with a barbecue fork.

"Oh . . . God . . . please," she managed to sob out.

"I'm not God, I'm Mickey . . . the king," he told her, smirking. He lifted a metal-toed boot and kicked

Noah's face, rolling the head away from them, further into the pool of blood.

"Please," Kelly begged. She was trapped in the cramped room, blocked by Mickey's body. The stench of vomit, feces, blood, and her own fear-sweat was overwhelming. For the first time she remembered Matt in the family room, innocently watching TV. *"Please,* don't hurt me."

"Are you done? Here. Don't say I never did nothing for you." Magnanimously, Mickey handed her a blue guest towel. With shaking hands Kelly took it, wiping her mouth. The vile taste of vomit permeated her throat. She thought she would be sick again.

Oh, God, he'd killed Noah! What did he want? The picture of the statue Mickey had made in the art room suddenly jumped in front of her eyes. Her own intestines hanging out . . .

She sagged toward the sink again, and managed a few more dry heaves, wondering if he was going to kill her and cut out her insides. Shock was beginning to overtake her now, and her skin felt cold and clammy.

"Well?" Mickey demanded. "Are you coming with me?"

Kelly struggled to emerge from her stunned state. The question made no sense at all.

"I *said,* bitch girl, are you coming with me? Because either you come or you're dead and that brat brother of yours, too. Just like this, bitch!"

To demonstrate, Mickey poked Noah's corpse again with his toe. He was holding something in his hands that looked like a set of Ford Motor Company car keys. It was monogrammed NR. "I really got him, huh? You know how it feels to cut skin? Skin's a lot harder than you think. It really slices, though, with this knife. It's a good knife. A butterfly knife."

These were more words than Mickey had spoken to

her in the entire past year. Kelly stared at him, seeing the madness on his face, the excitement that distorted his handsome features. He seemed as pleased and cocky as if he'd just done a show-off trick on his motor-cycle, rather than cutting a man's throat.

"Kelly?" piped Matt's voice behind them, soft, childish, and a little scared. "Kelly?"

Kelly froze, fear washing through her.

"Kelleee?"

All of Kelly's terror burst forth in a high-pitched, agonizing scream. "MATT! MATTIE! RUN, MATT! RUN OUTDOORS!"

"Kelleeee," the boy sobbed.

"RUN, MATTIE! RUN AWAY! RUN!"

Dinner was as romantic as their hostess: four tables for ten, each set with centerpieces of huge yellow tulips that had dramatic black centers, flanked by pairs of silver candelabra, a different type for each table. There was sparkly Waterford crystal and Spode china—all the elegant trimmings.

The menu was medallions of chicken in lemon-Dijon sauce, and latticed potato baskets that had been deep-fried then filled with fresh baby peas, and more items of *nouvelle cuisine*, all of which seemed utterly tasteless to Shay.

Something was wrong.

The more she sat at the table, answering questions about her work, in which a number of the guests seemed very interested, the more convinced she became that something at home had gone bad. She didn't even know why she had the feeling. Just that with every ticking seconds, it seemed to grow stronger.

Ben was seated across from her. Several times she tried to catch his eye, but he was absorbed in telling a story about the time he had entered the U.S. Clue

Championship and ridden a "Mystery Train" from Chicago to New York. He had loosened up as the evening progressed and now was obviously enjoying himself.

Two maids began to remove the plates, taking their time. Dessert and coffee would be next. Shay moved her watchband so that the face was on the inner side of her wrist. Then she glanced downward to see what time it was.

Oh, God, past eleven.

She wanted to phone home, but she had called only an hour ago, and Noah had been very reassuring. If she called again so soon, he would be offended and think she didn't trust him to take care of her children.

She didn't want to offend her friend.

Dan King, a bookstore owner, spoke up on her left. "Don't you believe that's true, Shay? That even arts agencies practice a form of censorship by default?"

Shay jerked her head up, mumbling an answer to the question. How long before dessert would be served? God, this meal was dragging on and on. Maybe she and Ben could leave after coffee, but by the looks of him, he wouldn't want to go yet. She felt a stab of guilt. He'd looked forward to this party, was making all kinds of contacts, and now she was acting like an anxious mother with a newborn, afraid to leave her children for even a few hours.

"You seem to be thinking of something else," said Dan, looking annoyed.

"Oh, I'm not, I'm not," she placated him. "Tell me about your views from the bookstore angle. Didn't you bookstore owners form a group against censorship?"

I want to go home, Shay was thinking. *I want to go home.*

* * *

The little boy froze in the hallway, his eyes goggling at them, his mouth quivering. A dark wetness spread across the crotch of his pajama bottoms.

"RUN, MATTIE! RUN! RUN!" Kelly screamed, pressing back against Mickey as if to stop him from moving toward the child. The hot pain of the knife point pressed into her side, and she could smell Mickey's sweat, sour and rank. She was terrified but she knew she had to get Matt out of the house.

The boy turned and darted back the way he had come.

Oh, thank God, thank God.

But then a horrible thought struck Kelly, tearing away her relief. Was he going to hide somewhere in the house? If he did, Mickey would find him. And she knew already that Mickey would not be kind to her six-year-old brother. He would carve him apart and look at his insides.

"RUN OUTDOORS!" Kelly screamed. "RUN AWAY MATTIE! GET HELP, M—"

Mickey slapped the words right out of her mouth.

"You bitch!" he snarled, dragging at her.

Kelly resisted, fighting wildly, her desperation working through her shock. She hit and clawed, digging her long fingernails into Mickey's arm. She wept from effort. The longer she delayed Mickey, the better chance Matt had.

He hit her again. "You fucking royal bitch!"

"RUN, MATTIE . . . RUN RUN RUN!"

Mickey slapped her again, the blow skewing her head to one side. For a second there was no pain, then agony rolled over her in waves. Mickey jammed the knife tip into her ribs, drawing blood.

"Okay, bitch girl, you're coming with me, get it? And you're gonna love every single goddamn thing I do, because if you don't, I'm gonna cut you open and pull out your insides, do you hear me? 'Cause I like a girl to watch me, see?''

''Yeah,'' she moaned, thinking that if she delayed Mickey, even a few more seconds, it would give Matt time to run across the yard and maybe even get help.

''Come on, come on, come on, enough of this crap,'' Mickey urged, hauling her across the laundry room to the door that led to the garage.

''Oh, please,'' she begged, dragging her steps, but he hit her and shoved her out through the doorway into the garage. She nearly fell down the step, but caught herself on the jamb of the door.

''Listen to me, bitch girl,'' Mickey said, grabbing a handful of Kelly's T-shirt and pulling up. ''You're gonna do what I say, bitch Kelly. Yeah, 'cause if you don't, I'm gonna come back here and grab that stupid baby brother of yours and I'm gonna cut off his little pink dick. Then I'll get your mom and you don't want to know what I'm gonna cut off of her.''

They stared at each other. Mickey's pupils, Kelly saw in a wild flash, had grown so big that his eyes looked solid black. She was so terrified she could scarcely breathe, and her muscles felt paralyzed.

''*Okay, bitch girl? I'll carve her up like a fucking-ass Thanksgiving turkey.*''

Mickey jabbed his finger on the garage door opener mechanism, then dragged her across the cement floor toward Noah's Spinnaker-blue 1989 Ford Tempo, which was parked in the garage. He yanked open the driver's door and shoved Kelly inside.

She fell forward, her hand hitting the gear shift lever between the seats with such force that she thought she'd broken a finger.

''Get over! Get over!'' Mickey screamed, shoving her. Kelly scrambled across the console and gear shift, briefly caught in the hanging shoulder harness. The car smelled of Noah, and there was a jumble of junk in the back seat, everything from old jeans and sweatshirts to crumpled packages of Fritos and a McDonald's sack.

Mickey sprang into the driver's seat and jammed Noah's keys into the ignition. He started the motor with a roar. Instantly there was a whine and the seat belt mechanism traveled forward along a groove on the door, fastening around them.

"What the *shit* is that?" Mickey yelled.

"Sh-shoulder harnesses," she wept.

He rammed the Tempo into reverse, backing out in a screech of tires. They squealed off down the street, gravity pressing Kelly backward against the seat. Where was Matt, she wondered as Mickey viciously accelerated. Had he run to get help for them?

She tried to close her eyes to pray. But the speed of the car was so violent as Mickey swerved around a corner that her eyeballs seemed dried, her terror so intense that she could not move them.

Matt sobbed as he ran into the family room where the TV set was still showing *Honey, I Shrunk the Kids* as if absolutely nothing had happened. Terror sprayed through him like water from the garden hose and he knew he'd peed himself, and he didn't even care.

The bad boy was after him and he had Kelly.

Matt knew the bad boy was going to come into the family room and cut his head off if he didn't hide.

But where? Where could he go?

His eyes darted frantically around the room, as he considered the couch, where he hid regularly from his mom when they played hide-and-seek, and the door-wall curtains, in which he sometimes wrapped himself when he wanted to play a prank on Kelly.

But that boy Mickey was *bad* and Matt had seen something on the floor behind him, too. Something with staring eyes and a bloody white beard that looked just like Noah. What if Bad Mickey found him in this room?

He ran toward the doorwall, squatting down to yank out the wooden broomstick that Shay used as a lock-bar. His small fingers scrabbled in the groove, getting purchase around the stick easily. He'd played with it before, when his mother was not looking, and he knew exactly how to take it out and get the door unlocked.

"RUN! RUN! RUN!" Kelly had screamed.

He got his fingers around the broomstick and threw it backward, jumping up to click open the lock mechanism. The *pulling* was the hard part—the door was old and was not a good slider, so sometimes Matt had trouble with it. He gripped the handle with both hands and leaned his entire weight into the effort of forcing the door.

As soon as it slid open far enough to create a space, he jerked at the screen, which was easier, and in a few seconds he had slipped through the aperture and was running barefoot across the grass.

Outdoors hit him in the face, wind cleaning out his ears.

The rain had started to fall in big, thick drops. Thunder rumbled and wind blew the grass and smacked at the branches of an old, overgrown apple tree under which Shay had built Matt a playhouse. Matt glanced west, toward the house where his best friend, Michael, lived. Usually Michael's house glowed with friendly yellow light, but tonight all the windows were dark. No one was home.

What should he do? There were terrible shadows of trees all along the edge of the property, and the shadow cast by Shay's studio was long and absolutely black.

Matt caught his breath in a hiccuping sob. Nobody was out here. Nobody would help him.

He glanced again toward the "apple tree house," as he called it. It was little and dark and the tree branches hung down, covering it. At night nobody would see it. He would wait there until his mom came home and she would come out in the yard and help him and hug him, and they would go inside the house together.

Grass squished under his toes as he raced across the lawn toward this sanctuary. He crawled inside like a mouse into a bolt hole. The tiny house was dark, and small shapes stabbed at his bare feet. He reached down and touched one. It was a piece of plastic Lego building block.

As he hunkered around, he heard the horrific squeal of tires as a car pulled away on the street. That was the bad boy leaving, Matt would bet. He clasped his hands around his torso, drawing up his knees so that he formed a small, tight, shivering ball. His pajamas were thin, and already he was feeling the cold.

Did the bad boy take Kelly with him? Matt shuddered, his eyes filling up with tears.

Coffee was now being served in the living room, both espresso and cappuccino. Guests milled around, deep in animated conversation. A young woman talked intently to Ben, her body leaning toward him. She threw back her head and laughed at something he said, lifting a pretty arm to ruffle one hand through her dark hair.

She was coming on to Ben, Shay knew. To his credit, Ben looked faintly bored. Shay loved him for it. She guessed she didn't want a man who became too interested in other women at parties.

She glanced at her watch again, noting that another half hour had passed, and decided to risk another call home. She threaded her way through the crowd, finding Eileen's writing room again.

Impatiently she dialed her own number. The telephone rang five times, and then her answering machine picked up. Kelly had recorded the tape several months ago. She listened to her daughter's sweet, breathy voice: *"Hey, dude, you've reached the Wyomings; we can't come to the phone right now but we really can't wait to get your cool message, so—"*

Shay hung on to the phone, puzzled. Were Noah and the kids so absorbed in the movies that they'd let the tape pick up? She called again, and again got the machine.

A tapeworm of fear wriggled inside her gut. It was quickly replaced by anger. What the hell was Noah doing, not answering the phone? Especially when he knew that she was anxious, and she'd especially wanted *him* to sit because she needed a mature adult, not a teenager. Blast him! Noah had his irresponsible moments, but she didn't think it would apply to her kids.

She tried one more time, hanging up just as Kelly said *Hey, dude.*

"Everything okay?" Ben came up and slid his arms around her midriff, his breath puffing warmly on her neck. "I was being attacked by a man-eating divorcée. Had to get away before she rolled me up in her web and hung me from a branch for her larder."

"Oh!" Shay jumped, the long, dangly earrings batting against her neck. "I was just dialing home. No answer."

"No answer?" Ben frowned.

"I called three times, and each time I got the answering machine. I hope you don't mind if we go home right now. I just don't like this."

''Maybe they went out to get ice, or Pepsi, or something.''

''He wouldn't do that.''

''He's not a professional babysitter, Shay. I wouldn't worry. . . . Okay, we'll go if you want to. I was ready to leave anyway. Let's go find Eileen and make our good-byes.''

''Let's make them short.''

Within five minutes they had left the party and were climbing into Shay's Cougar. She drove east on Lone Pine Road past the huge Bloomfield Hills homes barricaded behind stone fences and lush pines. Lighting crackled through the trees, and water pelted the car's windshield. She drove as swiftly as she dared, not wanting to skid on the rain-slicked curves.

''Rain,'' she murmured. ''Why would they go out in the rain? We couldn't have run out of anything; I keep that refrigerator stuffed full. If he's taken them somewhere I'm going to wring his neck, Ben. He's such a big old jerk, I should have known better.''

''Stop beating yourself,'' Ben said. ''Maybe one of the kids just turned off the phone ringers, did you ever think of that?''

''Not in our house. Kelly lives for the phone,'' she answered glumly.

Twenty minutes later they had pulled into her subdivision and she gave into her instinct for urgency, breaking the speed limit through the winding streets until she came to her own.

Her own house lights shone through the trees, looking delightfully normal. Almost every light was on, except in her studio, in which only her usual nightlight burned. She could even see the flicker of the TV screen coming from one of the family room windows.

Shay heaved a deep sigh of relief. She'd been a

paranoid fool. She'd worried herself sick, just like all the suburban mothers she sometimes looked down on.

"Hey, I wonder what they're watching," she said gaily to Ben, allowing relief to color her voice.

And then she saw that the garage door was up.

Noah's car was gone.

"Well, I guess he did go somewh—" She cut off the word. The Cougar's headlights had picked up a shape that lay flung on her grass, within inches of her driveway. Sparks of yard lights reflected off shiny chrome.

Mickey's Harley Davidson.

"Oh, Ben. Oh, God."

He had seen it, too. "Don't pull in," he ordered. "Stop down the street at one of the neighbors' and call the police from there."

But Shay was already slamming on her brakes. She skewed the car to a stop and scrambled out, running toward the house.

FOURTEEN

They went in through the front door, into the foyer which looked exactly as it had when they left, even to a Go-Bot that Matt had been playing with, still lying on the floor. However, the house seemed still, vacant, except for the mindless blare of the TV set in the family room.

"No," Shay kept saying over and over, her dry voice forming a dull, terrified monotone. "*No, dammit, no . . . no . . .*"

"Easy, baby. Easy," Ben said.

Ben was sniffing the air. His jaw muscles had knotted and there was a strange look on his face. "Shay . . . go back out to the car, will you? Wait there. I'll take a look around."

"No. I want to look, too. KELLY!" she suddenly called, her voice piercing the deathly silence of the house. "KELLY! MATT!"

"Don't. Go out to the car, Shay."

"I won't. I won't."

"Dammit—!"

Ben moved forward. Shay pushed after him, her pulse thudding as they entered the family room. On the TV, Rick Moranis was searching for his miniaturized children in the grass of his own backyard. The room was scattered with a litter of dirty plates, issues of *Teen Beat*, Pepsi cans, cookie crumbs, and pizza boxes. The sliding glass door had been opened about two feet, and a rainy wind flapped the curtain inward. Already the oatmeal-colored carpeting was damp with moisture.

"They went outside," Shay choked.

"Don't go out there. Don't do anything."

"But one of them must have gone out into the rain—"

"Switch off the TV set and just wait here for me," Ben snapped.

Numbly Shay picked up the remote and pushed the OFF button. The VCR and the television snapped off, and a heavy silence yawed into the room, instantly saturating every particle of air.

"I'm going to look around," Ben said, moving off toward the kitchen and utility room. An unpleasant smell was coming from that area, Shay realized. It smelled like—

She didn't want to think what it smelled like.

He was going to find something, Shay knew in that central, atavistic part of her brain where horror lives. And it would not be pretty, it would be very, very bad, and it would be something she did not want to see at all.

She felt a hollowness eating at her heart. She thought of a prayer but when she tried to say it, the words slipped away.

Then she heard a cry. It drifted through the opened door, where the damp curtain flapped.

"Mom," came the faint sob of Matt's voice.

* * *

Shay flipped on the outdoor lights and rushed into the yard, skidding on the wetness of the patio step and nearly falling. Rainy wind rushed into her face. "MATT! MATT! MATTIE!"

"Here, I'm in the apple tr—" The rest of his words were torn away by the wind, but Shay began running heavily across the grass, her three-inch heels digging into the sod.

"Matt!" she yelled, reaching the old, gnarly tree which smelled of blossoms. She squatted down to crawl under the branches, hearing a seam of her dress give way under the strain.

A small hand pushed open the door of the little house, and Matt's face peeked out. In the gray light Shay saw the tracks of tears and mucous that ran down her son's cheeks.

"Matt! What happened? What are you doing out here? Where are Noah and Kelly?" She pulled her son into her arms, and he clung to her, wrapping both legs around her, his fingers digging frantically into her skin.

"The bad boy," Matt blurted. "The bad boy came. The bad boy!"

All the hope washed out of her as if sieved down a sink drain. *"You mean . . . Mickey."*

"That bad mo'cycle boy, an' Kelly yelled an' screamed an' screamed an' she told me to run outside so I run outside, an' I hid in the apple tree house an' I got all wetted by the rain an' a bug bit me."

"Oh, Matt, oh, honey, oh, honey." She cradled her crying son, carrying him toward the house again. She was staggering, both from Matt's weight and her realization of what had happened. *Mickey had taken Kelly.*

But in that case, where was Noah? It made no sense. Had her friend caught Mickey trying to vandalize the house again, and gone after him in his car? Except . . . Mickey's bike was still in the yard.

"Shay," Ben said, coming out onto the patio to meet her. In the dimness of the gray, rainy night his cheeks had a hollow look and there was a grim line to his mouth. His tuxedo jacket was crumpled and there was a mark of something red on his shirt front—something that hadn't been there before.

Shay stared at that slight smear of blood. She gripped Matt's warm bony body so hard that the little boy squirmed.

"It's not Kelly, thank God, but it's Noah. He's dead, Shay. In—in the bathroom. He's . . . it's bad." For a moment Ben lost his cool and swallowed convulsively. Somehow that, as nothing else, pointed out the horror to her.

"*Noah?*" she repeated numbly.

"Yes, poor Noah."

Within minutes their house was swarming with police and within an hour an assortment of technicians roamed the downstairs area, especially the kitchen and bathroom, taking photos, collecting bits of hair and other scrapings in plastic evidence bags, and dusting ugly, dark fingerprint powder everywhere.

They conferred among themselves, and someone else was inspecting all the window and door locks. Two EMS attendants were waiting until they finished taking pictures of Noah, in order to take his body away. Shay caught a glimpse of the blue plastic bags they would use, similar to what she'd seen many times on TV, in news broadcasts about murders or shoot-outs.

She endured it numbly. It wasn't real. It was all an incredibly bad dream. Mickey had taken Kelly away. He had murdered Noah and abducted her daughter. She alternated between crying and a frozen paralysis.

A police detective named Salter seemed to be the one assigned to ask them questions. He was a tall, worried-looking man of forty who was running to plumpness and looked more like a systems analyst than a police detective.

"Son, tell me again what the 'bad boy' looked like," he said to Matt.

"He was black, he had a black—"

Salter sighed. He didn't seem to have much of a way with children and it seemed to annoy him that his eyewitness was a kindergartner. "Do you mean his skin was black? A black man like Bill Cosby?"

"No, a black *shirt*," insisted the child, leaning into Shay's knee and gripping her tightly. "I told you, a black shirt thing with a bird on it, a big bird, an' he had red stuff all over him."

Matt's own pajamas were covered with mud and bits of grass, along with pizza and chocolate stains. He drooped with exhaustion.

Shay swallowed, thinking about her one short look at Noah's body. There had been blood everywhere, a gore bath. Her bathroom had been turned into a slaughter pen.

Kelly! Where was Kelly? Was she dead, too, her beautiful throat slit like an animal's?

"Son. Did he say anything? Say where he was going to take your sister?"

"He said bitch," Matt quavered. He started to cry again.

"Please," Shay begged. Shock had made her voice hoarse. "He's told you everything twice—he's only a child, he's only six years old. It's past one in the morning; can I please put him to bed?"

"Okay, okay," agreed the detective reluctantly. "He can rest for now, but come back because I want to go over it with you again."

Shay carried Matt upstairs, and lugged her son into his bedroom, putting him down on his bed. His breathing had deepened into exhaustion. She decided not to change him out of his pajamas or wash his face tonight. It was better for him to sleep.

She didn't think that she was ever going to sleep again.

God, where was Kelly right now? Was she still alive?

She kissed the child's cheek, then went into the bathroom and urinated. Washing her hands, she gazed into the mirror. Her party makeup had worn off, giving her face a drained, ghostly look. One of her earrings had also come off, perhaps when she was in the yard with Matt, but the other one still dangled, twirling prettily. She took it off and laid it on the vanity. Her eyes filled with tears.

"Shay? Can I come in?" Ben came down the hall and pushed open the bathroom door, which she had left ajar. He had shed his dinner jacket and thrown off his bow tie. His expensive shirt looked crumpled, used, and the smear of Noah's blood had darkened.

They stood with their hips leaned against the vanity, arms locked around each other. She gave herself up to the comfort of Ben's physical warmth. His deep breathing, the way his skin felt, his smell . . . why had she never made love to this man? Now she wondered if she ever would. If anything happened to Kelly, how would she ever be able to make love or do anything again? Her daughter was her heart. It was that simple. Mickey McGee had stolen her heart.

"Ah, God, Shay," Ben groaned. "I'm so damn sorry about all this."

"She might still be all right. Do you think? I have to have some hope, Ben."

"There's a chance," Ben said after a hesitation. "There always is a chance. The fact that he didn't kill her right away but took her along with him gives us some kind of hope.''

"Unless something scared him off and he decided to kill her later.''

"Shay,'' Ben said, holding her and patting her. "You're shaking all over. Have you got any pills— some tranquilizers, anything?''

"I don't take pills.''

"You need something to relax you.''

She pulled away from him. Unreasonable anger filled her. "I don't *want* to relax! I want to do something. I don't have much faith in the police, Ben. They bungled the investigation when my parents were murdered. I want to be here for her. I have to go downstairs and answer more questions. Oh, God . . .''

They went back downstairs.

"Yes, yes, yes," Shay responded wearily. They kept going over familiar territory until even the questions ceased to have the same, sharp urgency they had the first time around. "He was a student of mine but only for one week. He had great talent, but his work was angry and so was he.''

A shudder racked her body and she gripped the arms of the upholstered chair in which she was seated.

"Mrs. Wyoming? Mrs. Wyoming?''

"I . . . sorry.''

"You say his work was angry? Angry at who?''

"I didn't have a chance to psychoanalyze him.''

Salter seemed to lose interest, turning a page in his notebook, in which he had scribbled detailed notes. "Tell me how often he rode his motorbike past your house.''

She went over *that* again, this time adding how Kelly had taken off her top in front of her bedroom curtains. No longer could she shield her child's privacy. Kelly's entire life would be opened for inspection.

Salter barely reacted, merely underlining something in the notebook. Shay watched his pen move, her thoughts scattering again.

Mercifully, at last Salter closed his notebook and rose to his feet. "Well, I think that covers it for now. We're going to put a recording device on your phone, and I'll contact a judge to get an order so we can put a tap on your line. You have call forwarding?"

"Yes."

"Well, if you leave the house, I want you to use call forwarding, and I want someone available to answer calls at all times. If you can't take a call, make sure someone is babysitting the phone. It's possible she might call. If so, ask her *where she is*—that should be the first thing you ask. Do you get it, Mrs. Wyoming?"

Shay shuddered. The instructions seemed chilling. "Yes."

"Always pick up on the first or second ring. Remember, if she calls, ask *where are you?*"

"All right." She rose, too, looking the man in the eye. "But I'd like to ask you, how big a chance is there that my daughter might actually call? Do you think she's still alive?"

The man's eyes flicked away, then came back to her again. Shay thought, something inside her freezing, *he doesn't think so*.

Salter said, "She could be. But we won't know for sure until someone spots them or they leave some kind of a trail."

After Salter dismissed her, she and Ben wandered to the living room, which was currently clear of technicians. Someone had been smoking, and the odor of cigarette smoke seemed stifling. But at least it masked those other, dreadful odors—the smells of death.

Ben turned to her. "You and Matt can't stay here tonight. This is a murder scene, Shay. These people are going to be here all night and probably half the day tomorrow, too. You can stay at my house until this is over."

She hadn't thought that far ahead. Her voice was hoarse as she said, "I can't drag Matt out of bed now. Besides, there's the phone."

"Gloria Adamson is my neighbor, Shay—remember, she's the assistant principal at Walton? I'm sure I can get her to help us with the phone if we need her."

"All right, tomorrow," she whispered. "But tonight . . . I can't leave here tonight, Ben."

He hesitated. "I'm staying here then."

They had never slept together before. She nodded, too weary and heartsick to argue.

He followed her upstairs into her bedroom, and waited while she switched on a small bedside lamp. The room was large, the wallpaper a muted pink and gold stripe, the bed a spill of comforter and pillows. Several of her early sculptures, female nudes, stood on white pedestals.

She stood gazing around the room, feeling as if it belonged to someone else, in some other lifetime. Then her gaze fell on the dresser, where she kept small photos of Kelly and Matt in matching pewter frames.

A pain stabbed Shay's heart, coring out her center.

"Shay," Ben said hoarsely. He seemed to feel her pain, too. His face looked tired, the stubble of his beard beginning to show. The clean, kind bones of his face looked very dear to her.

"I love you," he said.

She went into his arms and within seconds her body was torn with sobs. She fought them, gripping Ben's arms with all her strength but they still overtook her, and he patted her and hugged her and gave her his warmth.

"Dammit!" she sobbed. "Dammit! Why did it have to be Kelly? My beautiful little girl! I'm going to get her back, Ben. I'm going to find her and get her back."

"Shay, honey," he said, holding her. "Are you sure you haven't got any tranquilizers or anything?"

"No, nothing. I'll get her back!" She wept angrily. "I will! I'm not just hysterical. I'll do what it takes. I will. I will."

Her knees were suddenly sagging. Ben half-carried her over to the bed and laid her down. She felt his gentleness, his love, his caring, and another huge wave of sorrow moved through her, racking her.

"Darling," Ben whispered. "Oh, darling Shay." She felt his hands removing the white beaded dress, and although she wore no bra underneath, her nakedness did not seem sexual, nor did it seem to matter. Gently he lifted her, placing her under the sheets, and then he himself quickly stripped down to undershirt and navy blue briefs. He switched off the lamp and crawled into bed beside her.

"I'm going to hold you the rest of the night," he told her. "I'll just hold you. I'll be here, Shay. Try to get some sleep and in the morning we'll talk."

Dire Straits pounded out of Noah's car stereo speakers, the beat heavy and suggestive. Mickey drove slowly through the subdivision, which seemed to sparkle in the rain, the car headlights reflecting on the damp road surface. All the houses had windows that glowed yellow in the night, and everyone was inside watching TV and being happy.

Except her.

Kelly's body shook violently and she clapped her

hands to her mouth, forcing back her wild, terrified sobs.

Within minutes, Mickey pulled over on a cul-de-sac, where three or four colonials faced a tiny court. It all looked peaceful, serene. Forcing her back with the knife he began to masturbate.

"Watch me!" he ordered. "Watch!"

Kelly nearly gagged at the repellent sight of Mickey's penis being rubbed by eager fingers that were still streaked by Noah's blood.

She thought wildly about jumping out of the car and running toward one of the houses. But she was afraid she couldn't get away fast enough. She'd seen the way he had *sprung* toward the car in the garage. He was faster than she was. He would probably at least cut her, and then he'd jump out of the car and chase her down, and he would stab her, just as he'd done Noah.

Finally Mickey shuddered in spasms and uttered a high-pitched cry. She heard the sound of him zipping up his pants, and when she glanced back again she saw that there was moisture on his cheeks.

Had he been crying? Had he done that and cried after-ward?

She felt a horrible stirring of her heart, like sympathy trying to be born and then dying. Mickey had cried. What did it mean? How could he cry and want to kill her?

"What are *you* staring at?" he sneered, yanking the car into gear again.

"Nothing."

"You're staring. I saw you staring at me."

"You . . . told me to stare."

"I did not. I did not tell you to look at me. Do you want me to punish you, bitch dear? Bitch Kelly Wyoming, so rich and blond, who's got a big house and big studio and every fucking thing in her life exactly the way she wants it?''

It was beyond her. She didn't know what to say. She sat huddled in the passenger seat, alternately crying and praying.

God, she prayed. *Get me out of this. Please, I ask you. I don't know what to do, and I'm not a very good prayer, and oh, please, just help me get out of this.*

FIFTEEN

Just as Shay's mind had begun to drift and spin, preparatory to falling asleep, Salter knocked on the upper hall wall.

"Mrs. Wyoming?"

She struggled toward consciousness. "Yes?"

"We've blocked off the kitchen and laundry area. I don't want you to use them, or cross the tapes we've put up. Remember what I said about the phone, now. Call and let me know where you'll be, and keep in close touch. I'll be working straight through on this, and technicians will be by here later today. Oh, and don't talk to the press yet."

She said something, made some kind of response. Apparently it satisfied him, because she thought she heard him leave. She fell through layers of consciousness like a circus performer without a net. File folders fluttered and fell with her, twisting in a high wind. Ben's voice chanted, "*Removed, removed, remooooooved.*"

Then she was at Cedar Point with Kelly, standing in line for the Demon Drop rollercoaster ride. It was very windy, and the gusts battered at her daughter's hair, whipping out the long, honey-blond strands. In the sky a black funnel cloud swirled toward them, a thin, ominous vortex. No one in line seemed to see it.

"I don't want to ride," Kelly protested, clutching at Shay's arm.

But somehow they had reached the head of the line. The wooden platform they were standing on began to fall. It hurtled downward like an elevator in a two-hundred-story building, plunging fast and out of control.

Shay wrenched herself to a sitting position, gasping for air. The room had turned dawn-gray, and the numbers on her digital clock said 6:15 A.M. Beside her Ben snored lightly.

She realized that the bedside phone was ringing. It was probably what had awakened her.

She fumbled for it, having to reach several times before she managed to close her hand on the receiver. She was always groggy in the earliest hours of the day but this morning it was much worse. She felt as if she had been half knocked-out by some virulent form of sleeping pill.

"Hello," she croaked.

"It's me," said her ex-husband, Randy.

"Randy?"

What was Randy doing, calling her at this hour? Then she remembered. *Kelly.*

"I heard, the police left a message on my tape and I picked it up with the remote." Randy's voice sounded as hoarse as her own.

She shook her head, fighting the groggy, drugged-up feeling of nightmare. ''The police called you?'' she repeated stupidly.

''I know Salter, I sold him a couple policies. I'm in L.A. at the Hyatt Sunset,'' he added. ''I had a meeting with some Aetna people.''

She told him what had happened, the words emerging in short, grim sentences. She noticed that she was removing herself from it, her words far too calm.

Randy started to cry. Shay listened to his sobs, feeling a moment of stunning closeness to him that receded almost as swiftly as it had occurred. She couldn't afford the luxury of wallowing in grief—not if she wanted her child back. Already she knew this and accepted it.

''Oh, baby, why did you let this happen? Why did you let that boy hang around her? I can't believe you let this happen. . . . You caused this . . . living like a damn single woman; . . . the divorce would never have happened if . . .''

She listened to his hurt, grieving, angry ravings, feeling guilt sear her. Was he right? God, she should have done something about Mickey immediately. She'd assumed that because he was only seventeen, he wasn't dangerous.

''Shay?'' Ben murmured, turning over in bed.

''Randy,'' she said quickly into the phone, cutting into his accusations. ''I have to go now.''

He managed to stop the tirade. ''I'm flying home.''

''Call me when you get here,'' she said, hanging up.

Ben sat up. ''I assume that was Randy. Are you all right?''

''I'm fine,'' she lied.

Ben was watching her. The whites of his eyes glistened in the morning light, and his undershirt looked bleached. ''I don't think so. Can you lie down and catch a few more hours of sleep? The more rest you get, the easier this is going to be for you."

"Until she's found," Shay said flatly. "That's what you mean, isn't it? You think she's going to be found dead, don't you? Lying on some street somewhere, pushed out of Mickey's car with stab wounds all over her."

"Hey." Ben slid his arms around her, cradling her. "I didn't say that. Shay, don't think that. Damn that asshole for calling here so early in the morning. Come on, lie down again and I'll hold you."

"I can't."

"Try. Just try."

"No. I can't. I'm awake now. Ben . . . why do you think he took Kelly like that? Do you think he's going to use her as a hostage?" She shuddered, remembering all the TV news broadcasts of bloody police confrontations she'd seen over her lifetime, plus the hundreds of police dramas. *Law and Order. Miami Vice. Hunter.*

"He may plan that, yes. Or maybe he didn't plan anything at all. Maybe it was just an impulse," Ben said slowly.

There was a long silence, broken by the noise of an automobile turning onto their street, some nightshift worker returning home, or possibly another patrol car. Headlights briefly flashed across the window and were gone. Somewhere a dog barked. Had the technicians downstairs gone home? She didn't hear any sounds from below.

"Which do you think it is?" she said at last.

"I think he's impulsive."

"And what does that mean?"

Ben reached for her hand, pressing her fingers between both of his hands. "Shay, I've read about killers because of my books, an ugly part of my work I don't particularly like. But I do know there are two kinds of killers. One is what the FBI calls organized—they make plans, have contingencies. The other kind is what they call disorganized, very impulsive and spur-of-the-moment. Some are a combination of both. Mickey may fall into that latter category; . . . maybe he planned to kidnap Kelly all along, then killed Noah at the last minute because he got in the way.''

Shay moistened her dry lips. ''In that case we don't know what's going to happen next.''

''Maybe he's working toward some unconscious goal that fits in with his mental pathology.''

Shay threw back the covers and fumbled for a pair of jeans and a T-shirt. Turning her back, she pulled on the shirt. ''Well, I can't just lie in bed thinking about this. I'm going downstairs. We both need some coffee.''

''Shay. You can't.''

She looked at him.

''The police, Shay. They blocked off the kitchen, don't you remember? I'll make coffee when we get to my house.''

She went into Matt's room to check on her son.

''Mommy,'' he whimpered sleepily as soon as she walked into the room. ''Mommeeee. I want Kelly.''

Mercifully, his eyes fluttered shut again. She wondered how deeply this had affected him, if he was going to need post-trauma therapy after this was over. Yes, they all would need it.

She lay on the bed beside her sleeping child. She felt as if her entire body had been pounded, her stomach pummeled. *Is Kelly dead?* she wondered. *Did Mickey rape her? Has he cut her throat like he did Noah's?*

She thought of Kelly giving her the pink earrings, her face eager and open for once. You never knew how deep your love was for a child until something like this happened. How much a part of you they were. Bone of your bone. And she'd been reaching Kelly again, she knew she had.

No, dammit! She was *not* going to lose her beautiful child to a psychopath like Mickey McGee, not while there was still a breath left in her.

But what were her alternatives? Was she going to follow Salter's advice and wait passively by the telephone for the unlikely possibility that Kelly would call . . .

. . . or the more real and horrifying probability that Salter or some other police officer would call with news she could not bear to hear?

No, to wait without doing anything was to admit that it was all over—that her child was dead.

Mom, Kelly's voice said in her head.

Shay stiffened, realizing it was only her own mind playing tricks, but her daughter's presence, her panic and terror, seemed to flood the room.

When she emerged from Matt's room, she found Ben seated on the top step of the staircase, dressed in his black formal pants and his dress shirt from the previous night. The collar was open at the neck, making him look like a reveler after a particularly raucous Saturday night.

Morning light had begun to permeate the house, giving everything a pinkish cast. It was not kind to Ben's features, revealing every crease, crow's foot, and stubble of beard. She had never found him more attractive or appealing.

"We should go to my house now," Ben said. "You and Matt can stay with me until this is over. Separate bedrooms, whatever you want. I was just waiting for you to come out of Matt's room so I could tell you."

She hesitated a long moment. She had no really

close women friends. Noah had been her best friend—
he had been her refuge up until now. And going to
Marianne's in Connecticut was not an option.

"All right, but I have to do something," she told
him quietly. "I can't just sit and passively wait for
something to happen. Worrying, imagining the worst,
being deprived of the ability to act. That's never been
me. I can't stomach the victim role."

Ben gazed intently at her, as if trying to assess her
emotional state. "Then what, Shay? I assume you have
something in mind."

The idea came to her with such a flash that she
realized her unconscious mind must have been working on it half the night. "Yes, I do. Those case records—the ones you told me about, the ones that Dr.
Vigoda has. The police are going to want to look at
them, aren't they?"

"Yes, that'll be very important. They always trace a
missing perpetrator's relatives and friends. You'd be
amazed how often the guy goes right home to his
mother's or his girlfriend's. Some of them are incredibly stupid."

"I want to have a look at Mickey's case file, before
the police do. They'll impound those records, right? If
they do, then we'll never get a chance to see them."

Ben's surprise showed on his face. "They may already have taken them."

Shay shook her head. "In the middle of the night?
I don't think so. No, I think they'll go over to the
school today and collect his records, open his locker,
stuff like that. You have a key to the school, don't
you?"

Ben nodded. "As journalism and yearbook advisor,
I've got key privileges. But, Shay, I can't guarantee you
the records will be in Dr. Vigoda's office. She might
have taken them home. Besides, she keeps her office

locked and I don't have a key to that, so it's going to be breaking and en—''

''I don't care what it is. I'll take responsibility. Ben, I'm *not* going to be passive about this. I refuse to be.''

He pressed his lips together, the lines bracketing his mouth even more deeply. As a teacher employed at the school he was putting his job on the line if he helped her. ''All right,'' he said finally. ''I'll do it. But I can't guarantee what we'll find—if we find anything at all.''

''It'll be a start,'' Shay insisted. ''Please. I can see by your face you don't think I should do this. Well, I'm going to do it. *Kelly needs me.* That's the bottom line, Ben. She is out there and she needs me.''

While Ben punched the call forwarding code into Shay's phone and arranged for Gloria Adamson to come to his house, Shay went into her son's bedroom and packed a suitcase for him. She included several of his favorite Transformer toys, and a plastic bag full of his beloved Lego building blocks. She quickly washed him and dressed him in Guess? jeans, a shirt, and his new high-topped Reeboks.

''Where we goin', Mommy?'' he demanded sleepily.

Shay had already telephoned Natalie Goldner, Michael's mother, and left a message on Randy's answering machine, telling her ex-husband where she was taking the child.

She shook Matt awake. ''Honey, I'm taking you over to Michael's house for today. They're driving down to Cedar Point and want to take you with them. After that I've asked your dad to pick you up and he'll keep you with him until Kelly comes back.''

''Cedar Point,'' the six-year-old repeated doubtfully. Last year he had adored Cedar Point Amusement Park, in Sandusky, Ohio, but now everything was different. This morning he seemed pinched and anxious, unwilling to separate himself from her.

"Mommy has to try to get Kelly back," Shay said.

Her son's rosy lower lip went out. "I don't want to go to Michael's."

"Come on, Matt, hurry, see if there are any other toys you want to bring." She knew she wasn't giving her little boy the emotional support he needed—but dammit, what else could she do?

Her stomach knotted with guilt, she hurried her son through his packing and took him downstairs, avoiding the kitchen area, with its red and white police tape and its spills of dark fingerprint powder. Ben was waiting for them.

Silently they went outdoors, where Shay had left her Cougar parked in the driveway. The rain had stopped. The morning sky was pearl colored, layers of fuchsia clouds lying along the eastern horizon, suffusing the air with pink. The Sunday morning seemed muffled, the usual subliminal roar of weekday traffic disturbingly absent.

"It's too early," Matt wailed, balking.

"Please, honey. Come on."

"I don't want to!"

Dammit! Shay thought. She picked up her son and crushed him fiercely to her, smelling the sharp perfume of his hair and skin, mingled with perspiration. "It'll be okay, baby," she whispered.

They drove around the block to Michael's house, a white colonial with a floor plan nearly identical to their own. Ed Goldner, Michael's father, worked at the GM Truck and Bus facility in Pontiac, and his wife, Natalie, ran a package mailing shop in Troy.

Natalie greeted them at the door, wearing a blue chenille bathrobe and no makeup. She looked tired, but managed a smile for Matt.

"Hi, Matt, honey. Michael is just getting up; he can't wait to see you. He's upstairs getting dressed. We're going to play a video until breakfast. The *Muppet Babies*, I think."

Matt dropped his bag in the hallway and, without glancing back at Shay, scampered toward the stairs, instantly comfortable in the familiarity of his playmate's house. Shay felt herself sag with relief.

"Oh, Shay." Natalie Goldner moved forward.

The two women embraced but Shay quickly pulled away, afraid that she would collapse under too much sympathy. "I know this is terribly short notice. . . . Here's something to cover Matt's expenses." Hastily she dug into her purse for three twenty-dollar bills.

Natalie rejected the money. "Oh, I couldn't. Michael loves Matt. Oh, Shay . . . I can't believe this, I just can't believe this could have happened in our neighborhood."

"I can't either."

"A boy from the *high school* did this?"

"Yes."

"Somebody Kelly went to school with?"

Shay felt a sudden wave of anxiety. She didn't have time to talk! Every minute she stood here explaining things to Natalie was a minute she could not search for Kelly. "I've got to go, Nat," she said hastily. "Remember, I've left a message on Randy's answering tape, and he's got a remote, so he'll pick it up. You can call his tape, too, and leave a number where he can reach you."

"Thank God for electronics," Natalie said dryly.

Walton High School was Walton Hills' star high school, a long, low, brick building built near a beautiful stand of woods that, by some miracle, had escaped the builders who had turned most of the area, once considered "country," into endless subdivisions containing $180,000 to $350,000 homes.

Shay pulled into the circular drive that led to the huge, empty student parking lot. Hundreds of students drove cars, including lease cars provided by yuppie parents on the car plan from Chrysler, Ford, or General Motors.

The morning wind picked up a scatter of papers and Burger King wrappers, blasting them against a tree trunk. A pair of girls' pink bikini panties, Shay noticed, had been hung in the lower branches of a tree like a trophy. She shuddered, feeling as if she had entered an alien world of the young—a place that had bred Mickey.

"Okay," she said, shutting off the Cougar's motor. "We're here. Now I guess we sneak in, right?"

"No, we walk in like we own the place," Ben said. "Remember, I legitimately have a key. And I do know Eleanor Vigoda personally, in case there's trouble. Also, it looks like we're in luck—the maintenance service doesn't work Sundays and I don't see any police. Yet."

They let themselves in through a side door located near the auditorium. The halls, dimly lit with overhead lights, smelled of pine-scented floor polish. This was a new school, only six years old, and it had been equipped with all the upscale amenities. Here, by the 350-seat theater, the walls were hung with poster-sized photographs of the casts of various school plays. This year the school had done *Cabaret* and *The Mousetrap*.

Their footsteps echoing, they walked down an endless grid of corridors. Many had windows that looked out on a series of attractively landscaped outdoor atriums. Within minutes, Shay felt hopelessly lost in the welter of classrooms, labs, music rooms, computer rooms, libraries, and sound studios. Sprayed on the door of one of the classrooms was a swastika in yellow paint.

"That's recent," Ben muttered as they hurried past. "We do have a few skinheads here. The little bastards smuggle the paint in. Gloria expels them if she catches them."

At last they reached a side corridor that fronted on another atrium. Doors were labeled SCHOOL NURSE and PSYCHOLOGIST.

"Okay," Ben said. "This is Eleanor Vigoda's office. Are you still game?"

Shay fought the curdling sensation of doubt that had roiled her stomach ever since she had stepped into her daughter's school. They had no key for this room and she'd have to get in any way she could.

"Ben, why don't you leave now? If I get caught, I'll say that you knew nothing about this."

"No way. I'm here and I'll participate. Eleanor would have let us in if she'd been in town."

Shay nodded. She opened her purse and took out a slim, plastic I.D. card issued by the video store, expertly jimmying it between the door and the lock mechanism.

"You know how to do that?" Ben said, staring.

"My father taught me—we had to break into our house once. I also cracked his home safe after he died. He never told anyone the combination."

Within two minutes Shay had the lock open and they were inside the psychologist's office, a small room littered with case folders piled in stacks on the desk, chairs, table tops, and even on the floor, as well as on top of a gray file cabinet. Psychiatric books crammed a small bookshelf and spilled onto the floor.

"Oh, shit," Shay said, seeing the mess.

"Overworked, underpaid," Ben said. "You take the file cabinet, I'll start on the loose folders. And we'd better hustle. I don't know when the police will get here, and I might be able to make up some kind of an excuse, but I'd rather be out of here by then, if you don't mind."

Five minutes later Ben uttered a cry, lifting up a weighty folder that was bound to another one by a thick, grimy rubber band. It looked years old, dog-eared from handling, and had been stamped several times with various school logos.

"This is it, babe. McGee, Michael Daniel. A.K.A. Mickey."

SIXTEEN

Kelly's full bladder was swollen inside her with painful pressure. Despairingly she squeezed her legs together, fighting tears. Twice Mickey had stopped the car so he could pee out of the car door, but he had not offered her an opportunity to urinate. And she'd been afraid to ask, terrified to draw his attention in any way.

Now the crisis was becoming acute. If she didn't go soon, she was going to have an accident, she felt sure. Then what would he do to her?

They were on a two-lane, blacktop road north of the little town of Clarkston, a road that wound past farms, fields, farm markets, new subdivisions, and condo developments. Hours ago Mickey had switched license plates, stealing one from a car parked behind a 7-11, and was now staying on side roads where the county sheriff and police did not patrol.

Morning wind caught the leaves of the trees that grew on either side of the road, creating a green shimmer. The road looked vaguely familiar to Kelly. They'd driven out here last fall to attend the Renaissance Festival, she remembered. There'd been people in medieval costumes, jugglers, mummers, and parades.

It seemed like a lifetime ago. Now maybe she'd never get to go again. Maybe she was only going to live a few hours longer . . . or less than that, depending on Mickey's mood. He still hadn't bothered to wipe the blood stains off his hands—Noah's blood.

"So, what kind of a guy turns you on? I mean really *turns you on*?" Mickey was saying.

"I don't know," Kelly said, anxiously clamping down on her bladder muscles. Her side throbbed from the superficial cuts he'd made with the knife, and the blood-sticky fabric of the T-shirt stuck to her. Her finger hurt, and there were bruises all over her—bruises she didn't even remember getting.

"What do you mean, you don't know?" he badgered her. "You have to know."

"I don't."

"Fuck," Mickey snarled. "You're such a bitch, you know that? You and that bitch mother of yours. What's she do, pee ice cubes?"

"Please," Kelly said faintly.

"Yeah, I bet she pees ice water. She thinks she's hot shit, you know? She thinks she rules the earth. Where'd she get the money for that hot-shit studio of hers?" Mickey sneered.

"I—I think in the divorce, part of it. And some from an inheritance from my grandma and grandpa."

"They died?"

"In a party store robbery."

"Yeah . . . death, death, death," Mickey said, clicking his tongue. "Lookit those two old geeks."

Ahead of them, an ancient white Ford with fins

lumbered down the road. Inside were an old man and an old woman, dressed for church.

Kelly glanced at the dashboard clock. 6:45 A.M. Fresh despair filled her. How would the police ever find them out in Clarkston? Police never drove around in the country—they could drive for hours and never see a police car.

"Hey, we're runnin' on fumes," Mickey remarked, shifting in the seat with a raise of his hips. "Gotta find a gas station around here. Or else get a new car. What do you think of that?" They had turned onto another road—she didn't glimpse the name.

Her bladder pressure was so severe that she took a chance. "Please, I need to use the bathroom."

"Yeah? Can I watch?"

"*No.*"

"Oh, yeah? If I want to watch, I'm going' to, girl. 'Cause you and me, we're bound together, you know what I mean? It's just you and me, bitch Kelly. And pretty soon I got another surprise for you. A real good surprise you're gonna like."

She didn't want to know any of his surprises. "Please," she begged, trying not to whimper. "Please. Or I'll wet myself."

Mickey uttered an angry exclamation and jerked the car into the nearest driveway, a parking lot for a produce stand called Trager's Farm Market. The dilapidated wooden shed was still shuttered for the season, which didn't begin until July. A decaying sign said U-PICK.

He slammed the Tempo to a stop, its tires spitting up dirt. "Here, dammit. Get out and squat."

"H-here?"

"Yeah, *here*," he mocked. "Go on, squattey-do, but I'm not lettin' go of you." He waved the knife.

Kelly gazed at him for a horrified moment, seeing

the thin lines bracketing the sides of Mickey's full, pouty mouth. He was grinning at her, enjoying her fright. Had she ever really been in love with him? Daydreamed about him kissing her? Kelly shuddered convulsively. He was the most horrible and frightening person she'd ever met. And now he was going to force her to expose herself in front of him.

"*Pee*, goddammit!" he ordered. "Or I'll drive on— but I'm warning you, if you wet your pants, I'll kill you."

Shaking, Kelly reached for the door handle and pushed open the car door halfway, hoping it would partially shield her from the road. She climbed out and fumbled for the zipper of her jeans, lowering herself to a squatting position. She turned her back toward Mickey. A little breeze found its way underneath the car door, chilling her bare buttocks.

She thought she'd have trouble, but the urine almost burst out of her, spattering to the ground in a heavy, pungent stream. She listened to it splash on the dirt, her eyes stinging with tears of anger.

She had to get away from Mickey or he would kill her.

But how?

How?

Shay carried the heavy folder labeled Michael Daniel McGee to Dr. Vigoda's desk. Her hands shook as she slid off the rubber band. What horrid thing was she going to find in here? Would there be any facts that would help her to find Kelly?

"Hurry," Ben urged her, glancing toward the window which faced the parking lot.

"Okay, okay." She flipped open the folder, revealing an intimidating three-inch stack of test results, medical records, court reports, and social workers' reports. Some were professionally typed, while others consisted of only a few handwritten lines on a sheet. ''Oh, Lord,'' she moaned.

''Can of worms, huh?''

''Yes. Here, you take half.'' She handed Ben the second half of the file, and quickly began to leaf through the sheets.

It looked like a typical hard-core public assistance case record. Apparently the mother, Beverly, had been on ADC for years, enduring a succession of violent boyfriends and working at low-paying jobs. She had been hospitalized repeatedly for her injuries. However, one case worker had managed to obtain counseling for Beverly through Catholic Social Services.

From third grade on, Mickey had tested in the upper 3 percent on most of his tests. At six he had won a prize in a city art contest. A yellowed clipping showed a handsome young boy who gazed solemnly into the camera.

There had been two children. Mickey and a brother named David, a year younger.

''You'd better hustle,'' Ben urged, bringing her suddenly back to reality. He was looking out of the window. ''I thought I heard another car pull into the parking lot, Shay.''

For a wild instant Shay thought of snatching up the case record and carrying it out with them to the car, where she could read it at her leisure. But she knew the police needed to see this case record, too; she could not steal their resources.

''All right . . . I'm hurrying. I wish I had about another hour.'' Rapidly she continued to scan the pages.

The teachers' reports were not glowing. Mickey's crimes ranged from tantrums in class to absences from school—one stretching to nearly four months. Fighting on the playground. Spitting at a teacher. Slapping a teacher who attempted to discipline him. Masturbating in class. Chasing a dog with a knife and trying to cut off its tail. He wanted to ''see the insides,'' he had told a teacher named Judy Fisher.

And this was a *seven-year-old boy,* not an unruly teenager, Shay had to remind herself, turning pages. She thought of her own sweet Matt, whose worst crime was jumping up and down on his bed. She wished the case record were not so thick. Ben kept glancing out of the window, and she knew they did not have much time.

Then another sentence jumped up at her. *Mickey has poor emotional affect, and seems to have walled himself off from the fact that he killed his—*

She stopped, her heart pounding thickly, and reread the paragraph, then reread an earlier sheet, flipping backward in the file with a growing sense of horror.

Ben sensed her agitation and looked up. ''Find something?''

''It's . . . oh, God,'' she breathed. ''No wonder they kept these files secret. Oh, Ben, this is horrible.''

''What is it, Shay? We'd better move fast.''

''He killed his little brother with a handgun.''

''What?''

''His name was David. It was one of those awful firearms accidents. Mickey found his father's gun lying in a drawer and just shot David in the head one day while they were playing. Oh, Ben. The boys were only seven and six.''

Ben pressed his lips together. ''It doesn't surprise me. I've been reading, too. This is a hard-core kid.''

''But they were only children—''

''Charles Manson was a child once, too. I don't think all accidental deaths are entirely accidental, if you know what I mean. Even among children. I'd say Mickey has an aberrant personality, a real psychopathic bent to him, and it just surfaced early, that's all. But look, here's something else that's significant.''

Shay moved over to glance over Ben's shoulder. He pointed to another faded newspaper clipping.

''I *knew* there was something really screwed up in that kid's life,'' Ben said, slapping the top sheet. ''I mean, I *knew* it.''

Shay's eyes traveled down the small lines of newsprint, her heartbeat quickening until it became a heavy, smothering thud.

> . . . *Danno McGee, an apparent abuser of the mother for many years, barricaded himself, Beverly, and the 8-year-old Mickey in their house for nearly 14 hours where he repeatedly raped Beverly McGee in front of the child, and cut her with a knife, forcing the boy to watch. . . .*

''Oh,'' breathed Shay, feeling a surge of nausea.

> . . . *McGee tortured the child with cigarette butts, and also stabbed him in the ribs and side, causing the boy to lose nearly two quarts of blood. . . .*

The picture this brought to Shay's mind was horrific. She set the folder down without finishing the article, her hands shaking violently. Small dots spun in front of her eyes.

Ben sighed, ''Well, that's that. The kid's got a history of violence like you wouldn't believe. The police finally forced Danno McGee's hand—shot the guy three times when he crossed in front of a window. He lived, though. Did four to eleven at Jackson Prison. He's since broken parole and the authorities don't know where he is right now—but they'd like to find out. Seems he might be involved in some truck hijacks.''

They looked at each other. "His father," Shay said heavily. "Danno. That's who he really hates.''

"Can you blame him? The guy sounds like Attila the Hun."

They let themselves out of Dr. Vigoda's office, locking the door behind them. In the hallway, Shay clenched her hands into fists, forcing the tremors to recede. The letdown she felt was as pervasive as a shot of Demerol. God, was her naïveté never going to end? She'd thought she was going to find a clue in Mickey's case file, something that would help them. Instead she'd found evidence that he was even more vicious and dangerous than she'd imagined. A hard-core murderer.

Ben looked at her, sensing the downturn of her mood. "Hey, the police will know what to do about this. Come on, let's go somewhere and buy some breakfast.''

Food? When she was dying inside? "I . . . I don't think I can eat.''

"Yes, you can. Besides, we need to talk.''

They started through the maze of hallways again.

Before they left the market, Mickey leaned across the seat and rummaged in the pile of junk that littered Noah's back seat.

"Shit. This guy was a damn pack rat. And all his stuff has got paint and plaster junk on it. Great. Just great. We're gonna look like damn workmen.''

He found a pair of old, paint-stained jeans and a Detroit Pistons T-shirt for himself. He tossed a baggy button-down shirt with a missing button to Kelly.

She pulled the shirt on over her bloody T-shirt. It was huge on her, but it smelled of Noah's perspiration and gave her an odd feeling of comfort, as if Noah himself were somehow watching over her.

They pulled back onto the road again. Fields and little copses of woods dotted the landscape, and in the distance a white farmhouse was sandwiched between two huge red barns. Two big dogs chained in the yard were lying down, snoozing, not even glancing up as the car drove past.

"So what's your mom like?"

The question took Kelly by surprise. She turned to stare at him. For a few seconds Mickey's profile looked handsome again, his lips full but pressed together.

"I don't know," she mumbled.

"I mean what is she *like*. And don't give me no lies, bitch girl. Is she really as ice cold as she looks?"

"She's not . . ." Kelly swallowed, realizing anything she said could be dangerous. "She's just a mother," she finished.

"Bull*shit*. She doesn't look like no mother. And she thinks she's higher 'n the mighty. She thinks being a big, fancy, stupid *sculptor* makes her better than the rest of us. Well, I've got news for her. She isn't. She shits and sweats and fucks, just like us."

Kelly said nothing, hearing the anger shake in Mickey's voice as he talked about her mother. Was he jealous of Shay? She shook her head, her numbed mind refusing to think about it further. What did that matter anyway? She just wanted to get out of this car—to go home.

They drove fifteen or twenty minutes, then Mickey turned the Tempo into the entrance of a subdivision called Lake's Edge, located off Rattalee Lake Road. The sun was finally up. Yellowish light flooded the gravel road, picking up bits of mica that glittered like diamonds.

As they drove down a winding street, Kelly felt her throat close. The subdivision seemed drenched in Sunday peace. When a man appeared at the front door of one of the homes and started toward his mailbox to get his Sunday paper, Kelly opened her mouth to scream.

"One yell and I hang your guts out to dry," Mickey snapped, jabbing the tip of the butterfly knife into her side.

Kelly subsided, clutching at the fresh wound. She gasped, trying not to scream with pain. She was going to have *scars* . . . if she lived.

Maybe she wasn't going to live.

Why would he let her? He hated her. She stifled a sob, and sank back against the seat, trying to blot the trickle of new blood that ran down her side with the hem of the shirt she'd just put on.

Mickey had slowed the car and was staring out of the side window, as if searching for a particular house number.

"Hey, *hey,*" he crowed suddenly, sounding pleased with himself. "Right here, man . . . just where the phone book said."

Dully she looked up. The house was a tri-level. Three brick archways in front defined a long porch, on which tubs of geraniums, impatiens, and hanging baskets made a note of bright color. A vacant lot on the left gave it privacy, isolating it somewhat from its neighbors.

Mickey's breathing had changed, becoming hoarse and shallow. Kelly felt a terrible, premonitory twist of fear.

"Who . . . who does this house belong to?"

"You'll see."

He pulled the Tempo into the driveway and parked.

"Come on," he told her roughly, dragging her across the center console so that she was forced to exit the car on the driver's side. "And remember—one move and I do you. Hear that? You're gonna watch me. Get it?" he repeated, jerking her arm until pain shot through her.

"Yes, yes, yes," she whimpered.

"This is for you, babe," he whispered. "All for you."

She fought tears. Something horrible was about to happen, she felt sure. Oh, God, whose house was this? Why did she have the awful feeling that it belonged to someone she knew?

He dragged her up to the front door.

The flower containers on the porch were well tended, and the hanging pot was suspended by hand-made macrame hangings strung with ceramic beads that looked eerily familiar to Kelly. In fact, didn't Mrs. Goldman have some identical plant hangers in her art room . . . ?

Mrs. Goldman.

Mickey leaned on the doorbell, gripping Kelly by one arm so she wouldn't run away. He needn't have worried. Paralysis had taken possession of her, locking her knees and causing her breath to clog in her throat. *Oh, God, oh, God! This was Mrs. Goldman's house.*

They heard the chime of the doorbell echoing within the house, but there was no response. Mickey leaned on the bell while Kelly stared dully through the narrow glass pane that ran on the left side of the carved oak door. Inside, she could see part of a painting, and a shiny blue satin school jacket flung on the floor. Mrs. Goldman had three children, she remembered.

Mickey leaned again on the doorbell, and finally they heard a sound from within the house. Kelly saw that Mickey had the butterfly knife concealed in his palm.

"One scream," he hissed. "One scream . . . and you'll get what they get. I mean it. I'll cut out your insides, bitch. I'll cut you open."

A few seconds later, a man in a blue velour bathrobe opened the door. He had a sleep mark from the bedding across one cheek.

"Yes?" he said sleepily, staring first at Mickey, then at Kelly, a vague expression of alarm crossing his face. "Are you collecting for something? It's pretty damn early . . ."

"Mr. Goldman, right?" Mickey pushed the door open with his foot and stepped inside before Goldman, caught off guard, could react.

With a swift twisting motion, Mickey jammed the butterfly knife upward. It thrust through the opening of the bathrobe into bare, hairy skin that almost instantly gushed red. The man grunted, gazing down with a look of startled surprise. Instinctively he tried to push Mickey's hand back, but Mickey was already stabbing again, as if gutting an animal.

Each time he sliced upward, Mickey glanced at Kelly as if for her approval or admiration. He was breathing with orgasmic excitement.

Kelly felt a swoon of sudden lassitude. She tried to breathe but no air would come. Her head was buzzing with a horrible noise like electricity.

The blood-soaked velour robe fell open as Mr. Goldman staggered backward. His shriveled genitals were now covered with blood. He sobbed, staring down in horror at himself. Blood gushed from the wounds and spurted out from between his fingers.

"Ken?" came Mrs. Goldman's querulous voice from a hallway to the right. "Ken? Who is it? Is it the paper boy?"

Mickey flashed a murderous look toward the hall. "Ken?"

"*Don't, don't,*" Kelly begged, and realized she must have been saying it all along. "*Please don't. Please don't.*"

"*Just shut up, bitch, and let me do this.*"

Mr. Goldman had collapsed backward into a puddle of red, his naked legs sprawled apart. Mickey dragged Kelly around the corpse, toward the bedroom hall. She fought him, but he slapped her and thrust the bloody knife within inches of her nose, and she quickly realized that if she did not give in, he would kill her.

"Ken? Ken?" Mrs. Goldman's voice had become progressively more alarmed. Now the teacher herself appeared, a filmy peach-colored negligee robe clutched around her. With no makeup and her hair streaming untidily down over her shoulders, Mrs. Goldman looked unfamiliar, not like the teacher Kelly knew.

"Mrs. G—" Kelly attempted.

"Mickey? *Kelly?*" The woman stared at them, stunned. She shook her head, as if trying to grasp why two of her pupils should be in her house at 7:00 A.M. on Sunday morning. Then, as she took in the bloody knife in Mickey's hand, fright disfigured her face. She began to scream.

Mickey lunged forward, stabbing past the forearms the teacher had flung up to protect herself. Cutting off the woman's screams, he sliced into the hollow of her throat. A great rush of red blood poured out. Mrs. Goldman's head snapped backward and her mouth worked like a fish's, bubbling up with red. The gagging sound she made was the most terrible Kelly had ever heard.

From somewhere in the house, the whimpering of

a small child reached Kelly. But the sick buzzing in her ears had grown so loud that the sound had no meaning. Her knees wobbled and sank beneath her. Blackness overwhelmed her.

SEVENTEEN

Carillon bells were chiming from one of the nearby local churches as Shay and Ben reached their car. The sound seemed almost shockingly, grotesquely normal. While Kelly was in the hands of a murderer, people lived their regular lives, filing into church or getting ready to go out for Sunday breakfast.

In life, there is death, Shay found herself thinking.

When Shay turned on the car radio, a news flash was already on the air. *"Prominent local sculptor Noah Ransom was brutally murdered and a sixteen-year-old girl kidnapped last night from her Walton Hills home, by a suspect police believe to be a seventeen-year-old schoolmate of the girl. Police say—"*

Without asking, Ben switched off the broadcast.

"Please," Shay insisted. "I want to hear it."

"It's going to be running all day, Shay, and you'll hear fifteen versions, each one upsetting. Take my word for it, the media are only going to complicate things, not help. They're probably already swarming at your house hoping for an interview.''

They drove to a Denny's restaurant in the nearby village of Rochester, where Sunday breakfasters had already begun to gather, families with small children and grandmas, and couples.

Ben waved over their waitress and ordered Grand Slam breakfasts for both of them, two large orange juices, and coffee. Shay realized that she was freezing cold and had been for some time.

"I feel spacey," Shay said in a low voice. "I feel out of control. I feel so damn helpless, Ben. After I read that case file . . . I'm so scared for her. *What's he doing to her?*''

She had raised her voice slightly, and a couple eating in a nearby booth glanced at them.

"It doesn't look very good," Ben admitted.

Shay felt herself stiffen. "No!" she cried. "No, it's not hopeless. She is still alive. *She is still alive.* Dammit, Ben! Excuse me," she blurted, getting up and fleeing to the ladies' room.

In the washroom, she locked herself in a stall and gave herself up to a flood of hot, intense tears. But she stopped crying after only a few minutes, when another woman came in to use the facility. Tears were an admission that the situation was hopeless. She refused to allow any such admission. Never.

She blew her nose and wiped her eyes, then left the rest room. A phone booth was located in a small corridor near the rest rooms. She dialed her own number, and Gloria Adamson picked up on the first ring.

"Hello?"

"G-Gloria?" With force of will, Shay stopped the stammer, which occasionally bothered her in times of stress. "Did she call?"

"No, I'm so sorry. You've had a lot of calls from the

media, though, and from friends, but I'm trying to keep the line clear. I'm not leaving the phone even for a second, so you don't have to worry."

"Thank you. Gloria, I—" But she couldn't go on. She felt waves of gratitude that the woman would care enough to do this for her, more gratitude that Gloria was exceptionally capable, and would handle whatever needed to be handled.

"You don't have to thank me, Shay. We all want her back."

Shay hung up and immediately dialed Salter. She was put on hold and waited impatiently, reading the graffiti scrawled on the phone booth. DANA + KEVIN = TRUE LOVE.

At last Salter came on the line. His voice sounded tired and gruff, as if he had been up all night. It didn't sound like the voice of a man who had good news, she realized.

"This is Mrs. Wyoming," she began.

"Yes. Well, I've been trying to reach you. There's been a new development."

She gripped the telephone so hard that she felt the blood leave her fingers. "What—what kind of a new development?"

"A very bad murder of a family up in Clarkston. They were knifed—four people. A husband and wife, and two little girls, age six and eight. Apparently the wife was McGee's art teacher."

"You don't mean *Mrs. Goldman*?"

"Janice Goldman. Yes."

Shock chilled her, gripping her like skeletal, wintry fingers. She knew Janice Goldman, had worked with her to arrange the Michigan Council for the Arts classes.

"We also have a witness," Salter went on. "The couple's thirteen-year-old son was sleeping in a basement bedroom. When he heard the noises, he hid. He saw Mickey and your daughter leave.''

Shay fought the emotions that crashed in on her. First the raw, naked hope—Kelly was still alive! Oh, thank God, thank God. Mickey hadn't killed her yet. There was still a chance of getting her back.

Then came terror, equally raw, followed by anger.

Her voice rose. ''You're not saying that Kelly—that she . . . that she's somehow *involved* with this?''

''We don't know what to think. We're trying to find out. McGee drew on the Goldmans' walls with a felt pen—pictures of penises and testicles. And he wrote 'You're on our shit list.' Does that sound familiar to you, Mrs. Wyoming?''

''*Our* shit list?'' More shock. Was this nightmare never going to end? ''Oh, God. You do think Kelly's involved in this, don't you? Well, let me tell you, she is just as much a victim as any of the people he killed. Kelly is only sixteen years old. She's a quiet, shy girl— she gets A's and B's, for God's sake! She was a counselor at the Y day camp last summer. She's not—she would *never*—Ask her assistant principal. Ask Gloria Adamson—''

''Okay, Mrs. Wyoming, okay. I did ask her. I just got off the phone with her. Anyway, the good news is that the girl is still alive because a witness saw her.''

A waitress on her way to the ladies' room stared at Shay curiously.

''W-what are you going to do?'' she whispered.

''We still have the APB out, and now that we know that he's still in the area, we can target him even more. We're tracing his family and associates now. We're going to find him, Mrs. Wyoming, and we want to do it before he kills any more people.''

She said numbly, ''Yes.''

"Do you know anything about this so-called 'shit list' he wrote down?"

"No."

"Your daughter didn't talk about anything like that? Didn't mention it to you? Anyone else he might have a grudge against?"

"No," she whispered. "Mr. Salter, I've told you, Kelly barely spoke to him. She had a schoolgirl crush on him, but that doesn't mean they were friends. Don't you remember how kids are?" Moisture filled her eyes.

Salter instructed her to go to Ben's and wait until she heard from him again. "I'll be by later in the day to talk to you again if I need anything more."

She murmured something that Salter took as agreement.

"The guy knifed two little girls and left a damn bloodbath behind him. We're going to get him," Salter vowed, his voice shaking. "I want you to believe that, Mrs. Wyoming. We'll find him. He's *not* getting away!"

Shay hung up the phone and stood for a moment steadying herself. Her heart was pounding uncomfortably fast, and it seemed as if she could not get a deep breath.

Mickey had killed six people.

Could that really be true?

Feverishly her mind counted, coming up with the same total each time. First, there had been Mickey's little brother, David. Then Noah. Then the four Goldmans. That did make six, didn't it? And this was the boy who had her daughter in captivity and was forcing her to accompany him as he slaughtered children.

She knew she was deathly pale as she made her way back to the booth.

Ben looked up, his expression alarmed as he took in

her shocked face. Shay sagged onto the padded seat of the booth and gazed down at her breakfast plate that had just arrived. The scrambled eggs were flanked by brown sausage links, gleaming with grease. The food looked as unreal as a menu picture. She stared at it, transfixed.

"For God's sake, Shay, what is it?"

In short sentences, she told Ben what Salter had said. "He's killed six people," she finished dully. "And he's pulling Kelly with him—he's pulling her into it. I can't believe what a nightmare this is turning out to be."

"Shay, I can't tell you how sorry I am. She's a beautiful girl," Ben said, and she saw tears spill from his eyes, making a path down his cheeks.

They leaned toward each other and clung together, heedless of the fact that they were in a restaurant, with customers in other booths and uniformed waitresses hurrying back and forth with trays. Shay tipped her head close to Ben's, covering her face with her hands.

"Shit," he said at last, pulling away. His skin looked blotchy. "I didn't mean to break down. You don't need that."

"I need my girl back."

The teenaged waitress came around to fill their coffee cups and Ben made an effort to begin eating his eggs. It was obvious the action was purely mechanical. He chewed slowly, his gaze focused in the distance.

"What is it?" Shay asked.

"Nothing."

"I want to know. You've thought of something, haven't you? You're thinking something."

Ben stared at a forkful of egg. "Honey, it was brave of you to go to the school and look at the case file, but, you see, it didn't really do any good, did it? All it did was make you more scared and anxious than you already were. And now this latest news has really topped you off.''

''I had to know. I can't not know.''

''You're a brave woman. But you're not invincible. You hardly slept all night, and you're exhausted right now. Look, I have an internist. Why don't I call him and see if I can get you a prescription for—''

''*Don't push pills on me,*'' she snapped.

They glared at each other for a few moments, then both spoke at once. ''Jesus, I'm sorry,'' Ben began, at the same time that Shay said, ''I'm taking it out on you.''

Shay lifted her juice glass, taking several large gulps. She wasn't hungry but she was thirsty, her mouth and throat dry. A headache clanged inside her temples, beating with every pulse of her blood.

''Look, I told you,'' she said, ''I'm not the helpless type. I'm going to have four times as much stress if I just sit back and do nothing. Now, I want to know what I can do. You're a mystery writer, you've had dealings with the police, you've spent weeks riding around with them on calls. What would you do if this were one of your sons?''

Ben's face darkened. ''I'd find Mickey, and—'' He stopped, frowning.

''Why don't you say it?''

''Because I was reacting from the way I'd think about things, not the way you would.''

''And how are we different, dammit?'' Shay drained her orange juice and reached for Ben's. ''Can I have this?'' She looked directly into Ben's eyes. ''*I want to know what you would do.*''

''Well,'' he began uneasily, ''I guess I'd try to find Mickey and then I'd probably kill him with my bare hands . . . does that make you happy, Shay? I'd probably go berserk and become a psycho vigilante, and what good would that do anyone? I'd spend the next ten years of my life in jail.''

Shay seized on the one phrase. "But you'd find him, right?''

"Yeah.''

"Do you think you *could* find him?''

Ben carefully added the contents of several paper containers of cream to his coffee cup, making a ceremony of stirring the liquid smooth. He did not answer.

"You're not talking to me because you're afraid I might follow your advice,'' Shay went on hotly. "That's why you won't answer me, isn't it? Because I'm a woman and you're a man, and men track down their children's abductors, but women wait around for the police to do it.''

"Now, Shay—''

"You are *sexist*, Ben Lyte. You really are. You see me as helpless, don't you?''

"Let's not fight about this.''

"I'm *not* helpless. I'm a mother, I want my daughter back, and I don't have time for this stupid bullshit.'' Her voice rose. "Now, I want to hear your ideas.''

He hesitated, gazing at her as if assessing her emotional state, and finally sighed, giving in. "Okay. But let's talk about it after breakfast, all right? I won't talk any more until you've eaten something.''

"You bastard.''

His grin was brief and unutterably sweet. "Look, darling woman, I love you and I want you tough and strong, and if we're going to look for Mickey you have got to have some eggs and toast in you.''

After a breakfast she didn't taste, they paid their check and left, walking out to Shay's car in the parking lot. Ben took the key from her hand and got into the driver's seat. "Let's go to the park.''

"The *park?*"

"We have to go somewhere. I want to be able to think calmly."

A stream called Paint Creek gurgled its way through the rambling, green municipal park filled with big-trunked old trees. There was a large duck pond, populated by mallards and Canadian geese, most of which were clustered on the bank or quietly feeding. Gray mist covered the pond and lay in fluffy ribbons over the creek.

They parked near the pond and walked across the bridge, heading down one of the many winding walks. They were the only people in the park. Not even a jogger disturbed the quiet.

Ben took Shay's hand and held it tightly.

"This park does have a kind of peace," she said after five minutes of walking.

"That's why I brought you here."

"But we can't stay here long. I have to find her, Ben. That's what you would do, isn't it? You'd track down Mickey somehow—you'd use all the information you could find, and you'd bypass the police if you had to, or else find clues and give them to the police."

"Maybe."

They walked for another two or three minutes. On the water some ducks were paddling. Their quacks echoed hollowly.

"I don't trust the police," Shay said. "When my parents were murdered, they bungled most of the evidence and the perpetrators were never caught. Besides, if there's a hostage situation, the police usually make matters ten times worse."

"Now, not always," Ben began.

"You know damn well they do. They're macho types, all jacked up on adrenaline and carrying guns," she argued. "How many hostage situations have you seen on TV where the perpetrator gets shot, or the hostage, or even some poor little kid just sitting on a porch playing with her dolls?''

''Well—''

''Ben, you *know* what will happen if a lot of trigger-happy men get Mickey in their gun sights. Kelly could be shot by the police. I don't want that to happen. I want her back safely. I want to find Mickey before the police do.''

Ben turned to look at her. ''Come on, Shay, get real. I know you're upset but you're not talking realistically. The boy is psychopathic and extremely dangerous.''

''But he's also a seventeen-year-old, and he listened to me once before. If I find him first, then maybe there's a chance I can get Kelly away from him without violence.''

''And maybe Hitler didn't like lampshades made of human skin. This isn't anything to fool with! Mickey McGee is one dangerous boy, Shay. He's a—'' Ben cut off the sentence.

''What were you going to say? He's a what?''

''A spree killer.''

The word sounded terrible and clinical. ''A *spree* killer? Exactly what is that? What are you saying, Ben? What are you trying to say?''

''There's a picnic table over there, by the water. Let's go sit down, Shay.''

The table was situated on a slope that looked down on a section of the creek. Trees leaned over the water, branches trailing into the rilling stream. They sat down on a bench. Shay immediately felt the chill of the dew that had condensed on the wooden surface through the seat of her jeans.

''Let me tell you about a guy called Christopher Wilder,'' Ben began. ''He was an Australian-born businessman and race-car driver and in 1984 he traveled across the United States killing women. Some of his victims he found at shopping malls and some he met through beauty contests or dating services. The FBI classified him as a spree killer because he moved from place to place to do his killings, and there was no cooling-off period between them.''

''I see,'' she said numbly.

''That's very important, that lack of a cooling-off period. It makes the spree killer different from other serial killers or mass murderers—it puts a hell of a lot more emotional pressure on him.''

The way Ben spoke was ominous. For a wild moment Shay thought of jumping up from the picnic table and running away—not facing it. She wasn't nearly as strong as Ben thought. She did not want to hear her child's death warrant.

But she had to know what Kelly was up against. ''What do you mean?''

''I mean, because of the guy's fugitive status, a lot of tension builds. This gives him a feeling of desperation. His killings are open and public. The police are after him. There's lots of pressure, and it builds.''

''And?''

''Well, think about it, Shay. These types of killers aren't stupid—they usually have average intelligence or better. The guy knows he's going to be caught. And pretty soon the upcoming confrontation with the police becomes a part of his crimes—an element of them. He . . . well, he may put himself into a situation where he forces the police to kill him.''

A situation where he forces the police to kill him.

Shay stared at Ben, rocked by what he had said.

''The case record,'' she gasped.

''Yes.'' Ben nodded, as if delivering the worst possible of all news.

"Oh, God . . . Mickey's *already* got that kind of a confrontation in his background," Shay burst out. "It happened before, when he was seven—he knows all about it! He was there when the police shot his father. He saw him carried away." She felt the blood leech from her face. "That's why he's doing this, isn't he?"

"I'm afraid so."

"He—he really *wants* the police to kill him, doesn't he?"

"He could."

She moistened bloodless lips. She felt strangely flat and calm as she followed the logic to its conclusion. "God," she whispered. "It's all coming together like some sort of fatal puzzle. Salter says he'll find Mickey whatever it costs, and Mickey's already programmed for a police hostage situation. *He's going to force them to shoot him. Isn't he?*"

Ben said nothing.

"Ben? Ben? Say something!"

"I think we should go back to my house and try to relax a little," Ben said heavily.

"No," she said. "Dammit! No. I want to know more about this. Tell me more."

"It won't do you any good to know more."

"It will, it will!"

"Shay—"

"Tell me everything you know. I'm not leaving here until you do."

Mickey drove out of the Goldmans' subdivision, carefully observing the speed limit. No passerby glanced inside the car to see Kelly sobbing hysterically, or Mickey's hands and shirt again stained nightmarishly with red.

"Oh, God, oh, God, you k-killed all of them," Kelly wept. So many screams had caught in her throat that it felt as if her esophagus was bleeding. She could still hear the sickening retch Mrs. Goldman made as she died.

"And you *loved* it," he accused. "You watched every bit of it. You loved it. You came and came and came."

He returned to Rattalee Lake Road, then after a mile or so drove down a gravel side road that went past a condo development under construction. The project looked as if it hadn't been worked on in weeks, and was a confusion of dirt piles, foundations, and stacks of lumber and brick. Behind the mud and mess was a dirt trail.

The car bounced as Mickey pulled the Tempo into the rutted path. "I used to ride my bike here sometimes," he said. Low-growing bushes and saplings snapped at the aerial and batted against the fenders and wheel covers. Piles of trash and weather-beaten old garbage bags marked this as a place where people dumped junk.

"Our hideout," he told her.

She nodded. The signs of human habitation were encouraging. This was hidden from view but not entirely deserted. Maybe someone would find them.

They would wait here for a few hours, he said. He wanted to take a nap.

Sleep? In the middle of the morning? But she felt a wild rush of hope. Maybe she could jump out of the car. But Mickey immediately squashed her plan by taking a rope he'd found in Noah's back seat and using it to tie her hands together, then link her hands to the steering wheel.

When he had her trussed up, he took the butterfly knife and laid the tip into the hollow of Kelly's throat. "You got blood in here," he told her, his eyes glittering. "Say it."

"I . . . I don't know what you mean . . ."

"Say you got blood in you."

" 'You got blood in you,' " she parroted.

"No, no." He jammed the point in a fraction of an inch, only a tiny space away from where her jugular vein pulsed and surged. "You got blood in *you*," he corrected. "And you're gonna lose it all if you make one shitty, stupid move. If you even touch the horn of the car, or the car door, if you even cross your legs funny, then you're gonna get your throat cut, and you're gonna get some other things cut, too. You're gonna get fucking *dissected*."

Kelly's gasps of terror caused her chest to heave but she managed not to sob aloud.

"Okay," her captor announced, leaning back in the front seat and closing his eyes. "That's it. That's enough. Shut up now, all right? Let a guy sleep. I can't sleep with you howlin' like that."

To Kelly's amazement, Mickey actually did go to sleep within about sixty seconds. With his eyes shut he seemed smaller. She saw that he had very long, pretty, feathery eyelashes, almost like a girl's. There was a small, round, white scar beside his right eye. The T-shirt he wore revealed his bare arms, and she saw more round white scars, and several long ones, on which stitch marks could be seen. She wondered what had happened to him but it didn't seem to matter.

She sat rigidly, exactly the way he had left her, afraid to make a move. The rope Mickey had used was made of jute, and it had already abraded her wrists, scraping the sensitive skin. The wounds in her side throbbed, and her bruises were sore. But Kelly didn't dare relax or try to wriggle the rope into a more comfortable position. She didn't want him to wake up—not for a long time. Maybe while he was sleeping a police car would somehow enter the condo development and find the car parked here. Or a jogger or someone would come past, and she could wave to them and scream, and they would rescue her.

Oh, God, she thought. *Please, somebody. Please come.*

Mickey's breathing deepened, and he twitched, uttering a babyish cry that sounded like Matt in a nightmare.

Shuddering, the girl gazed out of the front windshield at their surroundings. The early morning moisture was beginning to burn away. The sky was a deep turquoise. Trees draped fresh spring leaves down on the hood of the car, and on the nearest branch, a green caterpillar crawled.

It was little and cute, and hunched itself earnestly forward like a cartoon animal, bumping its back up and down. She wondered how long caterpillars lived. Would it live longer than she did? She felt a stab of wild grief as she realized she might never see her mother or her baby brother again.

Mickey was a maniac, she knew. Just like Freddie Krueger, only a lot, lot worse. There was something wrong with him. He didn't even think like other people, and there was no way to know what he would do next, except that it would be terrible.

I don't want to die, she thought desperately.

Thinking this, she unconsciously shifted her legs. Mickey snapped awake like a jack-in-the-box. He thrust the knife under her chin in a motion so fast she didn't even see it until she felt the pressure.

"One move and you're dead, girl. Didn't I tell you that?"

"Yes . . . ow . . ."

"I mean *don't move*," he snapped.

"Okay!"

The pain in her neck nearly gagged her, and her nose burned from where his hand had bumped it. She didn't dare move. She sat tense, utterly rigid, waiting to die.

"Talk to me," Mickey ordered. "You got a father?"

"Yes," she managed.

"What's he like? He ever, you know, done time?"

She was too groggy from the long duration of terror to grasp what "done time" meant. "He sells insurance. He and my mom are divorced."

Mickey's laugh filled the car. "Yeah, I know all *about* divorce. Only my old man, he set it up so my ma and me, we'd never have no money, we'd always be in the shit house. You know what she did for money?"

He paused, indicating Kelly should say something. She forced herself to make an encouraging sound.

"She lived with this asshole liked to hit her with a belt. Isn't that great? He used to hit me, too. One time this guy turned my ass bloody, I couldn't sit down for two weeks. The world is full of jerks, know what I mean? . . ."

Mickey rambled on, telling her about all the people who'd done things to him, especially his father. He showed her scars on his chest, ugly white scars. He was almost crying, his cheeks burning red. The curse words he used were vile.

Kelly lost track. Her mind floated away, out of the car, focusing on a bird that had flown onto a nearby branch. She recognized it as a red-winged blackbird, which they had studied in fifth grade in a unit on Michigan birds.

Kelly focused her entire being on it, thinking how beautiful it was, with its glossy feathers and bright crimson wing tips. She would think about the bird, instead of Mickey. She would float away somewhere, forever.

"Bam!" Mickey shouted wildly, his voice filling up the car. He sounded like a seven-year-old boy playing a war game. "Bam! Bam! He got shot! He's bleeding and bleeding—BAM, BAM. He's dead meat!"

EIGHTEEN

Suicide. Death wish. On an unconscious level it's a lot more common than we think," Ben said pedantically. "Thousands do it every day. Late-night car accidents. Race-car drivers who push their cars a millimeter too fast. Drug dealers and crack dealers who take incredible risks. Alcoholics who drink a fifth of whiskey in three hours. People who get into bar fights. Police officers who—"

"Enough!" Shay cried. "I get your point."

She got up from the picnic table. "Oh, God," she choked. "I feel sick to my stomach."

Ben steered her to a clump of bushes where she bent over and retched violently, throwing up the breakfast she had just eaten. The taste was vile. "God . . ." she kept gasping. "Turn away, Ben . . . God . . . I have to help her, oh, Jesus . . ."

At last she was finished, and straightened up, wiping her mouth with her hand. She was shaking all over and her body was clammy with perspiration, the dampness at the seat of her jeans grown icy cold, creating shivers all up and down her legs.

"Here," Ben said gently. He reached in his pants pocket and handed her a tissue. "It's covered with pocket lint but it'll be good for wiping."

She leaned against him and wiped her mouth. "I want to go to the car now," she said in a shaking voice. "I'm going to find that little son of a bitch."

"Shay, no. This is way, way past anything that a lay person could do. You're not Bernard Goetz or Sylvester Stallone. Please, just come back to my house and we'll wait by the phone; maybe we can get pictures of Kelly and make up some posters to distribute. Gloria will help."

"Sure, posters are a good idea," she said evenly.

She pulled away from his support and walked down the path, her feet moving onto the bridge that arched over the stream where ducks paddled as if the world hadn't completely fallen apart.

Ben lived in an older subdivision, built in the early sixties before city water and sewer had been installed. The lots were all an acre or more, far larger than current lot sizes. Huge blue spruces adorned Ben's lawn, along with mature fruit trees. A long line of excavated dirt snaked across the grass, marking where he had just hooked up to the public water line.

As they pulled into Ben's driveway, he began to give her details of the digging procedures, and the contractor's opinions on when the heap of dirt would have sunk level enough to lay sod. Shay heard only bits and pieces of it. He was just trying to make conversation, she knew.

They went inside the house, which seemed large, dark and hollow, all the drapes pulled. Had Ben left the house only last night? Already last night's party seemed an eon ago. Hung on the living room walls were portraits of Ben's three children taken at their various high school and college graduations. One had graduated from Harvard. They were fresh-faced youngsters with Ben's good looks.

Shay went into the powder room and rinsed her mouth out, scrubbing her face and hands. Stress seemed to have thinned her skin, making her facial bones seem more prominent. There were violet shadows under her eyes, and her mouth looked bruised. A day or two more and she'd look haggard.

Gloria Adamson came out of the family room, carrying a book, Tracy Kidder's latest bestseller. She was dressed in jeans but still looked what she was—a professional, competent, warm woman.

"More calls, lots of calls," the assistant principal told Shay. "But none from Kelly. Most are just sympathy calls and I've written them down. Several people from the Bloomfield Art Association called. And your ex-husband called. He says he just got home from the airport and wants you to phone him as soon as possible."

"Thank you, Gloria."

"Shay . . . don't you think you should try to rest for a little while? I can stay here all day if you want me to, and if I get tired, I'll call in some of the other teachers to spell me."

"The teachers?" Shay said numbly.

"Everyone is grieving, Shay. Everyone wants her back."

Shay went into Ben's den, where he kept his computer and did his writing. The room was stacked with books everywhere, even piled on the floor behind the swivel chair. Empty glasses and Pepsi cans marked the long, early-morning hours spent here.

She dialed Randy's number, and within a few seconds the receiver was picked up—her ex-husband must have been sitting directly by the phone.

"Yes?" he responded shakily.

"It's me," she began. "Randy, I've talked to—"

"Oh, God," he said, breaking down as he had done before. "I heard. On the news. I saw her picture on the news. And *his*."

She clung to the phone, unnerved by the sounds of her ex-husband's sobs. "Our baby, our baby," he kept repeating. "Why did you let this happen?"

Her pity for him was sharp. He was suffering as much as she was. "Randy, I've dropped Matt off at Michael's house, and they're taking him to Cedar Point. They'll call tonight and let you know when they're back, and you can pick him up then. I told Natalie to leave a message on your tape; I told her you have a remote."

"Okay, okay," Randy said, pulling himself together. "I'll pick him up."

"And, please, keep the TV set off. You know how they sensationalize things, and I don't want them scaring Matt. And don't talk to the media, Randy." She knew the TV stations would play Randy's emotionality to the hilt.

"Maybe we could plead on the air, Shay. You know, beg him to bring our girl home?"

Her laugh was bitter. "This isn't the type of boy who'd listen to a plea, Randy."

"No," he insisted stubbornly. "The more people who see me on the news, the better. They might recognize him, Shay—they might know where she is and call the TV station."

Was he right? She realized that she was losing perspective. "All right," she agreed. "But I do want you to take Kelly's photo to a print shop and have them make several thousand posters of her—then get people to distribute them. And I want you to do one more thing.''

''What's that?'' he responded dully.

''Use your computer at work to see if you can find the address of someone named Daniel or Danno McGee. That's Mickey's father. It's a long shot but maybe he has a policy somewhere—car, boat, house, motorcycle—who knows? If he's still using that same name.''

''Mickey's father?'' Randy responded doubtfully.

''Maybe Mickey will go there, Ran. Please,'' she begged.

''Yeah, but it'll take some time. I'll have to search a lot of data bases, and get access to a number of companies.'' Hope colored her ex-husband's voice. ''Do you think—Shay, do you think we can find him?''

''You're a persistent guy, Randy—it's your best and worst quality. So use it,'' she said, hanging up.

Gloria Adamson had tactfully gone into the living room with her book, seating herself next to the phone extension.

Shay walked through to the family room, where Ben had turned on the TV. A movie was on, *Love Laughs at Andy Hardy*.

Ben picked up the remote and began flicking through the channels, catching portions of Jerry Falwell, Sesame Street, and a special called *Inside the PGA Tour*. *Babar* was running on HBO, and Showtime had *Hansel and Gretel*.

''A lovely time of day for exciting programming,'' Ben said. ''How about if I rummage through my videos, find something with a little sex and comedy? I taped some of those VH-1 comedy things; I've got a very nice library of yuks. With or without the X-rated language—your preference, my dear.''

His attempts to cheer her sounded hollow.

"News,'' Shay said. "I want the news.''

"Not on right now. It's Sunday morning, remember?''

"God, Randy just fell apart. He's so weak, Ben. How did I ever hook up with such a weak man?''

"Because you're strong and the weak are drawn to the strong. Maybe you're even stronger than I am, Shay. You're an indomitable woman . . . a survivor.''

"I'm finding Mickey,'' she said grimly.

"Baby, please, why don't we sit down and watch a little TV? I'll make you a drink. . . . I've got Bailey's Irish Cream, you like that, don't you? It's sweet and it goes down smooth.''

"After I just tossed my cookies? Will you stop?'' she said. "I have to think.''

Ben brought out a book he was reading, the latest novel by Michael Kube-McDowell, a sci-fi writer and friend of his who lived in Lansing. She could tell by the quick, jerky way he turned pages that he was absorbing only portions of what he read.

She sat on Ben's couch, forcing herself to watch the tape he had selected, the *Robert Wahl World Tour*. There was something she should be thinking about, she felt. Something important. Only what was it?

The different faces of Mickey filled her mind. The eager, responsive artist. The faceless motorcyclist who'd buzzed their house over and over. The vandal who'd masturbated and defecated in her studio. And the murderer.

She remembered her fantasy that she would be the one to reach Mickey. Had other caseworkers in his file had the same fantasy? But she had done better than most of the adults he came in contact with. At least she represented something positive to him—something he wanted.

She got to her feet and reached for her purse.

"Where are you going?" Ben said, looking up from his book.

"I'm just going to go home for a while, I want to go into my studio. I can think there. I'll call you."

"Shay, do you want me to come?"

"No."

He looked at her. "I love you."

"I know. And I . . . I love you, too." The words slid out in a whisper, but she knew they were true. She felt a vast wave of relief at having said it. The words would be something to hang on to, some kind of a lifeline.

It wasn't even noon yet—time seemed to have slowed down, creating an endless Sunday.

A van from Channel 7 was parked in front of her house. As Shay pulled up, a young man jumped out of the van and came running toward her, followed by a girl in jeans with a minicam. Shay waved them away. She had a horror of talking to them, of becoming one of those pathetic TV mothers. Let Randy play that role, if one of them must.

"Mrs. Wyoming! Mrs. Wyoming! Just a minute!"

They filmed her as she parked in the driveway. She got out of the car and walked around the house to the studio deck entrance, letting herself in with a key.

Noah died in this house, her thoughts skittered. *Was butchered here. Bled his life away in my house, doing a favor for me.*

The studio was exactly as she had left it, halfway cleaned up, her broken sculptures unmended, her En-tech project destroyed. But the light that streamed in the windows was clear and pale, the kind of light she liked best to work by. Despite Mickey's rape of the room, the studio still managed to exude a sense of peace and tranquility.

On a table she saw the sculpture she had done of Mickey's face on the night of the break-in.

She gazed at it, her heart pounding. She'd been upset when she'd modeled it—had slapped on the clay in a fury fueled by anger. But the results had been serendipitous. She'd managed exactly to capture the anger in Mickey that warred with his vulnerability—his need. It was some of her best work. She wondered what Mickey would say if he could see it. Would it stir him in some way, give them some common ground to talk, to communicate?

Shay felt a lift of sick excitement. This was what she'd come here to see, to find.

Finally, after only a brief hesitation, she went to the phone and dialed her sister.

"Shay? Are you all right? You sound awful." In the background Shay could hear Elton John. Marianne usually did her paperwork and case file dictations to the accompaniment of one of her vast collection of CDs.

"I'm . . . oh, Marianne." She stopped, unable to speak.

Marianne, always intuitive, said, "Wait, let me turn this thing down." The sound volume became reduced. "It isn't that Mickey boy, is it?"

"Yes. Marianne . . . he has her. He took Kelly."

Quickly Shay blurted out the story, telling her sister everything that had happened. She included Ben's opinion that Mickey was a spree killer, performing his crimes under high tension and programmed to self-destruct. And the fact that he seemed to be headed for a SWAT-type situation.

"Oh, God!" Marianne kept exclaiming. "Oh, Shay. Poor little Kelly—she must be terrified."

For an instant both sisters lost control and wept together, separated by six hundred miles of telephone wire. "I held that little girl," Marianne cried. "I held her when she was three days old. I gave her her first teddy bear. I took her to her first Broadway play. Oh, God. Oh, that *bastard*. That little *bastard*."

Shay spoke hoarsely. "Marianne, I reached him last year—when I taught him in the art class. Remember I told you about it? He responded to me, he showed some feelings."

Marianne was getting control of herself again. Her voice took on a professional edge. "So? What does that prove? He's a killer, Shay, but even killers have many levels and many feelings."

"I think I can talk to him. All I want is a few minutes to talk to him alone, without the police there. Somehow he was drawn to me . . . the artistic part of me. He responded to me once; maybe he'll do it again. And besides, I'm a woman. He wouldn't find a woman threatening. That's been proven. Women have the ability to use empathy . . ."

"Now wait a minute. Just wait."

Shay was too wound up to stop. "Mickey has a 'shit list.' He's killing people on that list. Logically, his father has got to be at the head of the list—he hates his father, I'm sure of it. If I'm lucky I can get there first. I want to get to Mickey before the police."

The decision seemed right and inevitable.

"Now *wait*," Marianne cried. "Just wait one fucking minute. Shay, this person is dangerous. He's killed six people. He's a psychotic, a spree killer, just as Ben told you."

"I want you to tell me how to talk to him."

"No, dammit. I'm going to call the airline and get

a ticket for Detroit—I'm coming to stay with you, Shay. I'll help you get through this.''

''Every one of my instincts tells me that somehow I hold a key to that boy, Marianne. The sculpture. The break-ins at my studio. His obsession with Kelly. God . . . I don't know how it all fits, but it does and I'm going to use it. If you don't tell me how to handle him, I'll call some other therapist. *I need to know.*''

''Mickey McGee isn't just a kid, he's a *dangerous psychotic.*''

''He's seventeen, Marianne.''

''He's as dangerous as Charles Manson. And you're trying to deal with this by fantasizing you can set everything right, just by talking to him. It's just a fantasy, Shay. A coping device. It can't work. You can't deal with this by—''

''No, dammit! Marianne! You've worked with people like him, you've defused their anger—you've told me stories about it. You worked for two years in that hospital in Norwalk. I want you to tell me what to say, how to talk to him.''

''What have you done to defuse your stress, Shay? Have you taken a few minutes to do some deep breathing? Some meditating? Why don't you play that tape I sent you—''

''A *tape!*'' Shay cried. ''Jesus, haven't you been listening to a word I've said?''

Marianne spent twenty minutes telling Shay how she had dealt with various psychotics at the hospital where she had worked and what she had done when several of her own patients had freaked out.

''You have to connect on some human level,'' she told Shay. ''Sometimes they'll respond to that. But it's not dependable. These people are not operating logically or rationally. They can lash out viciously. One of the doctors at the hospital in Norwalk was nearly killed by a fifteen-year-old boy, Shay. The kid jammed his thumbs in his eye sockets—it was very, very grisly.

"Be careful," was her sister's final warning. "And I'm still getting a plane ticket. You need me."

After she had hung up, Shay rummaged on a shelf until she found a small black tote bag with white piping that she had gotten as a premium from the Literary Guild. She wrapped the clay statuette of Mickey in tissue and put it in the bag. As an afterthought, she added the Tupperware container that contained the soft clay she kept for Matt.

Outdoors, three news vans were now parked in front, and as she walked to her car, several reporters came running up. They fired questions at her, all talking at once.

"Sorry. Sorry." All she wanted was to get in her car. Even talking to these people would be an admission that her daughter had been caught up in senseless, media-driven tragedy.

"Mrs. Wyoming—"

"Mickey McGee is a mass murderer, Mrs. Wyoming. How do you feel about—"

She jumped in the car and slammed the door, cutting off their voices. She backed up across the grass, her tires kicking up sod, and made a wild getaway turn in the street. They were vultures, she thought angrily. In one way they did care about Kelly, but in another way, all they wanted was to fill a five-minute news slot.

She drove back to Ben's. It was now noon. Children played on lawns, or rode bicycles equipped with training wheels. A man mowed his lawn, the mulching mower squirting out arcs of clippings. The sky was pale turquoise, and the day sang around her, alive with color and freshness. Only Shay wasn't fresh. She felt tense, every nerve and muscle in her body wired to breaking point.

Ben came to the door. He seemed relieved to see her. He had not shaved but had changed to jeans and a T-shirt from his tennis club. In the background she could hear another news broadcast, Randy's voice shakily saying *"Please, if anyone has seen my little girl . . ."* There was the distant whistle of a tea kettle in Ben's kitchen.

"Hi," Shay said tiredly. "I talked to my sister. I got mobbed by reporters."

He pulled her into his arms and gripped her tightly. He smelled pungent, his body odors betraying his tension. "God, I'm glad to see you. I hated to think of you going back to that house—your wild ideas about trying to find Mickey—"

She pulled back. "I still have those wild ideas," she said. "I came to ask you if you could help me figure out how to locate Mickey's father."

"Shay."

"Now, don't shit me, Ben. You know as well as I do that Mickey is going to end up on the doorstep of the man he hates the most. At least there's a damn good chance that he will."

Ben was silent for a minute.

"You know I'm right."

"All right," he admitted heavily. "If this is what you need to do, Shay. But if you get any information, you'll turn it over to the police, right?"

"Right," she said, wondering if she meant it.

He steered her into the kitchen, where he took the tea kettle off the burner. He spooned instant coffee into two cups, then added boiling water.

"I don't want any."

"Don't be such an ass. You need the caffeine, since you refused tranquilizers. Okay, we've got to go talk to

Mickey's mother first. I'm sure the police have been there already, but I flatter myself that we're smarter—maybe there's something they missed. She might be more willing to talk to you since you're Kelly's mother.''

''Am I only fantasizing, not accepting reality? That's what Marianne thinks.''

''Who the hell knows or cares?'' His smile was brief and crooked. ''As long as we turn over what we learn to the police—and don't do anything really stupid—I guess we can do this.''

Shay nodded, feeling a sudden release inside her, a thrill of her speeded-up heart. It was clear that Ben wrote about adventure but did not live it. While she—

She wanted her child back.

NINETEEN

While Gloria Adamson took a short break, Shay phoned Randy.

"I haven't found zilch," he said. His voice sounded stronger, more in control. In the background she could hear the click of computer keys.

"Nothing?" she said, disappointed.

Her ex-husband went on, "Not under the name of Danno McGee or Dan McGee. I've contacted a couple guys I know at other agencies—between us we've got great access to data bases, and he isn't in them. Well, there was an eighty-year-old Danny B. McGee, but he obviously isn't the one."

"Oh—"

"I have to see you," her ex-husband pleaded. "Shay, can't we speak face to face about this? We are her parents. She belongs to both of us. You sound so official. Can't you even talk to me? If we could just talk—"

Shay closed her eyes for a moment. He was pathetic, using his grief to try to reach her even now. The more Randy begged, the more she withdrew. Was she really as cruel as Kelly had once accused? Was it possible for ties of friendship to still exist between them?

Maybe she'd handled the separation from him poorly . . . but how did you handle such things? There were no instruction manuals for a kinder, gentler divorce.

Anyway, she needed him now, desperately—and she needed him functional.

"Randy, we might be able to work out a friendship, I'm not discounting it, but right now Kelly needs us. Can you keep searching those data bases? Can you do that for *her*? And not fall apart?"

She heard him breathing.

"Okay," he agreed. "But Shay—"

"Yes?"

"Just say *something* to me—give me one little straw of hope. I'm a person, Shay. I'm real."

Shay thought for a few seconds, feeling her eyes suddenly prickle with tears. He was pleading with her to recognize his humanity—his feelings. Perhaps that was what he'd wanted all along, not her love so much as her recognition. A wave of forgiveness flowed over her like a softening June rain. Randy's humanity still existed—despite his drinking, despite the pain they had shared. God, had she become cold and hard, just as Kelly accused?

"I care," she said softly, and hung up.

Putting Shay's things into Ben's car, including the Literary Guild bag, they drove to the home of Beverly and Mickey McGee. An elderly woman in a blue pants suit, her wrinkled face twisted sourly, told them to go to the side door. "They've got the basement apartment—you ring out back. *She's* home. She gave her notice today, and she owes me eight weeks back rent.''

They rang the bell, then heard slow, tired steps climb the basement stairs. Finally a tall woman appeared in the half-glass pane of the back door. She wore acid-washed denim jeans, a blue plaid camp shirt, and a cheap-looking pearl necklace. Her face was startlingly ugly, her nose bumpy at the bridge as if it had been broken several times, her cheekbones flattened. A scar curled the corner of her lip.

''Yes?''

Shay was shaken by the woman's battered appearance. It reminded her of the New York editor, Hedda someone, whose face had been beaten beyond recognition. Why hadn't she gotten plastic surgery? ''Mrs. McGee?''

''Who're you? More reporters? I don't want to talk,'' Beverly said sullenly, turning to close the door.

''Wait!'' cried Shay, springing forward. ''Please! We're not reporters! I'm Kelly Wyoming's mother. And this is Ben Lyte, one of Mickey's teachers. I have to talk to you. Please. Can we come in?''

''I don't want to talk to you. I've already talked to the police. What do you want to do, condemn me?'' Beverly McGee added bitterly. ''I produced Mickey. I raised him. So it's my fault. Well, I'm sorry about your daughter. I really, really am. Now will you go away?''

''*Please*,'' Shay begged, throwing herself forward to wrench at the door. ''We just want to talk to you for five or ten minutes. We aren't blaming you, Mrs. McGee. I know Mickey's been a problem. I know he's been awfully hard to handle. It must have been rough, all those years.''

''Well . . .'' For the first time, Shay noticed the white scars that ran horizontally across Beverly's neck, partly hidden by the pearls. There were more scars on her hands and forearms. "Defense scars," Shay had heard them called. They occurred when a knifing victim raised her hands to fight off the blade.

"If we could just see Mickey's room, if we could just talk to you for a few seconds," Shay pleaded. "I haven't got anywhere else to turn. My daughter is sixteen . . . she's so pretty . . . here." She fumbled in her purse for her billfold and flipped it open to a school photo of Kelly.

Beverly McGee stared at the photo of a girl with shining, honey-colored hair and perfect, fresh skin.

"Oh, all right." She capitulated abruptly. She turned and led them down a basement staircase where a wooden stair rail had come partially loose from its wall supports. The steps were covered in different shades of shag carpet samples.

"I've had police here half the night," Beverly explained. "I told them everything. I kicked Mickey out, you know. I threatened him with a shotgun and told him never to come back. He's abusive, just like his father. I won't tolerate physical abuse any more. I've had therapy. I told him that and I told the police that. You see my face? I can't afford plastic surgery. Men did this to me," she spat viciously. "Bastards, every one of them. My son is a bastard, too, Mrs. Wyoming. He's one of them and I won't take it. They are done hurting me and that's final."

The basement looked like a welfare apartment. Partially carpeted with garish carpet samples that must have been twenty years old, it smelled of cooking, mildew, and laundry odors. A humidifier motor rattled in a far corner. Cardboard boxes were stacked along a wall, and some looked as if they were in the process of being packed.

Mickey had breathed in this stale air, Shay thought. He had watched TV on that pathetic, frayed couch.

"Don't worry, we haven't got roaches," Beverly said bitterly, sensing her judgment. "I spray it every week. But it's cheap and I do the housework for old Mrs. Butera upstairs—she can't do heavy lifting any more. Not many places will take a kid with a motorcycle. They can't take the noise."

"I understand." Shay's mouth was dry. "Could we—could we see Mickey's room?"

"I don't see why not. Everyone else has seen it. The police took some stuff. Some of his notebooks, his scribblings and junk—but you can look, I guess."

Beverly led them to a small room, its door crudely cut in the paneling. The room was just barely large enough for the sagging twin bed and cardboard dresser over-flowing with jeans, sweatshirts, jockey undershorts, candy bar wrappers, Pepsi cans, and back issues of *Easy Rider*, a motorcycle magazine whose covers featured plump pinup girls straddling huge, chrome-laden Harleys.

A one-board wall shelf held various sculptures, many of them obscene. There were genitals with open, yawning mouths filled with sharp teeth. Renditions of female genitalia, again with teeth. A statue of a naked girl who clutched her own ripped-open abdomen, from which snakelike intestines spilled.

Shay stared at this, feeling her gorge rise.

"I didn't touch his room," Beverly said behind her. "He would have killed me if I did. You didn't mess with him. He's as mean as his father—and that's damn mean."

Beverly McGee went into the other room and turned on a portable radio, leaving them alone.

"Jeez," Shay muttered. "I can smell him." She took an unwilling step inside. The room smelled of a combination of dirty clothes, spoiled food, and dried semen. It almost reeked of unclean thoughts.

"Well, we might as well look," Ben said, investigating the closet.

Gingerly, Shay began rummaging through drawers. A bottom cardboard drawer would barely pull out, the weight of its contents dragging it down. It was stuffed full of porno magazines.

Shay shuddered as she looked at magazines picturing women tied up with leather thongs, or handcuffed, being entered by wet-eyed men with enormous red sexual organs that glistened with fluids.

Mickey had read this vile material, then gotten on his Harley and driven past their house looking for Kelly. It seemed monstrous to Shay. She swallowed back a rise of stomach acid and was relieved when Ben came over and shoved the drawer shut.

"It's pretty standard," he told her. "Most guys like Mickey have their pornography collections. It's part of their overall clinical picture."

Overall clinical picture. Was Ben trying to distance himself by using medical phrases?

Shay noticed a small patch of pencil scribbling done in a corner over the bed where the ripped wall paneling revealed patches of dingy basement wall.

"What's this?"

"What's what?"

"He's written on the wall here." She crawled across the unmade bed in order to read it, trying not to breathe the stale whiff of old semen that drifted up from the unwashed sheets.

SHIT LIST had been printed in grotesquely squarish capitals that looked as if each one had taken hours to create. Beneath were a number of even smaller words written in illegible printing.

"Damn," Shay muttered. "I can't read this."

"It's prison writing," Ben said, leaning over her to peer at the scribblings. "Some felons have amazingly aberrant handwriting, lots of backward slants and really weird letter formations. I'd guess those are the names on Mickey's shit list. I can't read them, either—which is probably exactly the way he wanted it. However, we can bet the police have seen this, too."

Shay thought one of the names said Danno McGee. A rampant penis had been sketched by that name.

"Come on," she urged Ben. "Let's go talk to Beverly again."

Beverly McGee was seated on the couch, a textbook opened on her lap, when they returned to the living room. She stared dully at the book, not turning pages. In the dim basement light her complexion seemed sallow.

"My son was sick," she told them as they emerged. "I knew it and the school knew it and the caseworkers all knew it and nothing was ever done. Now he's gone, and I don't ever want him back here."

Shay stared at the woman. There was something awry about Beverly, something creepy. This woman had pulled a gun on her own son. She had also allowed herself to be battered to the point of disfigurement. It was as if she always went to extremes, as if she didn't even know a normal, safe, settled middle ground.

"Beverly," she began, forcing a smile. "Could you tell us where you think Mickey's father might be? Do you have any idea?"

"Somewhere far away, I hope." The woman's lips formed a grim line. "If I ever see him I'm going to shoot him through the head."

Disappointment stabbed Shay. "I *have* to find him, Mrs. McGee."

"I told the police everything I know."

"Think," Shay pleaded. "Are there any people you know who might know where he might be—any other names you could give us? *Anyone* we could talk to?"

The woman stared down at the opened pages of her book, a text on law office management.

"Kelly wants to be a nurse someday, she wants to go to nursing school. She's very intelligent, Mrs. McGee. She's such a good girl." Her voice cracked again. "I love her so much. Please, talk to us."

Beverly's eyes darted from Shay to Ben, to the door, to her book, and then back to Shay. She seemed to make a decision. "A guy, Nino, Danno owed money to. He works down on Gratiot, owns a garage down there. And Danno's old girlfriend, she's in the phone book."

She scribbled the names on a piece of paper, and rose. "I got to go to a computer lab now. I'm in school to be a legal assistant. I'm going to work in a law office. I'll have a good job by next summer. Be careful," she added. "Mickey is just like his father—even looks like him. They're both sons of bitches."

"Thank you," Shay said faintly.

But Beverly McGee wasn't finished. She rubbed two fingers across her battered, smashed nose. "Oh, yes . . . and one more thing. Mickey does know where his dad is."

"*What?*"

"Yeah, I'm pretty sure he does. He was boasting to me. I think he's found out where the bastard is. He threatened to tell him where we are, too." The woman's eyes narrowed and a grim look clenched her ugly features. "That's why I told *her*, this morning, told her that I'm moving. I'd die before I'd stay here for that son of a bitch to find me again."

* * *

Shay slid behind the front seat and unfolded the sheet of paper Beverly had given her, quickly reading over the two names the woman had written down in a script that, also like a felon, slanted weirdly backward.

"That apartment gave me the creeps," she gasped. "The anger, the evil. Oh, Ben . . . what kind of woman could she be to raise a boy like Mickey?"

"There are a lot of strange people in this world," Ben said as Shay started the motor. He eyed her. "Shay. You've been this far, you've talked to that woman, now are you beginning to rethink this a little? The boy is a damn monster. When are you going to admit it? You don't try to talk with a monster. You don't reason with one, you certainly don't give one any warm fuzzies."

"Warm fuzzies? Warm *fuzzies?* Do you really think that's what I'm trying to do?"

She started the car and accelerated along the subdivision streets, going too fast.

"I think you're in way over your head, deluding yourself that you can accomplish what policemen, probation officers, social workers, counselors, and teachers couldn't."

"If I'm in over my head, then so be it," she snapped. "And now that we've come this far and I've got the names, why don't I drop you off home? Thank you for your help but you have responsibilities of your own."

Ben's head jerked back as if she'd slapped him. Maybe, emotionally, she had.

They glared at each other.

Then he snapped, "Slow down the fucking car, dammit! You're driving at forty miles an hour, you're going to hit some kid and then where will you be?" Ben reached out and grabbed the steering wheel, forcing her to pull the car to the curb. He snapped the gear lever into park. "Shay Wyoming, you are one stubborn woman, aren't you?"

"I am."

"Well, you're going to promise me something before we go one foot farther, or I'm going to call the police and tell them every goddamn thing you're doing."

"You wouldn't," she gasped.

"I wouldn't? Lady, I love you and I don't want to go to your damn funeral. I refuse to sit in some damn church pew and cry for you. You are going to locate that boy's father and then you are going to turn over the information to the police and let them act on it."

"No."

"Promise it, Shay, or I swear I'll call Salter and tell him you're hindering the investigation."

Her eyes blurred with hot, angry tears. "Dammit, Ben . . . I don't want the police in on this."

"Well, it isn't up to you. You've appointed yourself some little god, deciding how best to help your daughter, when you have no expertise in the matter at all, and you're going to end up getting yourself and Kelly in more trouble than ever. Listen to me, Shay. I'm not just any dork. I've researched crime, for God's sake. I've ridden on dozens of police calls. I have some expertise in this."

She stared at him. Love was written all over his face, and frustration. He wanted to be a knight in shining armor for her and he couldn't, because he was just an ordinary man, not a hero. But she couldn't think of his ego now. She felt the pull of the addresses she held in her hand . . . a certainty that she was at last on the right track.

She put the car back in drive. "I'm doing it, Ben. Whether you agree or not. Now, I'll drive at the posted speed limit but I'm taking you home."

"Wait." Ben fumbled in his jacket and pulled out an object. Shay gasped. It was a gun. A .38 revolver, perhaps—she had only seen a gun up-close twice, and each time it had made her feel weak and nauseous. "I brought this, just in case."

Shay drew in her breath sharply. She could see her mother and father's bodies lying on the floor by the cash register, her father's eyes still open, glazed and vacant in death.

"*No*," she cried. "*No!* I don't want that. I won't kill—I can't. I hate guns."

Ben's eyes speared hers. "Well, don't deceive yourself. The path you are taking leads to guns. If you're crazy enough to try to find Mickey McGee, then you're crazy enough to kill, or to put yourself in a situation where you *have* to kill. Better to have a weapon than not have one."

"I'm *not* going to be violent," Shay said, gesturing for him to put the gun away. She started the car again. "My only chance with this boy is on the level of talk and feeling—assuming we can find him." She glanced at the first name on the notebook paper. "Shit—her handwriting is awful—I can barely read it, but I think the address is in Detroit somewhere near Gratiot."

"Near Gratiot?" Ben began in that way of males reading maps.

She looked at him. "I can find it."

"I'm with you, Shay." He touched her hand, squeezing her fingers. "I'm no Rambo, though. Please remember that. And I hate getting powder burns on my hands—it plays hell with my typing."

The trip to the auto shop on Gratiot Avenue near Seven Mile was not productive. Nino Ughetti, owner of Nino's Brake and Bike: We Do Great Work, had a trimmed beard and hair pulled back in a ponytail. He was dressed in a baggy army surplus coverall obliterated with engine grease, but still managed an aura of biker good looks.

"Danno McGee?" he said, grinning bitterly. "If I could find him, man, I'd get him to pay me the five thousand he owes me. I heard he's using a fake name now. You find out where he is, you give me a ring, hear?" He handed Shay a soiled business card and followed this with a leer. "You call me, hey, girl? With or without the word on McGee. I'll give you a ride on my chopper."

Then they drove to the still mostly white neighborhood in working-class Ferndale where Danno's ex-girlfriend Deena Roberts lived. The street was lined with shabby bungalows built in the forties and fifties. The balmy afternoon had drawn out a collection of children who were rollerskating on the cracked sidewalks. Mongrels barked in backyards, and in the driveways, men peered into the opened hoods of cars.

Deena was apparently about to leave for work. A trim, washed-out blond with overpermed hair, she was hurriedly fastening a waitress apron around her waist. Shay could imagine her in black leather and high-heeled boots, riding on the "sissy seat" of a big 1200-cc motorcycle, with her arms wrapped around the waist of someone like Nino Ughetti.

"No . . . no . . . please. . . . I saw the news; I don't want to talk."

"Just for a second," Shay begged, but the woman slammed the door in their faces. A few minutes later they heard the screech of car tires.

"I guess she doesn't want to talk," Ben shrugged, but Shay forced her foot down on the accelerator, following Deena's rusted-out Toyota to Woodward Avenue, then onto the 696 Expressway, and finally to the Elias Brothers restaurant in Troy.

They took a booth. When a frightened Deena appeared through the kitchen door, balancing a tray of Slim Jim sandwiches and Belgian waffles, Shay got up and went to meet her.

"What do you *want?*" the woman gasped.

"I'm trying to find Danno McGee. I need to know where he might be—do you know anything about him? Like where he works? Anything?"

Deena had turned as pale as the crockery on her tray. "I can't tell you."

"I'm going to sit here all day until you do," Shay threatened.

"I don't know where he is. He leaves me alone now, thank God. He put me in the hospital twice. He's got some other woman to beat on now."

"Deena, nobody will know that you told us anything."

Another waitress barged past, glancing curiously over her shoulder at Shay. In a moment, Shay knew, the manager would be out. "Where does he work?" Shay begged. "Give us something—anything."

"He drives a truck," Deena said sullenly. "Or he did two years ago, and he hops from job to job a lot. I don't even know if he's in the area any more." She gazed defiantly at Shay. "He uses another name now, and I'm *not* telling you what that is. I'm not *stupid,*" she hissed. "The manager's coming, so you'd better get back to your booth. I'll send out your waitress."

Shay stood her ground. "We need to know his new name if we're going to be able to find him."

"Tough shit."

Shay improvised. "If you don't tell me, I'm going to tell the police that you have information you're withholding—that's a felony, Deena."

The woman looked frightened, and stepped closer to Shay. "Sparling," she whispered, her eyes avoiding

Shay's. "Dan Sparling. He used that before. But for God's sake, don't tell him I told. *Please.*"

Shay and Ben sat in their booth, going over the brief notes that Shay had made.

"Just great," Shay sighed. "I told Randy to go over his computer for the name Danno McGee and now we have another name to feed in—and it might not even be the right one. I don't trust that woman. She looked like a biker chick to me."

"I don't think any of Danno's associates are going to be exactly trustworthy," Ben remarked. "Why don't you give Randy a call right now?"

Shay went to the telephone in the outer lobby. She seemed to spend her entire life making phone calls from lobbies.

"I have a new name for you to plug in," she told Randy as soon as he was on the line.

"What is it?" The office noises in the background were louder now, people talking and phones ringing. Randy must have called in his coworkers to help with the search.

"Dan Sparling. Randy, can you drop Danno McGee and get on Sparling right away? Call me back at this number. Oh, yes, and they say Danno is working as a trucker now. Maybe—"

"Stay on the line; I'll plug it into the data base right now."

He put her on hold, and suddenly the elevator music version of "The Tears of a Clown" was playing in her ears.

Shay waited. A family with three small children trailed past her into the restaurant. They were all dressed in church clothes. The father carried a pretty six-month-old baby girl. The baby gazed over his shoulder at Shay, her eyes limpidly innocent.

Shay averted her eyes. Kelly had looked like that. Kelly had been as pretty as the infant Brooke Shields. She could feel the tears starting again. Despite her vows, they were becoming uncontrollable, like a reflex.

"Shay!" Randy came back on the line. He sounded excited.

"Yes?" Hope galvanized her.

"I could have something—a health insurance plan through a place called Ypsi Trucking." He pronounced it the local way, Ipsi. "And there's a home address; it's in Ypsilanti, too. Do you think this could be Danno?"

Ypsilanti, an hour's drive away along I-94, was almost a twin city of Ann Arbor. It had achieved fame during World War II with the Willow Run bomber plant. "We'll have to find out," she said, scribbling down the address.

"*Now,*" Ben began sternly when she returned to the booth. "Now is the time to take what you have and call the police, Shay. You have a name, you have an address and a place of employment. Or something to go on, anyway."

"No," she insisted. "Not yet."

"Why not? Surely you aren't planning to confront the man yourself? Don't be ridiculous." Red spots of stress decorated Ben's cheeks. "The man is an ex-con—he's well known for beating women. What do you think he'd do to you?"

She nodded. She'd been thinking about that, too. "I'm going to call Ypsilanti and see if I can raise anyone at that trucking company—I'll say I'm an insurance investigator or something."

Ben groaned. "You mean like they do in detective novels? Very believable on a Sunday afternoon, kid. Look, let me do it. They usually have Sunday dispatchers at places like that—and it'll be a man. He'll respond better to another man.''

Five minutes later Ben hung up, smiling. ''He's on a run, thank God—off to South Carolina with auto parts, then to Texas. They don't expect him back until Thursday—which is very, very good news, Shay. It means that Danno won't be at his house when Mickey gets there—*if* he's headed there. So Mickey is going to have to wait, too.''

Shay got up and grabbed her purse. ''I'm driving over to Ypsilanti right now. I want to look at the house.''

''You mean we. *We're* going there.''

''Ben—'' She knew he didn't want her to do this, and he would drag her down, attempting to force her to be sensible. ''I told you. You should stay—''

Ben said, ''If McGee was in the area, I wouldn't let you go, but since he's away—''

''I don't have to ask your permission to do this,'' she told him.

''I know. Oh, baby, I know. If driving past that house will help your pain—come on, I'll drive. You're stressed out. Why don't you try to sleep in the car?''

Shay suppressed a nervous laugh. Ben was humoring her. Sleep? It was like asking a hyperactive four-year-old boy to take a nap. She knew she wasn't going to be able to sleep a wink. Was this a wild goose chase she'd embarked them on? Did Mickey have something else in mind; had he already left the state with Kelly?

She shivered with both fear and anticipation.

Somehow, she didn't think he had. No, she thought, he was right here in Michigan, somewhere in the Detroit area, looking for the next person on his shit list. With any luck it would be Danno McGee.

All they had to do was intersect his path.

TWENTY

At noon, Mickey untied Kelly's hands and backed Noah's Tempo out of the narrow, rutted trail.

"Where . . . where are we going?" Kelly whispered, her throat dry. *They were going to kill someone else. She knew it. Oh, God. . . . He was going to make her watch more murdering, and he would force her to pretend she liked it.*

"I'm hungry," Mickey responded, spinning the wheels. It was a lot harder to back out than it had been to drive in, and there was no space to turn around.

"Oh."

He jammed his foot on the accelerator and the car finally bounced over the rut, throwing Kelly against the door. Mickey put his face next to hers, so close that she could see a scar near his left eye, the bristle of his beard hairs, and dark spatters of dried blood he had not cleaned off.

Blood from the Goldmans.

"We're gonna pick up some ribs, see? And you're

going to be a very good girl, aren't you, bitch Kelly? *Aren't you?''*

She nodded, terrified.

"Say it," he snapped.

"I'll be good."

"You're the king, Mickey."

" 'Y-you're the king.' "

"You're *my* king. And I love to watch you use your blade, Mickey, I love it love it love it."

Miserably she repeated the words, managing to get them right. She had to do what Mickey said. The only thing that was keeping her alive was the fact that somehow, for some horrible, scary reason, he wanted her around. To watch.

He's totally freako, she told herself, fighting back tears. She knew tears were very dangerous. Her crying angered him because it made him see that she didn't want to be with him. If he thought she wasn't going along with the program, he'd cut her throat with that awful four-inch blade, just as he had cut Mrs. Goldman's.

The sun was overhead now, glaring through the windshield of the car and heating up the interior. Mickey had turned the air conditioning on. She knew he didn't want the car windows open because he was afraid Kelly might yell out.

They drove south on Ortonville Road. He was rambling on again, telling her about all the awful apartments he'd lived in with his mother and how she'd been on welfare for years. About all the sculpture stuff he wanted, and the big studio he never got.

They rode past several expensive homes that had big barns and two or three horses. This was horse country, Kelly remembered. In one of the paddocks a girl about Kelly's age was putting a lead on a chestnut-red, skittish horse. She smiled and stroked the animal's glossy neck, happy in the beautiful Sunday afternoon.

Kelly gazed at the girl longingly as they sped past. God, Kelly had always wanted a horse. Now she might never get one. She could hardly believe that she had once thought Mickey cute . . . romantic.

He didn't seem handsome to her any more. His shock of dark hair now needed a shampoo and hung greasily in his face. His nose now seemed short and pug, disgusting to her, and every time she looked at the spots of congealed, dark red blood on his face that he'd never bothered to wipe off, she felt nauseous.

Get me out of this, she kept thinking. *I want to go home. Please, let me go home. I'll never be an asshole to my mom again, God, if you'll just listen this one time.*

I swear it, she added.

A pickup truck was approaching them from the opposite lane, hauling an aluminum horse trailer. It swerved slightly in their direction, as if the driver had momentarily lost attention.

Kelly's eyes widened and she tried not to show the terrible thought that had leaped into her brain.

What if she could make Mickey have a car accident?

If somehow she could get the car to hit something, not badly, then the police would be called, or a passing motorist might help her.

Mickey was talking about Danno again, repeating all the horrible things the man had done, the cigarette burns, the knifings, the beatings, the way he forced Mickey to polish his motorcycle for him, kicking him and calling him stupid if the chrome didn't look good enough. His words were full of hatred and obscenities.

Kelly let it all slip past her ears.

Cause an accident? Terror washed through her. The accident she'd been in two years ago with her father at the wheel had been traumatic. A shocking crunch of metal and assault of pain, and the agony of her dislocated shoulder. She'd been in the emergency room for six hours. What if she got hurt again—only worse? She didn't have her seat belt on. If they hit something, she would fly right through the windshield. Broken glass would cut her face and scar it or maybe even cut her throat. Jesus . . .

"Asshole!" Mickey was yelling, as if he thought she'd been hanging on every word. "Damn fucking asshole—thought his fucking bike was more important than me—"

She sneaked her hands down to her waist, fumbling for the buckle of the seat belt which she hoped to fasten. Mickey didn't seem to see her. He was too busy hating his dad and braking for a stoplight as they came into town.

She managed to click the buckle into its fastener. If they crashed, she'd be protected. She was breathing rapidly, the shallow air not giving sustenance to her lungs. The town of Clarkston had old houses with porches shaded by big, spreading trees. It looked cozy and happy, the kind of town Kelly had always wanted to live in.

They drove several blocks. Nobody was paying any attention to the Tempo at all. Why should they? It was an ordinary car, nothing special. Also, Mickey was scrupulously following the speed limit, and he had a different license plate on the car.

She moved her eyes back and forth, calculating. How was she going to manage an accident? What should they hit? If they hit another car, she might kill someone. Maybe a little kid like Matt. Oh, *God*, she could never do that. Maybe she should try to get her foot on the accelerator and push down real hard, forcing them to hit a tree.

She smelled her own fear, the sweat of terror, as she pondered these questions. What if it didn't work?

What if they hit the tree and Mickey wasn't even hurt and became so mad he took out the knife and stabbed her to death?

He could do it.

He would do it.

Her bladder suddenly hurt, and she had to pinch her legs together to keep from wetting herself in sheer terror.

"What's on your mind, bitch girl?" Mickey suddenly rasped.

She jumped guiltily. "N-Nothing."

"You're thinking something. I can tell. Well, let me tell you something, kid . . . *don't think it*. I ain't about to get caught, not yet, not until I get down to the bottom of my list and I got something right here in my hand that's gonna keep you sweet, hear me? Nice and sweet and quiet."

He didn't have to flash the butterfly blade at her. Kelly knew what he meant. He would stab her if she did anything. He'd enjoy doing it.

"I'll be quiet," she quavered. "But—"

"Yeah?"

She wanted to ask if she could call home and talk to her Mom—just for a few seconds. Shay's voice, her cool good sense and sympathy, seemed suddenly like a lifeline to the normal world.

"Nothing," she whispered.

The rib-and-chicken shack was located in what had once been an old gas station. It emitted a strong odor of barbecued meat and deep-fat frying oil. The greasy smell made Kelly feel sick.

The counter girl barely glanced at them as Mickey ordered two full slabs of ribs, four orders of french fries, and two 32-ounce containers of regular Pepsi. She was a chubby high school girl with mousy hair pulled back in a ponytail. Even if Kelly screamed, this girl would never be able to help her. In fact, Mickey would probably kill her, too.

"And add two orders of chicken dinner," Mickey specified. "Three piece dinners. White meat. An' lots of salt."

"Two chickens," said the girl, waddling off to fill the order.

Cautiously Kelly looked around. They were the only ones standing in line—which was one reason Mickey had chosen the place, Kelly knew. He stood close to her, a jacket of Noah's slung over his arm. The butterfly knife was underneath it, jammed into her.

Maybe if someone else came into the rib shack—a couple of men. She could run to them . . . throw her arms around them . . . cry . . . beg them to help her.

She felt tears sting her eyes again.

God, what was wrong with her; she was daydreaming like some kind of a fool. It wasn't going to happen. And if it did, Mickey would probably kill everybody, not just her. The realization struck her like a punch to the center of her chest. He didn't care who he killed or what he did because he himself wanted to die.

"Two chicken dinners, two full slabs, four fries, two 32-ounce Pepsi's," said the girl, returning with their order.

Mickey pulled out two twenty-dollar bills from his pocket and thrust them at the girl. The money had spots of blood on it. The girl barely glanced at the bills, just stuffed them into the cash register and handed the change to Mickey.

"*You* carry the shit," he ordered Kelly, indicating the greasy cardboard box that contained the ribs, and the two bulging white paper sacks. He shoved the knife into her rib just a fraction harder, causing a sharp spasm of pain.

Kelly tried not to gasp. Like an obedient servant, she reached for the order and balanced the fragrant sacks in her arms. She wondered who was going to eat all the food. She wasn't hungry at all.

"Eat it," Mickey ordered, shoving a greasy section of rib bone into Kelly's face. "Eat it or I'll shove it in you—and I can't guarantee which end." He giggled, pleased with himself for the gross joke.

They were again parked on the trail behind the partially built condo development. This time Mickey hadn't pulled the Tempo so far up the rutted trail, so it would be easier to back out. No one was around and the air was sweet with the smell of new leaves and earth.

"Eat your fucking share or I'll ram it up you," Mickey repeated, gnawing noisily on several pieces of the sticky, greasy meat. He grabbed the paper bag that held the french fries and stuffed four long ones past his lips. He chewed without closing his mouth.

Kelly shuddered and looked away, forcing herself to take a small bite of the spicy barbecue. The red sauce reminded her of blood, and she immediately retched, clapping both hands over her mouth.

"Don't barf," Mickey ordered. "If you fucking barf I'm going to kill you right now, hear? I'm gonna cut out your intestines and see what they look like."

"No," she begged. She swallowed back sour splashes of acid, struggling not to throw up. God, when was this going to be over? *Mom,* she prayed weakly. *Mom . . . I'll be good.*

"You ever see your own guts, girl?"

"No," she gasped.

"I bet yours are pretty, know what I mean? All pink and glistening—I seen a picture once in a magazine, of an operation, like. These surgeon guys were reaching into this woman and everything was right there for you to see. It was incredible. A real rush.''

Kelly fished out some fries from one of the sacks and nibbled on them, pretending to eat. Longingly she thought about her mother—about the way her mom's face had lit up when she gave her those pink dangly earrings from All That Glitters.

''Drink some of this fucking Pepsi. I ordered it for you,'' Mickey shoved the big sweating plastic container at Kelly. Numbly she took it. She sipped the too-sweet liquid, tears filling her eyes. She'd had two chances to escape while they were in Clarkston but she hadn't taken them. She hadn't been brave enough.

She wondered if she was really going to die.

It was already past 6:00 P.M. Hazy light diffused the air, turning the sun pale. It would not get dark until nearly 9:00 P.M., the day unnaturally suspended. This had been the longest day of Shay's life.

They took I-75 south, and merged onto I-94, the area's oldest expressway with the road surface beaten down, pulverized by the thousands of cars and semi trucks that traversed it every hour. Ben had slipped a Glenn Miller tape into the deck.

As ''Pennsylvania 6-5000'' jitterbugged through the car, Shay leaned her head on the head rest and let her mind drift. For an instant she seemed to sense that Kelly was crying, but that didn't require any psychic connection. Her daughter *was* alive. Shay believed that with every particle of her being.

What if Mickey didn't show up at his father's at all?

That was the problem . . . that was the real worry.

But he will, she thought, remembering the contorted scribblings on the wall, and what Beverly McGee had said about him knowing where his dad was.

It all really boiled down to one thing: was Mickey

reachable? That's what she was gambling on. Because if he was, if she could talk to him, if she could somehow penetrate his shell with words and reach that eager, creative, positive side of him—then she could get Kelly back. The police would bring out the terrible side of Mickey, but Shay knew she could touch that other side of him, the good side.

She felt it, deep in her gut, and she'd decided to trust that gut instinct.

They passed signs for Metro Airport, a jet coming in low for a landing. Her mind immediately did an about-face, remembering what Marianne had said about psychotics being unpredictable, quick to blow. Perhaps Mickey operated only on twisted emotional instinct—as vicious as a wild animal. She remembered Marianne's story about the fifteen-year-old boy who had tried to rip out a doctor's eyes.

Chilled, she glanced over at Ben's profile as he drove. He was in this, too. He had made it clear he believed she was wrong, but that would mean nothing if Mickey decided to stab him. She would have the responsibility of Ben on her shoulders.

Well, she could solve that by making Ben leave once they reached Danno's house. He could have the car, she'd take a cab. She sighed, recrossing her legs and shifting herself in the seat. This was her fight, not Ben's, and wonderful as he was, she could not risk him.

If she went into the house. That would be taking an enormous risk, but if she did not take the risk, and Kelly was found later—she'd go through the rest of her life, knowing she hadn't done everything she could, she had not gone the final mile.

No, she couldn't back out now.

Ben would have to understand.

*　*　*

Mickey tossed the food wrappers and sizeable portions of untouched meat and fries out of the car window into the bushes, where birds swooped down to investigate the leavings.

Kelly shuddered as she saw that Mickey had turned south. They were headed toward the more heavily populated area of Pontiac-Waterford.

Why? Where were they going? Apprehension filled her stomach like cement.

Within twenty minutes he had pulled into a convenience store called Pizer's Parties. When Kelly saw the sign, her blood iced through her veins.

Pizer's party store!

This store was owned by Kimberly's mother and father! Kimberly from art class! The Kim who Mickey had supposedly pulled a knife on, and who he'd been raving about half the morning, all the crap she had pulled on him.

She felt a wave of faintness flood over her, and gasped shallowly.

Kimberley was on Mickey's shit list.

Mickey's entire body had gone into overdrive, hate and joy vibrating through him like high-octane gasoline.

The more Kelly showed her fear, the more he got off on it. It was so incredible . . . such a sweet high. . . . He was king. Dammit, he was, and this proved it! He could hardly wait for what would happen next.

He pulled the Tempo into the party store lot. It was an ordinary brick dump, plastered with signs advertising the Michigan Lotto and Keno games, potato chips, milk, and Stroh's beer.

A red LeBaron with a woman and three children in it was just pulling out. Mickey saw that there was only one other car, parked in the back. He'd hit the store just right, during a Sunday lull. Any minute now another car could pull into the fucking lot, or some asshole would come strolling up on foot to buy a six-pack. But for now, the coast was clear.

The danger excited him. He was already hard, his groin aching.

He fastened the rope around bitch Kelly's wrists again and dragged her out of the Tempo, jabbing the knife into her side.

"You dare scream and I'll do you, too . . . get it?"

She stared at him, wide-eyed. "You aren't . . . *not again*?" she whispered.

He growled, *"And you're gonna watch every second of it and you're going to come and come and come. And if you don't, I'll kill you, too."*

He frog-marched her into the party store.

Kelly stumbled ahead of Mickey, pushing open the door with her bound hands. He crowded in after her, his eyes darting around the room.

In a swift glance he took in the emptiness of the aisles. Nobody by the microwave heating a sandwich. Nobody opening the refrigerator for a cold beer. No dumb little kid standing in front of the candy counter. And—he could tell by the half-open door to a storage room—nobody unpacking boxes, either.

Well, hot damn. Luck had held for him all day because he *was* king and kings were in power. Yeah, he was set, he'd bought a ticket. It was meant to be and he was going to ride until the ride ran out.

The seventeen-year-old girl standing behind the cash register looked up from writing something down on a price sheet. She was stocky, solid, with reddish hair and very pale, milky skin splotched with freckles.

"Hi," Mickey said jauntily.

Obviously bitch Kimberley had seen the news. The color drained from her face. She took a small step backward, her hands gripping the worn formica counter top as if to keep herself from falling. She was too paralyzed to scream.

"Hey," she said faintly. Mickey heard the sound of air gulping in her throat. "Hey."

"You're on my shit list, sugar."

Feeling the warm sexual heat of Kelly's horrified gaze, he waved the butterfly knife, opening and shutting it from alternate sides in a snick-snicking, deadly display of skill.

This was going to be fantastic. Yeah, he'd show both of them what he was made of. Maybe this time he'd fuck both of them.

Kim uttered a sob and hurled herself backward, cowering behind the bulk of the cash register. Mickey *loved* it . . . *loved it*.

"Kim," Kelly blurted urgently. *"Kim, push the alarm."*

Shocked, jolted down from his fantasy, Mickey turned to her. How had she known that party stores keep burglar alarm buttons under the counter? And probably guns, too. The little bitch!

But then he swiveled his eyes back to Kimberley and knew he was fucking safe. She wasn't pushing any button. She was totally into her fear, mesmerized by the sight of the knife.

"Press the button!" Kelly screamed. *"PRESS IT PRESS IT!"*

But it was too late.

TWENTY-ONE

At a Shell station, they found an attendant who recognized the street address Shay had scribbled down. He directed them north of town to a subdivision near the Green Oaks Golf Course.

"You can't miss it," he said.

Shay jotted down the directions, then went to a drive-up phone located at the edge of the station, near the curb. First she dialed Ben's house.

"No calls," reported Gloria Adamson. Traffic sounds made it hard to hear her voice. "I've been within two feet of the phone this entire time."

In spite of the fact that she hadn't expected Kelly to be able to call, Shay still felt a tightness in her temples.

"Any other calls?"

"Two or three calls from Detective Salter. Calls from Kelly's friends, a girl named Heather Schoenfeld, especially. She sounded very upset—something about a fight she and your daughter had. I'm keeping a list."

Shay immediately hung up and dialed Salter.

"There's been another stabbing," she thought he told her, but a semi truck was passing on the street, its engines roaring so loudly that she could not hear.

"What?" she said, putting a hand over her left ear.

"Where are you calling from? A phone booth? I said there's been another stabbing. At a party store, a girl called Kimberley Pizer. She's at Pontiac General Hospital right now in critical condition. Her parents owned the store; she worked there part-time. Some kids came in to buy beer and found her, or she'd be dead."

"Oh, my God," Shay breathed, gripping the phone. *Another one.* "Was . . . was Kelly with him?"

"Yes. Kimberley I.D.'d her. Says she had her hands tied in front of her."

Shay made a moaning sound. She felt a wave of terrible, vile hatred. She wanted to take Mickey and stand him against a wall—and drive her car into him. Back up and hit him again and again, until he was obliterated.

The murderous wave receded, leaving her shaking and stunned.

"Will Kimberley be all right?" Shay whispered.

"She's in surgery now. She's critical but she does have a chance. Mrs. Wyoming," Salter went on. His voice sounded intense, Rambo-angry. "I want you to know that we do have some leads on McGee's father that might pan out. We think that's where he's going. We're going to get the son of a bitch. Believe it."

She'd heard the macho note, the aggressiveness, just what she feared.

"Does that mean that you'll risk the life of a hostage—my daughter—in order to get Mickey?"

"Calm down, Mrs. Wyoming. I know this is rough. We're doing our best, believe me. Just go home and wait. We'll get in touch as soon as anything else breaks.''

She thought of a dozen sharp replies, but bit back all of them. ''All right, good-bye,'' she said.

She slammed down the phone, taking out her helplessness on that inanimate object. She leaned against the booth, trying to gather the shreds of her courage. A teenaged girl stabbed—a girl Kelly's age. It was all horrible and senseless and it had to stop.

Walking toward the car where Ben waited, exhaustion flooded her. She decided not to tell Ben about Kimberley Pizer. He would only pressure her further to give up, to turn it all over to the police. She loved him, but she didn't need his pressuring right now. Kelly was not his daughter, and Ben still held faith in the justice system, a faith that Shay realized she no longer possessed.

''You didn't tell him we've found Danno's address, did you?'' Ben began sharply when she reached the car.

''No.''

''When are you going to, Shay? You have a lead to this case. You have concrete information and you're not sharing it. You're playing God. Don't you think—''

She slid into the passenger seat and slammed the door shut. ''I think,'' she said carefully, ''that I've got to play this out. I've got to trust my instincts, Ben. I know what the police SWAT bullshit can be like and I don't think they can help Kelly. Ben, I think we should separate right here and now. You drop me off here and I'll call a cab and do this on my own.''

He stared at her, red mottling his cheeks. ''Dammit, you really mean it, don't you? You really mean it.''

''Yes.''

''He's done another one, hasn't he?''

The sudden question caught Shay off guard. She felt the color drain from her face.

"I could tell by the way you reacted when you were on the phone. Shay, the kid is a monster; when are you going to face that? He can't be reasoned with, he can't be fixed or helped. He's as mad as a dog with rabies. Dammit, as much as I love words and earn my living by them, I know one thing, Mickey McGee is not going to be stopped with words. That's reality, Shay."

"Well, if that's true, I don't like reality. I don't like it one damn bit. Now let's start the car and get out of here. I want to find Mickey's father's house."

"He won't be there," Ben said softly. "If he's done another killing, he'll realize he's too hot now. Danno's is the last place he'd be."

"And it's the only place I know he might be," she said, "so I'm going to go to the house and at least drive past it."

"We are, you mean."

She gazed at him for a long minute. "Are you sure?"

"I've come this far, haven't I?"

Ypsilanti was filled with blossoming fruit trees, and had the pleasantly shabby aura of a university town. Students from nearby Eastern Michigan University strolled the sidewalks, clad in trendy T-shirts, tank tops and shorts, on their way to movies, restaurants, or other Sunday evening amusements.

They didn't speak on the fifteen-minute drive through town. There wasn't anything to say. They'd each given their position and each thought the other was wrong. But Ben was still supporting her—for which Shay felt a numbed gratefulness. He was no ordinary man, she realized. He was special. Why couldn't he have come along at a time when her life was calm and her daughter wasn't in danger of being murdered?

The subdivision looked painfully new, a cheap builder's special. There were spindly saplings planted in yards and amateurish landscaping that had barely begun to flourish. A skinny boy in a Sister Soulja T-shirt skateboarded down the street in front of them, zigzagging back and forth, unwilling to let them have the right of way. Ben cautiously maneuvered the car around him.

The address Randy had given them—1734 Stony Stream Court—was a yellow colonial sitting on a lot devoid of trees or any sort of shrubbery. Its lawn was so newly sodded that seams showed between the strips of green. A plastic Big Wheel lay overturned on the newly cemented walk. At the sight, Shay wavered. It seemed impossible that Mickey could be headed for a place as stultifyingly ordinary as this.

They drove past four times, each time slowing up to stare at the house. Once, Shay thought she saw a child staring out of the curved living room window.

"Park in the driveway, Ben. I'm going up to the door."

"Shay, you said you just wanted to drive around the block."

"Did you think I came here just to look at the house and go home again? I know what I want to do. Give me a chance. Don't stand in my way. I mean it, Ben. *Please.* Or else drop me off here and I'll manage on my own, and I mean it."

Ben looked at her and opened his mouth to say something, then closed it. "Okay, but I'm coming, too. We can be encyclopedia salesmen. I used to sell them. I still remember the pitch."

The front porch of the house was scattered with a collection of run-down toys. The worn objects gave the place the battered look of a home day-care center.

Shay stepped around a soiled pink teddy bear in order to ring the doorbell. A TV set, turned to the shopping channel, could be heard inside, along with the howl of a squalling toddler.

"Yeah? Shut up, Donnie, shut up, can't you see I'm tryin' to answer the door? Shut *up*, I said!" The harassed young woman who came to the door looked like one of the E.M.U. college students they'd seen earlier—only she was seven months pregnant. She wore baggy gray sweatpants and two tank tops, the bottom one black, the top one a faded blue—the garb of a frazzled young mother coping with too many demanding small children. A charm on a gold chain around her neck spelled out MISSY.

But it was the bruises that drew Shay's horrified and fascinated eye. Around the woman's throat they were purplish, dotted with dark red marks of fingernails. An irregularly shaped, greenish-yellow mark marred her left cheek and still showed the shape of the hand that had made it.

All the things Shay had read about battered women spun into her consciousness. The way they were kept physically and financially helpless, living in a constant cycle of terror and reconciliation, always striving to please a tyrant who never could be pleased. A hundred or so of them rose up every year and killed their batterers. And thousands more ran away.

"Yes?" Missy Sparling repeated. In the house, a second child had added his sobs to the howls of the first.

Shay made a split-second decision. "Mrs. Sparling? Missy?"

"Yeah?"

"Is your husband's first name Danno?"

The woman looked frightened.

"Does he ever go by the last name of McGee?"

Missy's hand flew to her battered neck, and by the quick dart of her eyes, Shay knew that they were in the right place. This was Danno's wife or live-in girlfriend. "Please. If I could just have a second. My name is Shay Wyoming, and this is Ben Lyte. I'm the mother of Kelly Wyoming, the girl who's been on the news. The girl who was kidnapped by Mickey McGee."

"Please, go away."

Impulsively, Shay fumbled on her finger for the diamond cocktail ring she'd worn for the party and, in the long hours since Noah's murder and her daughter's abduction, had not removed. It had belonged to her mother and contained twelve stones totaling three carats—not terribly expensive, but still costly enough to be worth something to a woman who probably was kept without any spending money.

"Here," she said, handing the ring to the woman.

Missy Sparling's shock was obvious. She took the ring, staring down at the dome-shaped setting of stones that caught and refracted the late afternoon light. She held it with reverence as if she had never touched such a ring before. Then she looked at Shay again. "Why are you giving this to me?"

"This is probably worth $5,000, maybe more. And I can give you money, too." Shay opened her purse and pulled out all the bills she was carrying—about $125. She pressed these into Missy Sparling's hand.

"I want you to leave your house for a couple of days."

"Shay," Ben said warningly beside her.

Shay ignored him. "Missy, your husband is on a trucking run until Thursday. He won't know you're gone and I need to be able to wait here for Mickey. I know he's your husband's son by a previous marriage, and I think he's coming here, Missy—maybe he's on his way right now."

Missy looked startled.

"He's a very, very dangerous boy. He's——" Her voice was shaking and she steadied it. "He's already killed six people, Mrs. Sparling, and he's kidnapped my sixteen-year-old daughter. You and your children are in danger if he comes here; . . . take my word for it."

Missy's hand clutched at her throat. A child screeched again from within the house. "I don't know."

"Go to a motel, Missy," Shay said urgently. "You have babies, Missy, and another one coming. This is none of my business but you could take that ring and get out of here and find someplace safe for yourself and your kids. But whatever you do, could you stay away from this house for at least three days? Here"——she scribbled her own address on a slip of paper—"take this. I'll help you, Missy. Later. After this is over. I swear it. Please, give my daughter a chance. I just want to stay here and talk to Mickey."

Missy nervously fingered the cocktail ring, gazing down at it with a combination of fear, greed, and longing.

"Or you could keep the ring and hide it from him as your own little nest egg," Shay suggested desperately. "Please—just three days, Missy."

"Okay," Missy said. She slid the ring on her finger and pocketed the bills. "But only two days, okay? He's callin' me on Wednesday night and I got to be back here for that. God," Missy sighed, "if he calls here early and I'm not here——"

"He won't," Shay said recklessly.

"I got to trust you, don't I? But there ain't any other way I can get any money. He won't let me work. And he won't let me take the pill."

* * *

They left Ben's Cierra parked six houses down the block and walked back. The life of suburbia surged around them—dogs barking, kids playing boom boxes, a newborn baby's distant mewling wail, the sound of a chain saw cutting into the early evening.

Missy packed suitcases for the two toddlers, one nineteen months and the other about three years old, and then drove away in an ancient Subaru that had a loudly rattling muffler and a squeaky fan belt.

"Well, I hope it doesn't die on her in the next mile," Ben remarked as the muffler sounds faded away. "Do you realize, Shay, that makes three battered women? I wonder how many children he's abused. The guy's chronic. No wonder Mickey is so fucked up—look at the background he comes from."

Shay looked around the living room. A brown lounge chair and brown couch faced the TV set and cable box. A playpen with a torn plastic pad dominated the center of the room, filled with chewed stuffed animals. A used Pampers decorated a table top. There were no books, no pictures, no throw pillows, no plants, no coffee table, and only one lamp. The soiled white walls were scarred in unexpected places, as if someone had hurled heavy objects at them.

Shay murmured, shuddering, "This place reeks of violence and unhappiness. That poor woman."

There was no cable remote. Restlessly Shay walked to the set and switched it on from the box, then realized that Mickey might hear the TV from the street if he were to come, and turned it off again. The eye of the cable box glowed red.

She glanced at her watch. It was now 5:20 P.M. Was Ben right that Mickey would consider this house too "hot" to risk?

And did it even matter? At least she was here—she was doing *something*. She would not sit home and be passive; she would not let her daughter go without a struggle.

An hour passed. At first she and Ben talked quietly, but their disagreement hung between them. Several times Ben suggested calling Salter, but Shay vetoed it.

She paced about restlessly, thinking what a contrast this barren house was with her own, which overflowed with books and art and warmth. Without television, there was little to do, but in poking through the kitchen she managed to find a copy of the *Ypsilanti Press* in the trash can. She and Ben split the sections, reading about the rape of a female student in one of the E.M.U. dorms, and about a fraternity house mother, sixty-seven years old, who was about to receive her B.A. degree.

But Shay kept having to read a paragraph three and four times. Finally she put the paper aside and went to peer out of the front windows. The sky had clouded over, and a skittery wind picked up scraps of paper in the driveway, hurling them across the spongy sod. In a few hours, it would be dark.

Chilling questions swirled in her mind, torturing her with the threat of unknown answers. Would he come? And how? Would he just knock at the door as they had done, or would he try to break in, later, after dark? And when he did arrive, would Kelly be with him?

Would she be tied up? Screaming? Wounded and bleeding? Had he stabbed her with the knife? Or . . . oh, God . . . had he raped her? *Tortured her?*

She closed her eyes, squeezing the lids. *Hang on, Kelly,* she thought, forcing her entire being into the phrase. *Hang on, honey, because I'm here and I'm waiting and I love you, baby.*

* * *

The wait stretched on. The light that streamed in the living room window turned grayer as clouds moved in from the north. The house uttered its own private noises—the hum of a refrigerator motor, the pop of joists somewhere inside the drywall, the abnormally loud tick of a cheap K-Mart wall clock shaped like a goose.

Ben had settled down on the couch and was actually napping, his lips fluttering loosely as he breathed. Shay thought it was amazing, the way he slept, escaping into unconsciousness where he would not have to deal with problems but could simply drift.

She wished—how she wished—that she could do the same. But, although exhaustion yoked her with leaden chains, and caused her eyes to burn, Shay could not relax. She supposed she was unconsciously afraid that if she did, she would somehow be giving up on Kelly—consigning her to death. Only her motherly vigilance could keep her child alive, she thought bitterly, wiping her grainy, hot eyes. It was a crock, of course. But still she felt her muscles tensely ready.

She folded up the playpen and moved it to a side wall and paced restlessly, afraid to turn on the TV set or the small radio she'd found, for fear that Mickey would hear these noises and get frightened away.

If he came.

For the fiftieth time, she stared out the front window. It was streaked at toddler level with the fingerprints of Missy Sparling's children. On the front walk, three four-year-olds were still racing Big Wheels up and down, the hollow plastic wheels rumbling on the cement. A car drove by playing loud rap music, the sounds fading slowly down the street.

Shay shivered, feeling the chill reach all the way down into her. That could have been Mickey, reconnoitering, checking the place out. On the other hand, maybe Mickey was far away by now, targeting some-one else for his bloodbath; maybe he would not come here at all. Maybe this had all been useless from the beginning.

God. Was this a wild goose chase? An ego defense, busy-work that she'd manufactured for herself, to keep her brain from going totally insane with worry and rage?

She moved away from the window and sank down in the lounge chair. When she leaned her head back, the tiredness crept around her like a gluey fog.

She jerked herself awake again. It was like driving when you were tired, falling into those tiny, microsec-ond naps that could be so fatal. She had brought the Literary Guild bag into the house, and to distract her-self she pulled out the small bust she had done of Mickey.

There he was. God, she'd caught him. Had she ever. The handsome, yet soft face with its anger and vulner-ability, and the force of creative, vibrant life that ema-nated from the boy, totally beyond his control. Good, bad, evil, she mused. We all had it in us in varying amounts.

Did the worst, the most murderous psychopaths still have value in them, some spark that was worth saving? A tiny section of their soul that was pure?

Darkness was closing in, the soft, violet dusk. A hatch of insects danced through the air, their wings silvery.

Mickey was feeling a rush . . . a flow of wild excite-ment that seemed to get stronger with each turn he made, each intersection he drove through. Yeah, he was nearly there now and it felt good, so much better than he imagined.

Things were gonna pop—soon.

Things were gonna happen. And it would explode all around him and he would be in the thick of it. He'd show them once and for all who he was . . . the king.

They were driving past a McDonald's, and he could see cars lined up at the drive-through window, some guy pulled up to the mike, ordering his Big Macs, fries, and shake. Mickey felt saliva fill his mouth, but he knew he had to keep on driving. There was no more time for food. He had important things to do and they did not include stuffing his face.

He glanced to the passenger seat, where Kelly sat curled up like a little girl, her knees drawn up to her chest, her bound hands clasped around them. Honey-colored hair fell around her face, and her color was pale, her eyes screwed shut.

Shit . . . she was afraid of him. She didn't get off on things the way he wanted—she wasn't going with the program. In fact, the way she sobbed and carried on made him angry.

He didn't want to be angry, he wanted to soar above it all. He wanted to let things flow, let them go, make them happen. But he didn't know what he was going to do with her. Maybe she was like all the others, just a piece of shit that hated him and blocked him and caused bad things to happen to him. Yeah . . . maybe that's exactly what she was.

"Wake up," he called roughly. He reached over and smacked the girl across the face, jerking her head to the side. "Wake up, bitch Kelly, I don't like you sleepin' on me."

She didn't make a sound, even though he had hurt her. "I wasn't sleeping."

"You *never* sleep when you are around the king."

"Sorry. I'm sorry, Mickey."

"Yeah, bitch, I bet you're sorry, I just bet. You don't care, do you? You don't give a rat's ass."

"I . . . I do," she faltered.

"Bull*shit* you do."

He was on Prospect now—almost there—passing the subdivisions, all the bullshit houses that he and his mother had never been able to afford to live in and never would. Right now he could see one that had added on a greenhouse room to the back, jammed with plants. He could have used that space for his own work. There was never going to be any place for him, was there? The son of Danno McGee, a filthy con, a dirty kid-abuser, did not become a great artist . . . now, did he? *That* was the real bullshit, wasn't it? That he even should have thought of it at all.

"Sorry," Kelly quavered again, her whole body vibrating. He could hear the quake of her breathing, almost like a dog panting. Her fear stunned him. Shit, she was only doing this because she was afraid. That totally spoiled everything.

He wanted her to want it, that was part of the fantasy, and she didn't.

"*Shut the fuck up!*" Mickey snarled at her savagely. "*Or I'm going to show you what your insides look like, get it? I'm going to ram it and jam it.*"

She shut up. He gripped the steering wheel so tightly that he nearly bent the wheel. He was going to teach her a lesson, all right. He would teach everyone a lesson.

He was the king. Nobody stopped him.

Nobody.

TWENTY-TWO

The children with the Big Wheels had gone indoors, called in by a heavy young woman wearing Bermuda shorts and a big shirt that flapped over her thighs. Shay used the bathroom, where damp training pants were hung over the shower rod, and a child's potty sat in a corner. A section of wall near the tub had been dented as if hit by a hammer. Shay could picture the scene that had created it, and shuddered. Danno's *three* battered women. Two had gotten away. If Missy Sparling had any sense, she would never come back to this house.

She found a half-clean towel to dry her hands on. Being in the center of someone else's flawed world made her feel destructive—a force that had come into this house and would change it forever. Or was it Mickey who would change this house? She could feel him coming now. He was very close.

Stop being so damn dramatic, she ordered herself.

But the feeling did not leave her. She left the bathroom and walked down a hallway with walls marred by toy scratches and baby-smears. A wall phone near the dining room had phone numbers scribbled beside it on the drywall. On impulse she stopped and picked up the receiver, listening for the dial tone.

The tone repeated emptily. Slowly she hung up.

She'd almost dialed Salter.

Suddenly she did not want to be alone.

"Ben," she said, shaking him awake. "Ben."

"Wh—Wha—" He shook his head groggily.

"Ben . . . wake up, will you? I have a feeling . . ."

"What time is it?" He sat bolt upright, lifting his left hand to look at his watch. "Seven-thirty? How long did I sleep? Jesus, I feel as if I've got airplane glue in my mouth. Has that Missy woman got any Pepsi in her refrigerator? I'll even take Kool-Aid. I've got to have a drink."

He got up, starting toward the kitchen, as relaxed as if this were his own home.

"Ben!" Shay pulled on his arm. *"Ben!"*

He looked at her. During the day, his beard had grown a fraction of an inch longer, and now covered his face in a dark stubble. Wasn't stubble supposed to be "in" among movie-star hunks? It only made Ben look tired, and unutterably dear.

He said, "It's only a can of soda, she's not going to mind, Shay. She can always tell her husband that one of the kids drank it, it's no big deal."

"Ben . . ." Her voice sounded hoarse, stretchy. "I have a feeling, just this feeling, I think he's on his way here now. I really think so."

For a second the smile froze on Ben's face. Then he said, "Hey, honey, I was thinking while I slept. I know you're upset and I know this is terrible for you, a real ordeal. We've inconvenienced that poor wretch Missy, but it's been in a good cause because it's helped you to get through all of this. You've felt like you were doing something, you've felt useful and you haven't fallen apart. But now let's go home.''

''What?''

''You've done as much as you can. Call Salter, and then let's go home. We're both exhausted. You need to sleep. And I'd like to catch that movie on HBO—the Steven Seagal thing.''

She stared at him. Her daughter was kidnapped and he wanted to watch *television*? Or was he acting casual just to deceive her and relax her? Probably the latter, to get her out of here.

''I can't watch a movie,'' she said coldly. ''I want to stay here, Ben, how many times do I have to repeat it? This is the only place I could go where he might be, and *I have to be here.*''

He stood up, shaking himself, but his eyes on hers were equally chilly. ''You're deluding yourself, Shay. Why won't you admit it? This whole trip to Ypsilanti was just a psychological device—a way for you to cope with this thing. I went along with it, but Mickey isn't coming here. In fact, if you had called Salter or let me turn on a TV set, you probably would have found that they've already picked him up.''

''No.'' She shook her head. ''No, they haven't picked him up. He still has her. I feel it, Ben . . . dammit! Damn you! I feel it. I know it.''

''So you're a psychic now? A seer who can see into the future?''

Was he sneering at her? This man who had insisted on coming with her and being supportive? Who had said he loved her only twelve hours ago? His betrayal burned her.

''Why are you being like this?'' she cried. ''Why? You wanted to come here with me—you insisted! I offered to let you go home, to do this on my own, but no, you had to come with me. You knew what it would be like, but now you're bitching. Make up your mind, Ben. One thing or the other!''

He looked away from her, his body language betraying unease.

''Well?'' She sat quivering, her anger like hydrochloric acid. Oh, God . . . she was so strung out.

''I don't know,'' he muttered. ''I guess I'm being a royal asshole.'' He hesitated. ''I guess I'm getting a funny feeling, too.''

For prosaic, practical, pragmatic Ben to admit *that* was like a sword point to Shay's stomach. It stabbed in and twisted with almost palpable pain.

''You are?''

Ben glanced urgently out of the front window, where a car was rolling toward the house—a blue Tempo exactly like the one Noah drove.

''Look,'' Shay said, pointing. Her voice came out as a whispered gasp.

''Jesus . . . maybe we've made a big mistake,'' Ben said.

It was another subdivision, not nearly as nice as the one the Wyomings lived in, and the sight of it struck terror into Kelly's heart. Every time they turned down a street with houses, something awful happened. Mickey had turned the car radio to a rap song by Soul II Soul, but Kelly barely heard the pounding lyrics.

''Where is this? What are we doing? Where are we going?'' she cried, the words exploding from her. Wedged in a corner of the passenger seat, she glanced frantically to her right and left. ''Oh, God . . . I can't believe this . . . I'm not here. I'm not here! This isn't happening!''

''Well, it is happening. What are *you* shaking for?''

Mickey snarled. "You're shaking like a goddamn leaf."

"W-what do you expect?" She was past caring now what he said to her or what he thought. He was going to go to another house and kill some more people, and he would force her to watch. Then he was going to kill her, too. She'd sensed it—a subtle change in the way he talked to her. She wasn't acting the way he wanted her to act, and he didn't like it, and that was going to be the end of her.

But she didn't want to die yet.

She couldn't die! She was only sixteen—she hadn't even gone to college yet. She hadn't even started nursing school, and she was going to take care of premature babies and she would never get to do that if she died. And her mother—and Matt. She would never see them again if she died now. And her dad. God, she loved them all so much.

Grief stabbed her. She knew that she was going to go up to heaven, probably within a few minutes, and she would hate being there because she would be all alone. She didn't allow herself to think of how it was going to hurt, and how horrible it would be to see her own insides coming out the way Mickey promised. Those were things she could not allow into her mind because it would kill her to think them.

Dazedly she noticed that he had driven around the same block two or three times. Her mind struggled. Maybe there was time to save herself, maybe she could still convince him she liked him.

"M-Mickey," she stammered. "Mickey . . . I . . . I want to be with you . . . I . . . I think you're brave . . . you are the king . . ."

If she'd said these things an hour ago, he would have listened or perhaps jeered at her, or sworn, or hit her, but now he didn't even reply. He was scanning the houses, his eyes flicking toward the cars parked on the street—a Cutlass Cierra, a Toyota Corolla, an Aerostar van, a—

Kelly's eyes riveted on the familiar blue Cierra parked to the right, wheels turned into the curb. Her heart gave a strangled jump.

That was Ben's car. The vanity license plate said LTRC—Ben Lyte's lame-duck way of spelling *literacy.*

Kelly used every ounce of willpower she possessed to wrench her eyes from the car. Her pulse was hammering so hard she thought she would throw up.

Oh, God, what was Ben Lyte doing here on this nerdy street in Ypsilanti? It couldn't possibly be a coincidence. What if her mother was with him? Oh, God, was this a good thing or a bad thing? She didn't see any police. Not a single police car. Mickey was here, though, and she knew what that meant: blood and stabbing and slit throats that made horrible gagging sounds as they bled.

"Don't hurt anybody this time," she blurted. "Don't, Mickey. Don't."

"What do you mean? Are you afraid? Are you chickenshit?" Mickey's mood had surged, and he seemed almost drunk now, his eyes glittering as he scanned the houses.

"I j-just don't want you to hurt anyone."

But he wasn't listening as he rounded the block for the third time and then pulled into the driveway of a yellow colonial, about eight houses away from where Ben's car was parked.

It's the wrong house, the wrong house, it's too far away, Kelly sobbed inside her head, silently. *Ben, Ben! I'm sorry I thought those terrible things about you! Mom . . .*

"Heeeeere we are," Mickey announced cheerfully. "This is it, kid, this is where the king is gonna do his thing. Come here!" He grabbed her by the rope that tied her hands, jerking her across the gear shift so roughly that something metal cut a long swathe down her left thigh.

Kelly stifled a howl.

In a few minutes, she was going to be dead.

Time broke down into tiny pieces. Even her breathing seemed to take forever.

Shay stood behind the cheap curtain, angled so that she had a view of the street although her body was mostly hidden. She saw the car turn into the driveway, and she saw Mickey's face through the windshield— looking grim yet exalted, like a pumped-up soldier going into battle. Ben was at the telephone dialing 911.

She heard him saying something—she didn't catch the words—didn't have to. It didn't matter any more, nothing did. Mickey was dragging her daughter out of Noah's Tempo, the knife at her throat. He yanked her across the cement, dragging her as if she were a crash-test dummy, or a store mannequin.

She saw that her daughter looked like an accident victim, her eyes holes of horror. Kelly was weeping, bloody mucous streaming down her chalk-white face. Her hair was tangled, and blood soaked the too-big T-shirt she wore, staining her jeans as well.

Mickey marched her toward the house and the two disappeared from view, blocked by the jutting angle of the house. Then Shay heard breaking glass from the small window in the top of the front door. He was breaking in.

He was here and it was time for her to do something, time for her to move, and she couldn't. Her knees were locked in place, her breath clogged in her gullet, her muscles unable to move.

''MOM!'' Kelly screamed. ''MOM, MOM, MOM . . . !''

* * *

"It's all right, honey. Stop crying. Hello, Mickey," Shay said, by some miraculous act of will forcing her voice to come out warm, even, and calm. It was the most incredible achievement of her lifetime, her finest hour.

The seventeen-year-old boy who had killed six people stopped short, staring at her incredulously. It was obvious that he recognized her. His eyes seemed almost to suck into hers, as if they were lovers. She sensed Ben standing behind her at the archway that led to the dining room, still by the phone. But she didn't have time to think about him now. She only had a few seconds to break Mickey's pattern, to somehow talk to him.

"Mickey," Shay began, using the exact tone of voice that her sister had told her to use—soft, slow, easy, not accusing, not judgmental. *Reach him on a human level*. "I see that it has been a long day for you."

He shook his head angrily back and forth. "Long day? It's been a *shit* long day." His mop of black hair fell forward. He had spots of crusty dark red on his skin . . . blood?

Her heart sank. Seen up close, Mickey seemed so coarse; he reeked of sour body odor and blood. How could she have thought there would be some good in him? Terror froze her. Had she killed them all with a stupid, naive idea?

He snarled, "Get in the room, bitch Kelly! Go! Go! Go!" He gave the girl a push and she stumbled into the end table, then caromed onto the couch, sobbing. In pushing her, Mickey had stabbed her a long, glancing blow with the knife. Bright red blood seeped out of a fresh cut in the back of Kelly's T-shirt.

"*Mom, Mom, Mom,*" the girl sobbed, raising her bound hands. She didn't seem to feel the cut. "He killed Mrs. Goldman—he killed her kids—he killed

Kim. Mom . . . he's going to kill all of us! He's going to cut us up!''

At the sight of her child's fresh blood, Shay felt such a torrent of fear and hatred that it rocked her backward. She felt a shriek welling up from her stomach, but she fought it down.

''Shay,'' she heard Ben say in the background.

He had called the police after all, what he'd wanted to do all along. Now within a few minutes the police would be here, and Mickey would have what he'd wished for. Violent confrontation. He would live out his life-scenario, the ending programmed for him since he was eight years old.

Distantly she heard her own voice emerge, carrying the calming peace of a trainer crooning to a skittish colt. ''You must be bothered about a lot of things. You must have a very long shit list. Would you like to talk about it?''

''Shay!'' Ben shouted. ''Don't—''

It was a mistake.

''Would you like to eat shit?'' Mickey yelled. Within seconds he was across the room. The butterfly blade flashed out to sink itself in Ben's white cotton T-shirt.

''NO, NO, NO, NO!'' Kelly screamed, a hysterical broken record.

Shay's scream was clogged in her throat.

She gazed at her lover in horror. A stabbing was a terrible thing to watch because the person did not just drop down the way it showed in the movies or on TV. He fought. In dreadful slow motion, Ben's features twisted with surprise and pain. He looked down at himself, at the blood gushing out. His fingers tried to push it back in. He stepped back, as if trying to run backward into the kitchen, balancing himself with difficulty.

Then he sank downward like a man going through the ice. Ben weighed two hundred pounds, and the sound he made dropping to the floor was loud. Once on the floor he continued to writhe, and a soft, wet gargle emitted from his lungs. *Shay*, he might have said.

"Ben!" The scream pushed out of Shay's throat. "Ben!" She realized that Kelly was screaming, too, both of their voices curdling together.

"SHUT UP, BITCH!" In two steps Mickey was back to Shay, the knife dripping red. He grabbed the lamp, cut off the cord with one swipe, and used it to tie both Shay and Kelly to the lounge chair.

Although it seemed that an eternity had passed, it was actually only a few minutes. Mickey danced through the room, pleased that he had both women hostage to his power.

"Look! Look!" he cried, strutting. "I'm the king. Mickey the king."

He leaped into the center of the room like a black belt karate master, twirling the butterfly blade at them. No, at Shay—that's who the display was for. Every time he snicked the blade his eyes sought hers. Again she had the loverlike feeling, his sexuality smoking the air with heat.

The knife clicked, blade flicking from one side of the handle to the other, snapping out, then into his palm, then out again. A street fighter's display of bravado.

Shay watched Mickey show off for her with a feeling of doom. How could this possibly end well? Ben needed a hospital trauma unit—and fast. Every second was vital. As for herself and Kelly, he would kill them, too, once he'd strutted for them, milked them of their terror.

Kelly quivered as she squirmed up against Shay,

desperately attempting to make some kind of physical body contact. "Mom . . . he likes you, Mom. He kept talking about you. Once he thought I was you."

Shay leaned into her daughter's side, thinking what a fool she'd been—what a crazy, selfish fool. If it had not been for her vanity and her deep psychological need not to be passive, the police would have been waiting here when Mickey arrived and Ben would not have been stabbed.

"Lookit! Lookit!" Mickey twirled the knife some more. "This is a butterfly knife, see? See the shape it makes? Like a butterfly's wings. My dad taught me that. He taught me a lot."

"You . . . you are very good," Shay managed.

"I'm the greatest! Better than my dad. Better than anyone."

"Better than anyone . . ." she repeated, belatedly remembering Marianne's instructions to repeat and reflect back whatever Mickey said.

"Better than *him*! He called 911, didn't he?" Mickey added, prancing over to where Ben lay breathing stertorously. "That bastard Mr. Lyte called 911 and now we're going to have a lot of pigs over here, aren't we? Lots and lots of 'em!"

His eyes devoured Shay's like a lover's.

The lamp cord had an extension attached to it, and the extension's rectangular socket pressed agonizingly into the center of Shay's spine.

Could she hear sirens in the distance? She craned her neck, trying to listen, but her own heartbeat was so loud, Kelly's whimpers so shaky, Ben's breathing so ragged, she could not hear anything. *What was taking the police so long?*

"Mickey," she began desperately. "I brought

something for you . . . something you might be interested in.''

"What?" He laughed, the sound wolfish. "What'd
you bring, bitch Shay? Yeah, you're the beautiful blond
bitch, aren't you? The lucky bitch. You got it all and
you don't even know it, do you? You're just a woman.
Just a stupid, fucking, dumb-ass woman.''

But his hot look belied his words, searing across the
space that separated them. Shay realized with a horrid
twist of her gut that this boy was sexually turned on by
her, that he had been all along, that Kelly was only a
substitute for her.

"I brought you a gift," she forced out the words,
trying to stop her voice from quivering. "There—on
the table—in that black tote bag. I made you something.''

He stared at her warily, his lip flaring, as if unsure
whether or not she was lying.

"I don't want nothing," he jeered. "You're my hostages, get it? I've got you and they're gonna stand
around out there and eat their hearts out, see? I got it
all planned!''

Ben uttered another moan and repeated her name
again—or was it that of one of his children? At least he
was still alive. Shay dragged her mind away from him.
If she did not think now, none of them would survive.

"The Literary Guild bag," she repeated.

"*Literary Guild!*" Mickey yelled. "What the fuck!
What the fucking *hell* are you talking about? Books?
Are you crazy, woman? What's fucking Literary Guild?
I'm Mickey, I'm the fucking king!''

Shay stiffened, trying to work through her despair.
God, how did she talk to a person like this? He did not
want to be reached. He wanted to be *worshipped* as some
kind of a grisly, prancing king. Beside her, Kelly was
stifling small hiccupy sobs.

"It's a tote bag; I've put it on the table in there—" She jerked her chin toward the dining room. "I made something for you, Mickey. It's in the bag."

"What fucking bag. What *fucking* bag." But Mickey danced through to the dining room, returning with the canvas tote which he swung carelessly, as if it had no value.

"Careful with that," Shay snapped. "It'll break."

"What'll break? What . . ." Shay had packed the Tupperware container into the bag, along with a few simple tools. Mickey threw these on the side table. Then he pulled the sculpture out. "What the hell." He stared at the clay piece, hefting it into his hands in stunned amazement. He shook his head, staring at it as if it were a miracle come to life.

"It's . . . the king," he whispered.

"It's you."

The boy touched the forehead of the small bust, his hand running down the contours as if he could only experience it by touching. "Me?" He was trembling. "Me? No . . ."

"It doesn't look like you," Shay suggested, remembering what her sister had said about reflecting. Did she hear the sirens now? Yes . . . surely she did. A chorus of them whining in the far distance.

"No . . . not me, not me, *not me*." With every word Mickey's voice got louder, his eyes more glaring and furious. "No, no, *no!* It's not me at all, it's him. Him! *Him!*"

"The sculpture doesn't look like you, it looks like your father."

"FUCK!" Mickey screamed, lifting the clay piece high over his head. He hurled it downward, smashing it onto the carpeting. The head crumbled in half. "FUCK! FUCK YOU! FUCK YOU, DANNO!"

To her shock, Shay saw that Mickey was crying.

Savagely the boy crashed the clay down, beating it against the floor while bits of dried clay flew. It was as if he were beating it to death. The *whup-whup-whup* of the sirens grew louder, converging on the neighborhood. There were three or four of them. Fainter ones howled in the distance.

"Mom . . ." Kelly whispered, gulping. "Mom . . ."

Mickey had heard the sirens, too. He looked up from his demolition of the clay bust. His eyes ran with tears. For a second he looked like a terrified eight-year-old. "It's happening," he said, wiping his upper lip, where mucous was dripping from his nose.

Whup-whup-whup-WHUP-WHUP-WHUP.

The police cars were in the yard now, car doors slamming, blue lights strobing. Mickey looked around the room wildly, his eyes lighting on the TV set. He raced toward it and flicked on the cable box. The shopping channel jumped onto the screen, female hands demonstrating a gaudy ruby ring while an announcer cajoled viewers to call in.

"Shit! Shit! Shit!" Mickey cried. He flicked the channel button until he reached Channel 7, which was showing a golf tournament.

"Yeah!" he cried. The brief weakness he had shown was gone. He seemed to regain his bravado as the screen showed a male golfer chipping toward the seventh hole. "Yeah, yeah, YEAH! Guess what's gonna be on here, huh? In a couple minutes. Just guess what! Mickey the king! That's who's gonna be on TV! Mickey the king!"

Shay sank against the back of the lounge chair, seeing the gleeful triumph in the boy's eyes.

TWENTY-THREE

Mickey had yanked the curtains shut, blocking their view of the street and the more than ten police vehicles and ambulances that waited out there. Using another extension cord, plus a rope he'd found, he'd trussed Shay and Kelly side by side in the lounge chair like twin prisoners.

"*Shiiiiit,*" he cried, pacing toward the window where he flipped the finger toward the flashing blue lights, jamming his hand violently up and down. "Fuck YOU, assholes!" he shouted. "Think you're so smart, don't you? Think you're so DAMN smart!"

He bounded over to the cable box and switched from Channel 7 to 4 and then 2, where sporadic news breaks had been detailing the situation.

"*. . . has been barricaded inside the house of his father, Danno McGee, also known as Dan Sparling, for more than two hours,*" came the familiar voice of Rich Fisher on Channel 2. "*With him are believed to be at least one, possi-*

bly three hostages. Seventeen-year-old Walton High School student Mickey McGee is an alleged spree killer said to have murdered five people including two children in the last twenty-four hours, with another girl critically wounded.''

''That's Rich Fisher,'' Kelly whispered dully. ''I watch him all the time, Mom.''

''I know, honey.''

''Channel 2 is on the scene for an interview with a neighbor.''

The screen switched to a view of the heavy young mother in the Bermuda shorts who had shooed her Big Wheel–riding toddlers indoors. The woman looked excited, made talkative by the cameras and commotion.

''We didn't know nothing about any of this, until we heard the police cars drive up. Those people, the Sparlings, they kinda kept to themselves; she didn't mingle much with the neighborhood,'' the woman babbled. *''We have a good neighborhood here, no trouble. We don't have a neighborhood where these things happen.''*

''You do now!'' Mickey crowed, aiming his finger toward the set. ''You do now, BITCH! Fat, bitch woman! Fat and ugly! You think you're gonna get a ringside seat, don't you? Yeah! You think you're gonna watch it all in living fucking color!''

Noises from outdoors interrupted his tirade.

''MCGEE,'' repeated the police loudspeaker. ''MCGEE, LEAVE THE HOUSE BY THE FRONT DOOR, UNARMED, WITH YOUR HANDS IN THE AIR. REPEAT, LEAVE THE HOUSE WITH YOUR HANDS IN THE AIR, AND YOU WILL NOT BE HARMED.''

''Bullshit!'' screamed Mickey. ''Bullshit!''

Across the room, Ben stirred. His eyelids fluttered, his bluish lips moved, and he made pulling movements with his hands. A bubbly, bloody foam escaped his lips.

''Shay?'' he called. Shay felt a shuddering pang as

she realized he was calling for her in his extremity, this man who she had never made love to, and now never would.

"SHUT UP!" screamed Mickey, prancing over to kick Ben in the side.

Ben's head lolled backward as he lapsed again into unconsciousness.

"Oh, please," Shay begged. "He's severely wounded—don't hurt him any more. Can't you take him to the doorstep and leave him out there for the police to pick up? Push him out the door or something. They'll take him to the hospital."

"SHUT UP! SHUT UP! SHUT UP!"

Shay slumped back, and wrenched her eyes away from Ben's slow descent into death. Ben had brought his gun into the house—she felt sure of it—but he apparently was too ill to use it, and of course they could not get to it, since they were tightly bound to the chair.

For the past two hours, the nightmare had stretched on and on. It was like being locked up with a psychotic child. For a few minutes Mickey would pace the living room with violent energy, kicking at furniture. Furiously, he had upended the folded playpen, hurling it on top of the dining room table, then knocking it back to the floor again. It missed Ben's prone body by only a few inches.

Then he raged around the room again, giving them another knife display, each time twirling the blade closer, as if to show them how eventually he was going to jam it through their skin.

"You like the knife, don't you, bitch Kelly?" He had taunted the weeping girl, circling the blade up and down over her stomach and genital area. He laid the blade flat on Kelly's mons, laughing loudly.

Kelly shrank away from him, pressing herself into the cushioned chair.

"Hey, babe, what you crying for, huh? You gonna like it when I cut in here to see what you got, huh?"

"Mom . . ." Kelly sobbed, while Shay tried vainly to lunge out of her bindings, animal rage coursing through her until she was almost blind.

"I want to see what you got in your pussy, babe. I want to cut it out and use it for a purse, heh? I'll make a billfold out of you!"

While Kelly averted her face, sobbing pathetically, Mickey laughed again and pranced toward the window, where he engaged in a brief shouting match with the police outside, being careful to stay out of clear visual contact.

"FUCK YOU, PIG ASSHOLES! FUCK YOU! YOU WANT ME, DON'T YOU? WELL, YOU AIN'T GONNA GET ME, HEAR THAT? HEAR IT? BECAUSE I'M THE KING, I'M MICKEY THE KING! AND I'M GONNA GO OUT IN A BIG FUCKING GRENADE EXPLOSION, KNOW WHAT I MEAN? YOU AIN'T TAKING ME!"

Then the pacing and violence would be followed by a self-mutilating despair. In this phase, Mickey would fling himself down on the sagging couch and claw at his own face, ripping at his scalp with his fingernails until rivulets of blood ran down his skin.

"M-Mom . . ." Kelly whispered to Shay as they sat cramped together in the chair, the cords cutting into their skin. "Mom . . . he's *crazy*. He'll do it, won't he? He'll really do it!"

"No, honey, he's just showing off," Shay lied.

"He is scaring me. He—he's scaring me so bad," the girl gulped. "W-we're helpless, we can't even move, and B-Ben is going to die if he doesn't get a doctor. I don't want Ben to die."

"I know, honey."

"Mickey cried, Mom—I saw him cry when he didn't think I was looking. He hates his dad because he put cigarette burns on him and did a lot of horrible things to him.''

''I know.''

''Are we . . . ?'' Kelly's voice quavered. ''Are we going to die, Mom?''

Shay looked at her beautiful daughter, her face begrimed and bloody from her ordeal, her eyes huge and shiny with dread. She felt waves of love for her child—pure, hard, incredibly strong. At least they had reached each other. This nightmare had accomplished that much. She and Kelly weren't apart any more. But what could she say? *Were* they to die?

No.

No, she would not allow it. She would fight to the bitter end if she could . . . but *how,* came the immediate, despairing thought. She was tied up, trussed to a chair, and the police were outside. If Mickey did not surrender in another four or five hours, they'd begin thinking about charging the house, or sharpshooting Mickey through the window. Bullets would ricochet around in this small living room. If Mickey hadn't already murdered them, she and Kelly might get lucky and survive a shoot-out. But by then, Ben would be dead. In fact, Ben might only have a few minutes left—

Her eyes stung with tears. It was intolerable to think of Ben's death.

Ben. Kind, loyal, giving Ben, who was no hero and never wanted to be one, but who was just a decent human being who loved her. Ben was a man who could fill up the rest of her life, but it wasn't going to happen unless she did something, and did it now.

Mickey was fussing with the TV set again, trying to find himself on another news break. Dried rivulets of blood formed small trails on his cheek where he had dug at himself. He was feeling this stress almost as much as they were. How long could he go without cracking? Minute by minute his body language was becoming jerkier, more erratic, as if he were rapidly disintegrating.

He was another reason she had to think of something fast. Because if she didn't, he'd blow . . .

He'd already hinted at what was to come when he laid the flat of the knife on Kelly's pubic area. He was telling them he could go wild, go into a feeding frenzy of knifing.

She heard Mickey let out a cry. He'd found another newsflash—this one showing the Walton High School yearbook photos of Mickey, Kimberley, and Kelly. There were grade-school pictures of the Goldman's two little girls.

Then a photo of Noah flashed on the screen. Shay herself had taken it at a gallery opening last year in Royal Oak. Her old friend grinned into the camera, his white eyebrows quirked wryly. It was one of the best pictures ever taken of him, allowing his innate graciousness to come through, his vast, warm life force that had been so brutally quenched. But it still existed somewhere, didn't it? It had only changed.

Noah, Shay said in her head. *Noah, are you here somewhere? Will you help me? I don't know what to do. I have to reach him. . . . I thought I could reach him, but now I'm not sure I can.*

You can, came the thought, pitched in her own internal voice, but somehow she felt that it belonged to Noah.

But how? Noah . . . there's still something in him that isn't vicious!

Try, came the Noah response.

She shook her head, her eyes traveling around the room. Then she saw the Tupperware container she'd put the clay in. It literally seemed to darken, then brighten as she stared at it. Clay . . . sculpture. That was

Mickey's strength, wasn't it? His talent. His goodness, the beautiful part of him that God had created along with the evil.

"I love clay," said Shay in a soft, soothing voice that was quiet like a child's lullaby. "Clay is such a wonderful medium, isn't it? It's so pliable—you can make anything with it, do anything you want with it, you have power over it. You can put yourself into it, you can make anything. You can make a miracle if you want to."

Mickey didn't say anything. But he did glance over his shoulder from the TV where he crouched near the cable box to tune the channels, since the Sparlings did not have a remote.

She went on, delicately feeling her way. One wrong word and he might blow. "I've always loved to make things with my hands, to touch clay or wax and have it literally spring to life under my fingers."

She could tell he was listening to every word, even nodding, his body almost straining to hear her.

"I brought some clay," she continued softly. "I brought it here because I thought we might want to memorialize today, Mickey. Do you want to take the clay and try to make something? Would that help you? Wouldn't you like to feel the clay in your hands?"

He turned slowly. His eyes glittered, and there were spots of red staining his cheeks.

"It's in that Tupperware container," Shay dared. She wondered if she was pushing Mickey too far. He was so damn fragile, wasn't he? So brittle. Anything could make him explode now. Dimly she was aware that on the far side of the room Ben had come awake again.

"Tupperware?" Mickey repeated.

"Yes—there, on that table. The clay is soft to work,

and later it could be recast in metal. It could be a finished piece, Mickey. Not just a high-school project but a real work of art.''

As if inexorably drawn, Mickey moved toward the plastic container. He picked it up and stood staring down at the white plastic lid that covered the pale yellow bowl. He ran his fingers around the lip of the lid.

"Open it," Shay urged.

The boy pried open the tab that lifted the lid, and stared into the contents of the container. His face was gray, almost ashen, as if he looked not into a plastic bowl but into some other world, deep, hollow and endless.

His indecision seemed interminable. Outside the house, police radios were squawking, and another siren suddenly came to life, *whup-whupping* and then dying with a screech. They were readying themselves, Shay sensed, gathering additional forces. Perhaps a SWAT team had arrived, complete with armored truck and flak jackets.

Shay heard a slight sound and glanced toward Ben. To her shock, she saw that he was inching his hand along the floor, up toward the belt of his pants. *The gun.* He did have the gun! But the exertion was causing sweat to pop out on his forehead, and he slumped again, the brief, brave effort finished.

Mickey hadn't noticed. He was still staring at the clay, his eyes riveted on it. Shay felt a burst of hope.

"Take out the clay," she pressed softly. "Take the clay into your hands, Mickey. Start working it with your fingers. Play with it. See what you can make."

Outside, a siren suddenly squawked. "MICKEY MCGEE," began the police mike again. "MICKEY MCGEE, IF YOU DO NOT COME OUT IN THE NEXT

TEN MINUTES WE ARE GOING TO COME IN AFTER YOU.''

Mickey jumped violently. Like an angry bull, he swiveled his head toward the window and then his fingers reached into the Tupperware bowl and closed viciously on the clay. He wadded it up and hurled it across the room.

It landed only inches from Shay's head.

"FUCK!'' he yelled. "FUCK YOU, LADY!''

Electrical energy jacked maniacally through him. He sprang to his feet and lunged across the room to pick up the ball of clay and hurl it again. It slammed into the wall. Out of control, Mickey careened across the living room, kicking the couch, tipping over the end table, attacking the television set.

From the lounge chair, both Shay and Kelly watched in horror as Mickey went berserk.

"Mom,'' whimpered Kelly.

Sobbing, Mickey kicked the set, which tipped backward on its stand, the cable box falling separately to the floor.

"MCGEE, YOU HAVE EIGHT MINUTES TO COME OUT WITH YOUR—''

Mickey grabbed up the box and jerked at it, yanking its thick, black cable. When it failed to pull apart, he kicked the box, yelling vile curses. Then, in a frenzy, he stabbed the couch. The blade flashed and scraps of cheap fabric flew, along with chunks of foam rubber.

Kelly, Ben, and herself were next, Shay knew.

He'd stab them just as viciously as he was now demolishing the couch—he'd cut them to ribbons before he finally sated whatever demons drove him.

"Mom, Mom, Mom,'' moaned Kelly, her body jumping with each attack to the couch. "Mom . . .''

"SHUT UP, BITCH KELLY!'' Mickey whirled in front of them, the blade raised. His lips were pulled back from his teeth, his eyes wild. He stood above Kelly, ready to stab.

"Noooooooo," Kelly keened, totally undone.

Shay lunged against her bonds, not feeling the electrical cord cutting into her arms, or anything except the hideous certainty that these were Kelly's last seconds of life. *"Mickey!"* she screamed. *"Goddammit, Mickey, don't destroy! Build! Build! You're only seventeen! You have a chance for a life! They can't ever take that away from you, it's yours!"*

The boy had the knife aimed at Kelly's quivering lower belly. She had stiffened rigidly, her eyes shut, waiting for the cutting to begin.

"Mickey!" Shay screamed. *"Kill me if you have to kill someone! Don't hurt her! Let her go!"*

Mickey's eyes had widened, his pupils moving rapidly as if he had taken some drug, but he didn't plunge the knife—not yet. She'd stopped him for a second or two.

"Mickey! She's only sixteen. Let her live!"

Seconds ticked past. Outside, there were noises from the massed police cars—radio static, more car doors slamming, shouts, running footsteps, a squawk from the PA system they'd set up outside. They were preparing for an assault—to kill Mickey. That was what the sounds meant and Mickey knew it as well as Shay did. They would riddle him with bullets—they would kill the life in him, creating a pile of flesh-meat as dead as any sodden road kill.

Behind Mickey, as if sensing the end, Ben had become conscious again. Shay saw him struggling awake, a muscle jumping in his jawline. Again his hand crept toward his pants.

"Mickey," Shay begged. "Think, Mickey! You can still get out of this alive. But don't kill my daughter. Let her live. Let her have her life, Mickey."

The suspense was intolerable. Shay felt her body vibrate with the horror of it. Either Mickey was going to stab the knife down and kill Kelly, or Ben's hand was going to reach the .38 in his pants and he would blow Mickey away—or try to.

And if Mickey turned and saw Ben, it would send him back into his violence—with a vengeance. He'd turn the house into a bloodbath. He'd stab them all to death, slaughtering them where they lay in a spray of blood. The police would shoot him, and burst in only to find a room full of corpses.

Again she felt Noah in the room, somehow hovering, and there was a goodness in the air, a kindness.

"Mickey," she choked, verbalizing her thoughts, anything to keep him from bringing that blade down. "You have a talent that God gave you . . . a wonderful talent. I don't know whether it's really possible for therapy to help you. I can't promise you that. I can't promise you anything. You'll probably go to prison no matter what you do next. Is there any value to your life? I think there is. But only you can decide. Mickey, decide! *Decide there is good in you! Decide it!*"

Mickey stared at her, stunned. The silence stretched on, killing, cutting. It stabbed Shay to the heart far deeper than any knife.

"Mickey. You are valuable. But you have to decide."

Mickey stepped forward, the butterfly knife raised, and Shay's heart contracted, all the air sucked out of her lungs. But instead of stabbing, Mickey brought the knife down and cut through the cord that bound Kelly's wrists.

The girl screamed with terror and relief.

Tears ran down Mickey's cheeks. He sniffed, his mouth working crookedly. He was only seventeen years old, after all. Only a boy. A boy who would now go to prison for life.

"Mickey," Shay whispered as the cord fell away from her hands.

His eyes met hers. Pleaded with her for guidance.

A boy, she thought.

"I'll help you get through the police," Shay promised. "I'll tell you what to say to them—I'll help you get through this alive."

"I want—" Mickey began. "I want—"

"MCGEE," the police loudspeaker blared again, cutting him off.

He was never going to get what he wanted. But maybe he would get something—somehow.

The male EMS attendant wheeled Ben on a gurney to the big, chartreuse van. An I.V. was attached to his hand, and he'd been treated for shock. His face was still gray, but his eyes were focused. He reached out a shaking hand to Shay.

Mickey had been taken away in handcuffs in the back seat of a police car with a four-car police escort—to whatever fate his life would hold. Prison life would be hellish for a boy that pretty, that handsome, but perhaps being a murderer would give Mickey some status behind bars. Maybe there would be a chance for him to use his creativity . . . somehow.

"Ben," she blurted, running along beside the stretcher, trying to grip his outstretched hand. Would he make it? He looked so gray, so sweating. "I'm with you."

"Shay . . . God . . . a cosmic joke. I didn't have the gun. I left it . . . in the car. Didn't think . . . I'd need it. Could have . . . killed us."

"Ben, just rest now. You're going to the hospital, you'll be fine."

"Strange," he muttered, then, "love you."

"Oh, Ben," she wept. "I love you, too."

''Get another . . . book,'' he managed. ''In this . . . somewhere.''

Shay started to cry.

A mob of newsmen had converged on the scene, reporters and cameramen with minicams battling for position. Mikes bristled everywhere. Marj Jackson Levin, of the *Free Press*, was standing on tiptoe, waving her arm frantically, trying to get Kelly's attention.

They paused, arms around each other. Mother and daughter leaned into one another as if they were temporarily one. They were both grimy, bedraggled and bloody, like disaster victims, and some of Kelly's superficial stab wounds had started to bleed again.

''Kelly!'' A woman shouted. ''*What did it feel like, being enclosed with a murderer? Were you scared?*''

''*Did he stab you, Kelly?*''

''*Shay, as Kelly's mother, can you tell us what you feel now?*''

''*Kelly! Were you in love with Mickey?*''

''*Kelly—*''

The girl pulled herself upright, staring them down. ''We'll talk later,'' she said firmly. ''After we go to the hospital and comb our hair and wash our faces and look okay again. Right now my mother and I have to go to the hospital with Ben. My mother—''

Her voice caught.

''My mother is the best—''

She gulped again. She stopped, then finished with difficulty, tears running down her cheeks in a tribute that would be seen by one-and-a-half million people in the Detroit area and would be rebroadcast on national TV to several hundred affiliate stations.

''My mother is the greatest.''

THE BEST IN MYSTERY

☐	51388-6	THE ANONYMOUS CLIENT *J.P. Hailey*	$4.99 Canada $5.99
☐	51195-6	BREAKFAST AT WIMBLEDON *Jack M. Bickham*	$3.99 Canada $4.99
☐	51682-6	CATNAP *Carole Nelson Douglas*	$4.99 Canada $5.99
☐	51702-4	IRENE AT LARGE *Carole Nelson Douglas*	$4.99 Canada $5.99
☐	51563-3	MARIMBA *Richard Hoyt*	$4.99 Canada $5.99
☐	52031-9	THE MUMMY CASE *Elizabeth Peters*	$3.99 Canada $4.99
☐	50642-1	RIDE THE LIGHTNING *John Lutz*	$3.95 Canada $4.95
☐	50728-2	ROUGH JUSTICE *Ken Gross*	$4.99 Canada $5.99
☐	51149-2	SILENT WITNESS *Collin Wilcox*	$3.99 Canada $4.99

Buy them at your local bookstore or use this handy coupon:
Clip and mail this page with your order.

Publishers Book and Audio Mailing Service
P.O. Box 120159, Staten Island, NY 10312-0004

Please send me the book(s) I have checked above. I am enclosing $ _____
(Please add $1.25 for the first book, and $.25 for each additional book to cover postage and handling.
Send check or money order only—no CODs.)

Name _____

Address _____

City _____ State/Zip _____

Please allow six weeks for delivery. Prices subject to change without notice.

ADVENTURES IN ROMANCE FROM TOR